THE
UNSCRATCHABLES

Cornelius Kane

Scribner

New York London Toronto Sydney

SCRIBNER

A Division of Simon & Schuster, Inc.

1230 Avenue of the Americas

New York, NY 10020

First Scribner trade paperback edition July 2009

SCRIBNER and design are registered trademarks of The Gale Group, Inc., used under license by Simon & Schuster, Inc., the publisher of this work.

For information about special discounts for bulk purchases, please contact Simon & Schuster Special Sales at 1-866-506-1949 or business@simonandschuster.com.

The Simon & Schuster Speakers Bureau can bring authors to your live event. For more information or to book an event, contact the Simon & Schuster Speakers Bureau at 1-866-248-3049 or visit us at www.simonspeakers.com.

Text set in Weiss

Manufactured in the United States of America

1 3 5 7 9 10 8 6 4 2

Library of Congress Control Number: 2008029756

ISBN: 978-1-4165-9641-7

Stephen Jay Gould . . . says that we humans are neotenized apes—that is, we are apes that have maintained juvenile characteristics into adulthood, both physical and mental characteristics, and it is these juvenile characteristics that have been responsible for our success as a species. In selectively breeding dogs as we have, there is no doubt that we have neotenized them too. Both morphologically and mentally, dogs have been bred to maintain the juvenile characteristics of play, exploration, and subservience to the leader.

BRUCE FOYLE, *The Dog's Mind*

Let thy child's first lesson be obedience, and the second will be what thou wilt.

BENJAMIN FRANKLIN

THE UNSCRATCHABLES

THE JANGLER STARTED ringing as soon as I nudged open the door. But it was already past ten p.m. and I'd been on my legs for over twelve hours. I only wanted to flop.

I went to the kitchen cupboard and got out a can of Chump's. I peeled it open with a fancy electric gizmo—something I'd snared in a squad raffle—so I could eat straight from the can without jagging my tongue. I splashed some water into a bowl. I went to the sofa and hunted for the remote control, but it was buried so deep under soiled blankets and biscuit crumbs I couldn't even smell it.

The jangler was still hammering. Probably my ex, wanting to whine. Maybe Spike wanting to play ball. Maybe some prevention-of-cruelty charity begging for cash. But I was too sapped to care.

Sinking between cushions I felt the remote dig into my flank. I flipped it out, pawed at the controls, and the buzz-screen blinked on. Johnny Wag, famous quiz show host, was tossing the big-biscuit question to reigning champion Professor Thomas Schrödinger. But I had no appetite for brain-bait. I flicked the channel.

An electoral debate between President Brewster Goodboy and Buster Drinkwater. Goodboy was a cat's-paw, everyone knew it, but he'd win easily—I'd probably vote for him myself. Drinkwater used way too many big words.

1

The jangler just wouldn't shut up. I flicked the channel again.

Swinger Cat, a new sitcom from the other side of the river. Everybody said it was real funny—the laugh track sure said so—but I was in no mood for ribtickles.

A fawning documentary on the CIA.

A doomsday report on the Persians.

A horror movie, *The Unfamiliar*, so old I think it was in black-and-white.

A public service announcement warning us not to get scared by the fireworks on Democracy Day.

And finally something I could settle on—a ball game. The Bulldogs were eight runs up on the Hellhounds in the sixth inning. Not exactly tight, but something I could watch without needing to think. I could pick a team—the Bulldogs—and cheer them on. I could bark at the ump. I could gobble my Chump's. I could slurp my water and slowly drift into snoozeville.

The jangler stopped—finally.

But then it started hammering again.

Now I was really getting my tail up. I'd spent half the morning in court, giving evidence against the Airedale Ripper—a whitecoat who'd carved up his victims with a medical saw and buried the remains in his backyard. Then, before I'd even had time to wolf down my lunch, I'd been called out on a new case—bits and pieces of bone found in the sewer under Chuckside. A whole afternoon poking through doodah, and all we found were a couple of chalky knucklebones—not even good enough to chew on. When I got back to the station the chief ordered me to have a wash—my first in two months—and now I was feeling so clean I almost gagged. I reckoned I could hear fleas in the corner, wondering who I was.

The Bulldogs whacked one over the fence and the jangler was still clanging.

2

I considered ripping the cord out with my teeth. But all of a sudden the buzzscreen was showing an ad for Friday's prize-fight—a double bill of Leroy Spitz vs Deefa Dingo and Rocky Cerberus vs new sensation Zeus Katsopoulos. If Cerberus KO'd Katsopoulos in the first round, like everyone expected, it would make him the greatest southpaw since Butch Brindle. Everyone in San Bernardo was drooling at the prospect.

But here was the problem. The Reynard Cable Network had won exclusive rights to all UBF matches. And I didn't have RCN. So all of a sudden I started wondering if it was my old buddy Spike on the line, inviting me around to watch.

I fumbled the squawker off its cradle.

"Max McNash."

"Crusher—it's me, Bud."

Bud Borzoi was my fetch-dog at the Slaughter Unit.

I sighed. "What's up, Bud?"

"Coupla stiffs, Crusher. In Fly's Picnic."

"You can handle it."

"But you're gonna want to see this, Crusher."

"Why?"

"You're just gonna want to see it."

I sighed again. "Know what sorta day I've had so far?"

"Sorry, Crusher—I wouldn't be barking if it wasn't serious."

Fang it, the pup could make me feel guilty. "Okay," I huffed, "but lemme get my bearings first. Where in Fly's Picnic are you?"

"Slinky Joe's Sardine Cannery."

"That's right next to Wharf Twelve, ain't it?"

"You got it in one. See you down here in, say, twenty small ones?"

"Make it thirty. And Bud?"

"Yeah?"

3

"Do I need to bring a barf bag?"

Bud sniggered. "Make it a doggie bag, Crusher, case there's something you want a second nibble at."

It didn't seem long since Bud had been a wide-eyed rookie, hungry for cheap thrills. Now he was making all the quips.

"Sniff you later," I said. I tossed the squawker back in place and returned the half-eaten can of Chump's to the fridge next to the gravy pot. When I switched off the buzzscreen a brawl had broken out between the Bulldogs and the Hellhounds: teeth flashing, hackles bristling—the crowd was lapping it up.

IF YOU LOOK at a map of San Bernardo, Fly's Picnic is that rough chunk of the Kennels, about four sprints long and two and a half sprints wide, stretching from the mouth of the Old Yeller River along the shoreline of Belvedere Bay to the newly gentrified suburb of Staffordshire. It's a mixture of low-down industrial and rag-end residential, crumbling waterfront tenements, sagging storehouses, chemical storage facilities, smoke-belching factories, even an old boneyard.

But most famously there's the stink. Oily water, ash, refuse, fish heads, rotting timber, slaughterhouse blood, dead rats, raw sewage—half an hour in Fly's Picnic is enough to make anyone swoon. They say the flies get so drunk on germs in the Picnic they drop off walls.

When I pulled up at Slinky Joe's it was fifteen minutes shy of midnight. Flanked by factories, the wharf jutted fifty yards into the scummy water. Twice a week fishing trawlers docked here and dumped their loads directly onto the swollen wood. At night the whole area was a den of powder smuggling, offshore immigrants, sometimes carcass dumping.

I nodded to the guard-spaniels and ducked under the checkertape, rubbing my aching eyes. Ahead were a couple of police cars, red and blue lights spinning. Another car—a black-and-chrome Lupus, a gangster favorite—was in the middle of the wharf with its doors flung wide. And some crumpled forms on the ground. Two of them, in cheap black suits. At least it didn't look like I'd uprooted myself for nothing.

"What've you got for me?"

Bud Borzoi, gangly as a hat rack, was chewing on a toothpick and smelled eager.

"Two 'weilers, Crusher—recognize 'em?"

I surveyed the bodies. "Hard to recognize anything, way they are. Looks like they've been through a grinder."

Bud gave a chuckle. "The Ripper?"

"I spent the morning in court with the Ripper. Far as I know he's still in the clanger. Get someone to check anyway."

"Roger."

"But this don't look like the Ripper's MO." I did a slow circuit of the bodies, trying to find something still in one piece. "Any ID found?"

"None."

"Nothing embedded?"

"Nothing we can find."

"Figures." The previous year compulsory microchip embedding had been championed by some hard-nosed sections of the government and media. It was at times like this that I wished the law had actually passed.

"We did find weapons." Bud nodded to an officer holding up a couple of snaptooth bags—looked like Schnauzer .44s inside.

I grunted. "They won't be licensed, like the 'weilers. What about the tooter?"

"The plates were muddied, but we're checking the numbers right now."

"Registered to a dummy corporation is my bet."

"Gangsters?"

"All 'weilers are. Any witnesses?"

"Closest we got is a worker from Slinky Joe's."

"Where is he?"

Bud led me off to the side, where a mangy-looking mutt, a whippet by the look of him, was puffing furiously on a smoke-stick.

"Detective Max McNash," I barked at him. "Got a minute?"

"Sure." He was quivering, whippet-style, and stank of sardines.

"Got a name?"

"Flasha Lightning."

"Parents had a sense of humor?"

The whippet didn't know what to say.

"Okay, Flasha, what's the meat?"

"I don't want no trouble."

"Just get your snapper working if you don't want trouble."

The whippet glanced at Bud. "Like I said to the officer here, it didn't have nothing to do with me, nothing at all."

"Been in the pound before, Flasha?"

He looked wasp-stung. "M-m-maybe."

"How long've you worked here?"

"At Slinky Joe's? Nearly a year."

"Night shift?"

"M-m-ost times."

"Seen some interesting stuff 'round here, I bet?"

His tongue was sweating. "I guess so."

"Okay, let's have it. What happened here tonight?"

He swallowed. "It was break time, see—"

"What time?"

"Nine o'clock."

"Go on."

"And I came out here to suck some tar."

"No smokesticks in the cannery?"

"Uh-huh. So I came out here, see, like I always do, and I heard some guns woofing—"

"How many shots?"

"Two. And a splash . . . and a gut-clawing squeal . . . like I don't know what."

"Use your imagination."

"Like, I don't know . . . like something from a horror movie." His eyes were wide and yellow, like he watched too many horror movies.

"You're not much help to me, are you, Flasha? See anything?"

"I was too scared to look."

"You're telling me you saw nothing at all?"

"Just, I don't know . . . a whirl."

"An impression of movement?" That's what we called it in court.

"Uh-huh."

"Then what?"

"I waited awhile, then I crept out across the wharf for a look-see . . . and . . ."

His eyes had glazed and his withers were trembling.

"You saw the carcasses?"

"Yeah . . ."

"You called the police?"

He gulped. "I headed inside. The night boss jangled."

"You can't jangle yourself?"

"I was too . . . scared." He kept glancing at the bodies, like he half-expected them to rise up and attack him.

"No one else saw anything?"

"I was first out when the break sounded."

"Always first out, I s'pose?"

"I like my tar."

I made a show of thinking about it, then nodded. "Time to clock off, Flasha. You're heading down to the station with Officer Borzoi here."

The whippet whined like a creaking door. "I'm not gonna get my pay docked, am I?"

"Dock your pay or dock your tail—makes no difference to me, pal."

I was too dog-tired for this.

I WAS HEADING back across the wharf when I heard a yelp from behind the police cordon. It was Nipper Sweeney, sparkly-eyed newshound for one of the Reynard Media's info-rags. Nipper could be like an undigested bone at times—he'd been doing the crime beat for as long as I'd been in the force—but he could also be useful. I ambled over and cocked an ear. "What's on your mind, Nip?"

"You owe me, Crusher."

"What for?"

"For the tip on the poisoned Podengo. Who's dead?"

"I just got here. When I find out I'll let you know."

"Photo opportunity?" He nudged his photographer, who held up a flash-and-clink.

"Nothing you can use on a front page."

"You'd be amazed what we get on the front page these days. How about letting me through for a scope?"

"No deal, Nip. You know the run-through. Procedure first. Then happy snaps."

"Hoodlums?" Nipper nodded at the bodies.

"Maybe."

"Then who's gonna care?"

"Even hoodlums got mothers, Nip."

But I didn't wait for any more niggles. I headed back across the wharf with Bud at my heels.

"Reckon it might be him, Crusher?"

"Who?"

"The killer? Reckon it might be him?"

"Nipper Sweeney?"

"The whippet." Bud jerked his head. "Flasha."

Sometimes it surprised me how raw Bud was. "The whippet couldn't put a scratch in an egg yolk."

"He might be an accomplice or sumthin'. He smells nervous."

"'Coz I gave him the jeebies. 'Coz he's taking more than smokesticks out here, is my guess. But he's no killer. Bull terriers trust their guts."

A meat wagon was already arriving to load up the carcasses. Bud pointed out some bloodstains on the wharf, separate from the 'weilers.

"Have a sniff, Crusher."

"You've already taken a scent?"

"Yeah." He was giggling again.

I got down on all fours and took a deep draft over the blood. And almost immediately I gagged. *Fang it,* I breathed, rising.

"Matches the scent in the Lupus, Crusher."

"Fang it," I said again, and shook myself. I went over to the tooter and stuck my muzzle through the open door, careful to let not a whisker touch the upholstery. I sucked in a good sample. And it was the same.

"*Cat,*" I whispered, like a curse.

"A cat was in the car," Bud said, grinning.

I shook my head, not wanting to believe it. "It needs to be verified first."

"Course."

"Probably an alley cat—a stray."

"Hope so, Crusher."

11

"Just another rat-licking alley cat dragged down to the docks to get a bullet in the brainpot. Bang! The 'weilers toss him in the soup. And then they get killed themselves."

"That's the way I figured it."

I looked at Bud, staring at me like I was a hero. I looked at the whitecoats scooping the bodies onto stretchers. The police cordon. Nipper Sweeney and a few droopy-tongued onlookers, Flasha Lightning among them. And I felt it, for the first time—the gut sense, the animal instinct, that this case was going to be something different. And not in a good way.

"Gimme two shakes," I said. "I need time to think about it."

"Sure thing, Crusher."

So I mushed over to the end of the wharf, hearing the water lap beneath me, the roosting flies, the rustling rubbish. I looked north, past the hulking factories of Fly's Picnic, past the wharves and Amity Bridge with its sweeping searchlights, to the great skyscratchers of Kathattan, the glittering salmon-shaped island where the fat-cats lived—the stockbrokers and bond traders, the hedge-fund managers, merchant bankers, fashion designers, psychiatrists, lawyers, advertising executives, yoga instructors, architects, jewelers, feng-shui experts, toy designers, opera singers, and trapeze artists—the whole cream-lapping, wool-juggling, pajama-wearing, fence-sitting, bird-torturing, furball-coughing lot of them.

I prayed to Our Master that the alley cat wasn't from there. And I prayed even harder that the 'weiler killer had nothing to do with them.

I thumped my chest, dislodging something caught side-ways—a wishbone from yesterday's lunch. I spat a blob of saliva into the greasy water—*plop!*—and scratched a flea out of my ruff. I broke wind. I blinked my stinging eyes. And suddenly I just couldn't buy it; I just couldn't accept that it was anything complicated. It couldn't be anything to do with the fat-cats. It just couldn't. My brainpot was too overheated for anything else.

I turned back up the wharf toward Bud.

"Get the bodies to the bone house," I ordered. "Have the tooter towed to forensics. Call Amity Bridge—I want a report on all Lupuses that crossed from Kathattan today. Just in case."

"Sure thing, Crusher."

"And get the water dogs in. I want the harbor trawled. I want a carcass. I wanna see a dead alley cat."

"Where ya gonna be?"

"Not much I can do till I see those reports, is there? And then I won't be getting any shut-eye for a long time. So guess where I'm going?"

"Back to your blankets?"

I smirked on the way past. "You're sharper than your snout, Bud."

"What if the reports come in early?" he called out.

But I didn't even turn. "Let sleeping dogs lie, Bud, let sleeping dogs lie."

BUT I DIDN'T snooze well. I couldn't get the stench of cat out of my nostrils. There was something about this particular stink that wasn't right. I'm no expert, but I'd sniffed cat blood before, plenty of it. And apart from little things it's all basically the same: You can smell the fish, you can smell the cream, you can smell the superiority. But what was lingering in my muzzle was rawer than that. It was what a tiger might smell like.

I lived in the Tenderloin district, a few sprints from the Dog Force HQ in Dishlick. Across the road, on the site of an old sewage treatment plant, the government was building a massive stadium, Peace Park, future home of the Globe Games. But construction had fallen way behind and work packs were hammering and drilling right through the night. The biggest, half-finished grandstand oozed right across the street, throwing my tenement into permanent shade. Sometimes bolts and nails rained down on the roof and some idiot would jolt awake and start barking. Then someone else would join in. Before long the whole block would be yapping. Even worse, the activity attracted packs of hoondogs like moths, swirling around the construction site, snarling and snapping, trying to snatch tools, trying to sneak inside, trying to get caught—anything to beat the boredom of youth.

I rolled out of bed just before dawn. I was still in my shirt and tie. I did my usual 150 push-ups and sprayed some flea powder down my back. I went outside, puffing clouds of steam, and drained myself against a sapling. There were new scratch marks on my Rover, I saw, and the tires looked nipped. I told myself I'd get a new tooter, but I told myself that every week. I'd do a lot of things next week. When my pups grew up. When vet care was free. When things got better.

I stopped at an all-night pump. Gas prices had skyrocketed because of the looming Afghan-Persian war. I dribbled less into the tank than I'd sprinkled across the tree, counting on costs to drop a little overnight. Optimism, my pappy used to say, is like a rawhide bone—good to have around when you've got nothing else.

I took breakfast in a little muncheonette three doors down from the cophouse. The place was packed like an egg carton. I plucked the *Daily Growl* off the rag rack and settled into a smoky corner with a meatball and a coffee. The headline howled BLOODY SLAYINGS SCARE CITY. There was a grainy snap of me bent over the wharf, sniffing blood. Nipper Sweeney had put me in yap-marks: "Probably hoodlums." Not that I remembered saying that.

Chester White, an old buddy from academy days, greased past with a quip: "Look good in the scrapbook, Crusher."

"Gave up scrapbooks years go, Chesty. The glue was making me dizzy."

In the cophouse, still working his toothpick round his snapper, Bud Borzoi was waiting with a couple of folders and a shirt-eating grin. "Get a good snooze, Crusher?"

"Better than you is my bet. What've you got for me?"

"Registration check on the Lupus. Bogus plates. Got ID on the bodies, too. And we fished a victim out of the soup, just like you said we would."

"Settle down, boy." I dragged him into my office and shut

15

the venetians. "First things first. Did you check with Amity Bridge?"

"Uh-huh. No Lupuses fitting the description passed from the island in the past twenty-four hours."

"Good start."

"Then there's the cat carcass we hooked out of the bay, not far from the wharf. Smells like a real trashmuncher."

"ID?"

"None on him."

"From the Cradles?"

"Could be, Crusher. The body's in forensics."

"What about the 'weilers?"

"In there too. Dr. Barnabus is having a sniff."

"Barnabus? This early?"

"I called him out of bed. Figured you'd want the best."

I grumbled inwardly. Barnabus was the best, sure—problem was he knew it. "Anything turn up so far?"

"Tongue prints." Bud looked pleased with himself. "Sixty-percent match."

"Just sixty?"

"The tongues were sandpapered, gangster-style, but it was enough for a trace."

He handed over the files and I flipped immediately to the photos.

"Hell," I said, "this is Savage Brown and Lucifer Thorn. They used to do bite-and-grind work for Cujo Potenza."

"Cujo's dead, ain't he?"

"Run over by a car, well before your time. Ever since then Savage and Lucifer have been doing contract work in the Kennels. Anything for a cookie."

Bud sniggered. "No more cookies where they are now."

I snapped the folders shut and shoved them back at Bud.

"Two known hoodlums, a dead alley cat, and plenty of crime-scene blood—now all we need is a killer." I yawned and headed for the door. "I'm off to see Barnabus."

"Did I do good, Crusher?"

I looked back at Bud's dinner-table face. "You'll know you've done good when you don't need to ask, Bud. Go home and have a flop—it's your turn now."

"Sure you don't need me?"

"Can't see why. This is looking easier than I thought."

But in my ears, even as I said it, the sentence sounded hollow as a tennis ball.

I WASN'T HALFWAY across the squad room when the chief whistled me into his office. I scored an eye roll from Chesty White that said "the chief ain't happy." But I wasn't panicking. The chief and I went back to our airport days, when he was in luggage inspection and I patrolled the fences. We knew each other's dirty secrets.

"Close the swinger, McNash."

"Something wrong, Chief?"

"Call it an itch on my rump."

"Something I can scratch?"

"I sure hope so, McNash, for your sake."

When he got promoted the chief stopped calling me Crusher. He also stopped eating doodah in the local park. He got braid on his collar and a fancy spread in Baskerville with a backyard big enough to herd sheep in. He took a shampoo every week, had a coat trim every month, and got his nails filed every quarter. He got so much respectability that I even stopped calling him by his first name, Kaiser. But I never forgot what he was—a contraband-sniffing Kraut with a permanent ten o'clock shadow, a rheumy right eye, and breath that would kill a yak.

"Busy night down in Fly's Picnic, I hear." The chief had that show-day stiffness about him.

"It ain't over yet," I said. "I'm on my way to Barnabus right now."

"I've spoken to Barnabus. He told me Bud Borzoi had called him out of bed."

"That's right."

"Barnabus was surprised. And he has every right to be. Summoned to an autopsy by a junior detective?"

"Barnabus should get with the times." Inwardly, I cursed the old basset for stirring trouble.

"Really?" The chief was giving me his German Shepherd kill-stare. "A double murder? Possibly triple? And the detective-in-charge sends himself home for a snooze?"

"It was the best thing to do."

"Never heard of pouncing on a lead, McNash? While the trail's still fresh?"

"It was me who needed to be fresh, Chief. I hadn't flopped in hours."

"So you were happy to leave the case in the care of a toothpick chewer, is that it?"

"I trust the pup like a son."

The chief made a growling sound. "Well, did your pup happen to tell you about your choice-cut witness?"

"Flasha Lightning?" I made sure I didn't look surprised. "What about him?"

"Seems Borzoi didn't put a leash on him quick enough. Soon as heads were turned the whippet bolted out the swinger like his tail was on fire."

"No big deal," I said, quick as a flash myself. "He'd said all he was gonna say. And I figured the cophouse would give him the squirts, anyway."

"No kidding?" The chief grunted. "You should check his file—it's long as a dragline. Snatch-and-run work. Powder-dealing. Even tunnel work for Cujo Potenza."

"That a fact?" Some years ago Potenza had tried digging

a hole under the Old Yeller to Kathattan from an abandoned storehouse in Ribeye. All sorts of bony mongrels had worked day and night on the operation, only to have the river collapse on the tunnel, washing half of them away. "I figured he was a lowlife."

"Point is," said the chief, "you've got a prime witness who's gone to ground. You've got a case that's already growing mold— it's in the *Growl,* for Bacon's sake—and no leads."

I shook my head. "What you got is a dead Tom Doe in the slice-and-dice rooms. You got two 'weilers beside him who aren't getting any notices in the lost-and-found columns. And a detective with a fresh brainpot who's gonna get to the bottom of this or he never snoozes again."

The chief's eyes narrowed. "Sound pretty sure of yourself, McNash."

"With a clear head I'll back myself at any odds, Chief. With a furry one . . ."

But I didn't need to say anymore. In one of my first cases as a ranking detective I'd blown a crucial case by flopping asleep on a stakeout. A murderer had jumped clean over the back fence without me even noticing. But what could I do? I hadn't slept for three days. Not even smelling salts—not even six spoonfuls of coffee—could stop my eyelids dropping. But the fallout stuck to my shoes like you-know-what. The stink never really left the room. I still wasn't betting on any surprise promotions.

"All right." The chief's leaky right eye had flickered at the memory. "But don't count on any slack, McNash—not now. We've got elections coming up, case you hadn't noticed. Maybe a new law enforcement commissioner. Whatever. Word in the park is that the SU is in for a shake-up, maybe just for the fun of it. Know what that means? No more naps. No more oversights. Or we both could be back at the airport, sniffing for nitro."

"We always did make a dynamite team," I said, flashing my crocodile smile.

"On your way, McNash." The chief jerked a nail. "And don't show your fat snout until you've got some answers. I'm in no mood for jawback."

When I left him he was reaching for his rubber worry-bone. The thing was half the size it used to be.

MY DISLIKE OF Dr. Barnabus didn't make me any lone wolf. His droopy features matched his personality. His fully flared nose, which made him look constantly in the presence of a bad smell, put even close colleagues on edge. His wrinkly brow, his weary voice, his habit of peering over his half-moon spectacles—his whole air of superiority—gave everyone the feeling he was looking down on them. In short, he was a caustic old fleabag who'd spent far too much time sniffing at dead meat without taking a bite—the sort of discipline that'd send any breed 'round the bend.

"Teeth marks of 1000 psi in lower sternum . . . evidence of talon lacerations to esophagus and pylorus . . ."

When I entered he was hunched over the bodies, drawling into a hanging microphone. His assistant—a good-smelling Labrador bitch—was taking notes.

"Multiple fractures of the scapula . . . scoring of the humerus . . ."

I took a look over a huge chrome table where the 'weiler parts were pieced together like a jigsaw puzzle.

"Bit neater than when I last saw 'em," I said.

Barnabus didn't stop making notes, didn't even look up. "Observe the number of tooth incisions," he said to his assistant. "Thirty exactly. Notice the number of premolars—ten.

Notice the radius of the bite marks, the character of the scratch marks . . ."

"Got a fix on the killer?" I asked, tired of being ignored.

Barnabus finally raised his wrinkly bobble and stared at me. Ranks of fluorescent tubes glinted in his glasses. "Detective," he sniffed, "I've been here for three hours." Like it explained everything.

"And?" I shrugged. "Any theories on the killer?"

He took off his spectacles and folded them into his top pocket. "Perhaps," he said, "the detective-in-charge would care to avail us of his own theories?"

I could tell he was setting me up. "I got no theories. That's why I'm here."

Barnabus frowned like he couldn't believe it. "The Rottweilers were murdered at approximately nine o'clock last night." He glanced at a wall ticker. "That's over ten hours ago. And you mean to tell me the Slaughter Unit's prime detective has yet to formulate a theory?"

I didn't need to field any lip from a carrion-sniffer, but I didn't need to make trouble for myself either. "You want a theory?" I said. "Okay, cop this. Two 'weiler hoodlums take an alley cat down to the docks. They plug him. Then they get whacked before they get away. Probably an ambush. Any objections so far?"

"Who?"

"Who what?"

"Who killed the Rottweilers?"

"How would I know? That's what you do, ain't it? Sniff out clues?"

"But you must have some idea by now?"

I couldn't work out his game. "A rival gangster. A mad powder dealer. Someone with a serious beef. How would I know?"

23

"But a dog—you're definitely saying it was a dog?"

"So what?"

A smirk crept from under Barnabus's droopy basset jowls. "Detective McNash . . . these Rottweilers were killed by a *cat*."

I looked at the jigsawed bodies. I looked back at Barnabus. I glanced at the smug-looking Lab assistant. And I snorted. "Gumrot," I said.

Barnabus looked extra-waggy now. "The evidence is undeniable. The tooth incisions. The claw marks. The *musk*."

"Musk." I tried to detect something, but all I could smell was the nasty stink from my nightmares. "You're telling me this was done by a *cat*."

"Undoubtedly."

"A panther . . . a lynx . . . a wildcat?"

Barnabus shook his head. "A house cat."

"No . . ."

"Blood and saliva samples have already been dispatched to pathology. If you don't believe me perhaps the official reports will convince you. The killer you're looking for is a cat—a particularly large and powerful specimen, admittedly, possibly twice the usual dimensions."

"No . . ." I thought of the "gut-clawing squeal" Flasha Lightning had heard on the wharf . . . but I just couldn't swallow it. A worthless alley-cat victim was one thing. But a killer cat, on top of that, meant a major scandal. It meant a detective from Kathattan. It meant the FBI.

I shook myself. "What about the victim?" I tried. "The Tom Doe hauled out of the harbor?"

The gleam hadn't left Barnabus's eyes. "Ah yes, the fishing haul."

He waddled to a second chrome table, where a bloated cat

24

carcass—a common tabby, by the look of him—lay in tattered alley-cat threads.

"I'm afraid," said Barnabus, "that you're going to have to throw your nets a little wider, Detective."

"I don't get you."

"I mean my preliminary examination suggests that this cat here was not murdered at all."

"Drowned?"

"A stomach full of catnip and toxoplasma medications. I'd suggest suicide."

"No bullet holes?"

"Nothing that killed him."

"Contusions? Abrasions?"

"Nothing fresh."

"So you're telling me this cat has no connection to the 'weilers?"

"I hate to disappoint you, Detective."

But he didn't look disappointed at all. He looked as happy as a butcher. I felt like taking a bite out of his floppy ear, just for irritating me. But I reminded myself that my fighting days were over. So I could only steam, feeling my hackles stiffen.

"Seems like there's a lotta work to do," I said between my teeth.

"And I'd hate to hold you up," said Barnabus, already slipping his spectacles back onto his snout.

"Sure thing," I gnashed, "I got no time to yap with dry-nosed bassets anyway."

When I left the room I heard the old fleabag in the background, returning to his autopsy: "Massive trauma to the lower intestine . . . detached coccygeal vertebrae . . . deep fissures in the poststernum . . . hand me the buzzsaw, Blondie."

I SLUNK PAST the chief's office like I'd just wet the welcome mat. I stopped at my desk long enough to order a new search of Belvedere Bay. Then I called the beagles in Sensory Investigation, telling them to meet me at Fly's Picnic in thirty small ones. I thumped my chest—that wishbone still hadn't passed through—and was about to sneak off again when the jangler sounded.

"McNash."

"Crusher, it's me!" It was Spike, my beta-buddy, and he sounded waggy.

I kept my voice low. "I told you never to call me on duty."

"But it's about tomorrow's prizefight!"

"Listen, Spike, things have—"

"I got tickets—two tickets!"

"Tickets?" I lowered my voice again. "To Solidarity Stadium?"

"Twenty-second row! So close we might get some blood sprayed on us!"

"*Sheesh!*" I couldn't believe it. "Two tickets? How'd you get your fangs on them?"

"My number came up, Crusher, just like I knew it would!"

"A raffle?"

"The hiss and squawk. *The Dusty Dingus Happy Hour.*"

"You won a radio competition?"

"A sports quiz, Crusher! I knew all my study would pay off! You comin' or what?"

For a moment I pictured myself sitting high and mighty in Solidarity Stadium, chugging on a tingle-water, chomping on a chicken wing, cheering Rocky Cerberus. This was going to be the biggest fight of the year, the night when the doggies showed the kitty cats a thing or two. Every mutt in the Kennels would kill to be there; every cop in the force had applied for arena duty. And here was my best pal, telling me he had top-grade tickets. It seemed too good to be true.

But then, in a horrible flashback, I remembered the mixmastered bodies on the chrome slabs. The stink of cat in my dreams. The killstare of the chief. And I knew I couldn't commit myself to anything.

"Fang it," I said. "You know what I'd do to be there, Spike, but at the moment . . ."

"At the moment?"

"I don't know . . . there's something going on here, I can't say too much."

A chuckle from Spike, like he didn't swallow it. "You're kidding, ain't you?"

"I wish I was, pal. But there's a new case here, as curly as they come."

A hollow pause. "You really saying you can't make it?"

"I reckon not. I'm all tied up. So count me out."

Silence for a few seconds, then: "I can wait till—"

"Nah, don't wait for me, pal. I ain't gonna be there. That's all there is to it."

"Gee . . . if you say so."

"You go by yourself. Have a good time."

A pause, then a flattened voice. "I guess I'll see what happens, Crusher."

I felt like I'd swiped his blanket. Spike and I went way back. We'd been to the same obedience school. We hunted wild pigs. We chased bitches in heat. We even (not something I cared to remember) were prisoners of war together. But where I'd found something in the heat of the battle—pride, defiance, something—Spike had lost it. Even now he lived in a doghouse ringed with razor wire, jagged glass, and sentry lights, like he couldn't get his bobble out of the prison camp. The war had stir-fried his brainpot.

I got out of the building without the chief sniffing me and took a squad tooter down to the wharf. The air was clouded with flies: blowflies, green-and-blue flashers, bloodsuckers, maggot factories. The wharf was still sealed off with tape. A nervous young spaniel was doing sentry duty. The wetnoses from SI, the floppy-eared lot of them, were waiting for me obediently. I found my full barrel-chested voice:

"Listen up, doggies. Whatever you've heard about this case I want you to flush it from your bobbles right now. We got a murder scene here. We got a few pools of stale blood from the victims—two 'weilers and a cat, an alley cat most likely. Most important, we got a killer off the chain. And it's this killer I need you to track now. I want a scent trail, doggies, and I want it fast."

"Any idea of the killer's ID?" one of the beagles chirped.

"Make a difference?"

"There's gonna be a lot of trails here—it'd sure help."

"Okay," I sighed. "Word from the S and D rooms is that we're looking for a cat."

"A *cat?*" the beagle said.

"That's what Dr. Barnabus tells me."

There were grumbles—the beagles didn't like Barnabus any more than I did.

"All right, put a muzzle on it. At least you know what you're sniffing for. So give me a hard-target search. The whole district. Every doghouse, fleahouse, cathouse, and stinkhouse. And snap to it!"

As they went to work I headed into Slinky Joe's Sardine Cannery to ask about Flasha Lightning. But no one had heard from the whippet all day—he hadn't jangled in sick; he hadn't jangled in at all. But he was a scumlicker, and no one expected any better. I got his last-known flopdown and headed outside. To my surprise, the beagles were already waiting for me.

"What's the meat?" I asked.

"Nothing," one said.

"What do you mean, nothing?"

"No trail."

I looked down the fly-blown wharf. "You couldn't pick up the scent, through all this stink?"

"We picked up everything there was to pick up. Two 'weilers—"

"The heavies."

"—and a cat. The victim you were talking about. There's cat blood on the wharf, with traces of gunpowder, all the way to the edge. But nothing else. No trail of any other cat."

I frowned. "What're you talking about?"

"From the street to the murder scene is nothing but vehicle scent: styrene-butadiene tires and engine oil. Spots of diesel. Minute traces of saliva, urine, and scurf. A lot of loose hair. Most of it matches the files."

I knew the beagles kept detailed sniff-records of every cop and registered newshound. "Nothing else at all?" I asked. "No cats?"

"Only the one that went into the water."

"What about other dogs?"

"Fish packers, salty seadog scents—too many to count."

I tried to think it through. Did that mean that the murderer was a dog after all? One of the local workers maybe? His trace lost amid all the colliding stench? Or did it mean that the killer, cat or not, had escaped the scene by some other means?

I looked up. Even now a thwucker was heading out of town. When they needed to get from Kathattan to their resorts downstate, the pussies usually took a thwucker, a light plane, the high-speed monorail, or a luxury yacht—anything to avoid having to put a paw in the Kennels. But could one of them really drop out of the sky, dice the 'weilers up, and then vanish back into the clouds?

"Barnabus is getting old," the beagles said to me, and I could feel them—all the wetnoses—begging me to cast a slur on the old basset.

But I only growled. "All right, pack it up. I want a report on my desk by two. And speak to no one about this, that clear?"

As they headed back to their dogcart I took another look around the wharf, remembering Flasha Lightning's sweating tongue, his spluttering witness report. Clearly the whippet wasn't telling us everything. Because he'd seen the killer? Because he'd seen a thwucker?

When I reached the tooter the barkbox was hissing. I picked up the mike. "McNash."

A squeaky voice. "Detective? Forensic Pathology here. I was told to jangle you."

"Go ahead."

"The saliva samples on the dog carcasses show traces of FIV."

"FIV?"

"Feline Immunodeficiency Virus."

"A cat disease?"

"Uh-huh. Also evidence of endo- and ectoparasitical infections in the blood samples."

"Meaning?"

"The subject had fleas, Detective."

"A lowlife?" Nothing from Kathattan had fleas.

"Traces of flea medication are extremely minimal. I'd say very lowlife."

"Okay," I said. "I'll check in later. Over and out."

A lowlife cat. I sat for a long time in the tooter, thinking about it. Could Barnabus really be wrong after all? Was it possible there was only one cat all along—the victim, the trash-munching alley cat already in the S and D rooms? That he'd sprayed some blood on his killers before getting drowned? And could it be, like I always said, that the 'weilers themselves had been ambushed by a dog? Or dogs?

And could I still keep the case out of the paws of the FBI?

I gobbled a blowfly that was buzzing near my snout. I got the motor growling. I backed up the tooter and headed for the road. I needed to track down Flasha Lightning. But first of all there was a bar I needed to visit.

TOBY SHAW RAN a traditional Irish watering hole—Smell o' the Bog—with peatwater on tap and plenty of mashed potato on the menu. The place always drew a rowdy crowd, especially on Friday nights, when there were hoop-jumping and banshee-howling contests. What Shaw didn't advertise, but what was an open secret anyway, was that hidden in the basement was an illegal betting saloon—a smoky, windowless room, thronged day and night with all sorts of mutts, working dogs mainly, waging small fortunes on the grey races. I knew it, the chief knew it, the whole force knew it, but nobody did a thing, because Shaw was a priceless informer.

"Top o' the mornin' to ya."

"Still morning?"

"Always morning to an Irish Terrier."

"And always dinnertime to a bullie. Spare a minute?"

"To be sure, to be sure."

He was half Basenji, from which he got his smarts, and half Irish, from which he got his temperament. He played up the Irish half, though, kitting himself out in a waistcoat of green tartan and a shamrock-shaped tie, and smiling just about permanently with his eyes and snapper. He was as much a performer as Rin-Tin-Tin.

"How might I be o' help to you?"

I did a quick scope around the bar, where a couple of regulars

32

were eyeing us from the stools. "This ain't for general exhibition."

Shaw grinned. "You'd be wanting to visit the leprechaun's grotto?"

"If that's what you're calling it now."

"To be sure, to be sure."

We shifted to the rear of the joint, where Shaw maintained a little cubbyhole filled with mounted rabbit heads and paw prints of world-famous sprinters. A fire was always crackling, even in summer. From downstairs, seeping through the soundproofing, came the din of the gambling den.

"Mind if I smoke, laddie?" Sliding behind his desk, Shaw was already jamming a pipe with a blend of field clippings and cow dung.

"Go ahead. I won't be here long anyway. Just a few names I want to toss in the dish."

"Savage Brown and Lucifer Thorn?"

I blinked. "That's a good start."

Shaw released a cloud of smoke—it smelled like Sunday in the park. "I read the rags."

"The rags didn't name names."

"And I smell things on the wind."

"Care to divulge your sources?"

"Come now, laddie, you know the score." Shaw's network was more secretive than the CIA. "All I know is Savage and Lucifer met their Master last night in ways that might make an undertaker charge overtime rates."

"You don't look diced up about it."

"Savage and Lucifer lost their currency when Cujo Potenza got whacked. They became 'weilers-for-rent. No one'll miss 'em."

"Know who they were working for recently?"

"Wish I could say so."

"A biscuit under the table loosen your memory?"

"Come now, laddie"—Shaw actually looked offended—"I'm sellin' you no froth. Truth be told, Savage and Lucifer played muscle dog here a couple of years ago. But I had to dispense with them. They were gettin' a little snappy with the regulars."

"No good as bouncers?"

"No good at anythin', except whacking. If they made trophies for whacking"—he gestured to the sporting trophies—"their cabinets would be eternally full."

"So they wouldn't be working for charity, these two?"

"They'd be hired by someone who wanted to make sure the whacked stayed whacked, if you get my meaning. And had enough meat-tickets to pay for it."

I didn't like the sound of it. "So the fact that these two hippos got whacked themselves . . . that'd have to make some ears prick up 'round here?"

Shaw puffed out a cloud of smoke. "It's got tongues wagging."

"Any idea of who might be behind it?"

"Not the way it was done."

"What's that mean?"

"Casserole work's not the way of professionals. A professional puts a slug in the back of someone's bobble then bins the evidence. If he's desperate maybe he puts the body through a grinder. But to make a meat stew out of two victims and leave the mess steaming on the pier . . ." Shaw let the image hang in the air like his pipe smoke.

"What about Flasha Lightning—name meaning anything to you?"

"Sounds like a bunny chaser."

"A whippet. A fish packer. Sure you never heard of him?"

Shaw shook his head. "I can float his tag on the breeze, if you've got a minute."

"I'd be grateful."

Shaw left by the back staircase—a cloud of smokestick fumes blew in through the door—and I sat watching the little buzz-screen in the corner that was tuned permanently to the Reynard Sports Channel. They were doing a throat-lumping story on Rocky Cerberus in the lead-up to Friday's prizefight: Rocky frolicking with his pups; Rocky sparring with his four twin brothers; Rocky belting into a side of beef at the Chump's factory. "I kinda feel like I'm fighting for the whole of dogdom," he said. They were actually playing howl music under his words.

Then there was a news flash: the Persians had launched a massive terrorist attack on the Afghans, threatening global oil production. President Goodboy had issued an immediate condemnation of the attack and called for an emergency meeting of the United Breeds. When he spoke of world threats the prez seemed to grow a few inches, like he actually knew what he was talking about.

"Voting for Goodboy, are you?" It was Shaw, returning from downstairs trailing a shroud of smoke.

"Nothing'll change if I do or don't. I'm more interested in Flasha Lightning."

"A real buttrag, they tell me. Changes his tag with his lodgings. Called himself Jaws McGraw last year. But there's more bite in his name than his snapper."

"I can vouch for that. Any idea where he's flopping now?"

"Try the junkyard in Mongrolia. They say he snoozes there."

"Trash always returns to trash."

"Sounds like Scripture, laddie. Anything else I can do for you, 'fore you go?"

But I was already rising. "If I'm gonna make it to Mongrolia I'll need to get out of the starting box right away. But thanks for the meat. If there's anything I can overlook, just lemme know."

"I scratch your ruff, you scratch mine?"

I spared enough time to return his spud-licking grin. "To be sure, Toby Shaw."

WHEN I GOT back to the tooter I found the barkbox squawking again, but I dialed down the volume and took off at once. Mongrolia was at the rump end of town. I didn't have time for jawback.

It was afternoon already and a skywriter was puffing a familiar message in the blue: *Canem te esse memento.* Nobody in the Kennels was sure what it meant. Some said it was an ad for a new worm treatment. Others said it was a word puzzle with a million-biscuit reward. Still others insisted it was Latin for "Remember thou art only a dog." Whatever it meant, it didn't make us feel good.

The traffic in Pugkeepsie was nose-to-tail and moving about as fast as a garden slug. I swung into some twisty side streets (they said the cat planners of San Bernardo had created a maze of dead ends, loops, chicanes, and crescents just to keep us mutts occupied) but it only got worse. Approaching the Avenue of Freedom I got so hemmed in I couldn't even crank up the howler to clear a path. Ahead, a grizzly old collie was standing outside his tooter, chewing on a beefstrip.

I stuck my bobble out the window. "What's happening, pal?"

The collie shrugged. "Some sort of parade."

"Antiwar?"

"Antieverything. The Party of the Perpetual Underdog."

I gave a low snarl. The PPU was a ragbag collection of

37

disobedients who didn't want to answer to anyone and questioned the whole "pack mentality." I got infected with their ideas myself in that murky age between pup and dog. But I came to my senses eventually. More recently, the Reynard Media had done a good job of exposing them for what they were—mangy, ungroomed, distempered . . . bad dogs.

There was a Stinky Tex's Chicken Ranch by the side of the road and it was pumping out so many spicy aromas that I started drooling over the steering wheel. I hocked the tooter into park—no one was shifting an inch—and mushed inside to order a Crispy Skin Special.

"Any peppers with that, pardner?" The counter-jockey was wearing chaps and a cattle dog's hat.

"Skip the peppers, but I'll have a half-gallon of tank water."

Back in the tooter I wolfed down the lot, bones and all, in half a minute. I had a feeling I'd regret it—that wishbone was still refusing to make way—but as my pappy used to say, "If Our Master had meant us to eat mince, he wouldn't have given us choppers."

I hit Mongrolia at four p.m. It was a down-at-heel district, the inland counterweight to Fly's Picnic, full of bone-boiling works, rubber-toy factories, and sniffrag storehouses. Beyond was nothing but sooty trees and industrial waste all the way to Flickertail. I parked in the lot of the Mongrolia Municipal Waste Management and Recycling Lot—in the old days we called them junkyards—and sprayed some extra flea powder down my shirt.

The racket inside was like a war of harmonicas. Huge steam engines with pitbull jaws were munching into old tooters and dropping them into metal contractors. The shrieks weren't all of steel either—sometimes an old stray would get thrown in with the wash and no one cared to punch the Off button.

I fronted up to the site manager's shack and flashed my tags.

"Flasha Lightning—name mean anything to you?"

"Sounds like a hump-and-grind star." The manager looked half pug, with a pug's surliness.

"Might be traveling under the name Jaws McGraw."

"This ain't a hotel, you know. I don't keep no register."

"Good thing for you, stumpy. An unlicensed flopjoint could get you tossed in the cage quick-smart." I hooked a nail under his collar. "Come with me."

"I can't leave the—"

"I said come with me!" I wasn't fielding any lip from no yellow-toothed pug. "You're taking me on a little tour, gorgeous. And we'll start with the perimeter." I rammed him through the swinger.

"Whaddaya need me for?"

"Exit holes . . . tunnels . . . fence breaks . . . don't tell me you don't know where they are."

We headed for a huge mountain range of tooter wrecks. Puddles of rusty water were swimming with larvae. The rats were the size of raccoons. At the back of the mountain the pug found a hole in the chain-link fence you could've driven a dairy cow through.

I started dragging over a generator carcass. "Help me out here, angel face."

"What's this all about?"

"I can't outrun a whippet," I said, "but I can sure corner him."

We blocked every exit in the yard with an assortment of wrecks and metal sidings. Then I ordered the pug to bolt the gate. And I went whippet-stalking.

I upended trash, trundled over corrugated sheets, made sure everyone knew I was there. And there was no shortage of worthless mutts kenneled into the trash—"junkyard dogs," they called themselves. Fleabags on the lam, scumlickers without a biscuit to their name, curs with a taste for garbage. I glimpsed their slitted peepers and smelled their soaking filth. And I enjoyed scaring the ticks off them.

"Flasha Lightning!" I kept hollering. "I'm looking for a fish packer called Flasha Lightning!"

Eventually I heard a clatter of old pots, smelled a waft of sardines, and from the corner of my eye saw an eel-like figure spring out from a nest of old washing machines and streak for the fence like a genuine flash of lightning. I scrambled over a pile of spring mattresses and zigzagged after him. As he curled around a wall of busted shopping trolleys, I barked, *"Flasha!"* just to make him run faster.

There was a sound like a spoon gonging a dinner can—my mouth actually watered—and I knew I had him.

When I rounded the trolleys I saw him with his bobble in his paws: he'd bolted blindly for a hole and rammed headfirst into an old filing cabinet. I ripped out a choker chain and had it looped around his neck before he had a chance to whimper.

"Whatsa matter, Flasha, lost your thunder?" I jerked the chain so hard that he flew up into my face.

"I didn't do nothing!"

"You're coming with me to the cophouse, junkie."

"I don't wanna go back there!"

"Not like you got a choice, is it?"

I belted him on the bobble with my skull—nobody was around to see us—and dragged him to the tooter scratching and squealing like a poodle on the way to the vet.

40

"I DONE NOTHING wrong."

"Snip it, whippet."

"I got no reason to go back there."

"You'll be going to the pound if you don't play ball. And you know where they send you from there."

I shot a glance into the mirror. Chained to the security bar, Flasha was looking left and right, licking his chops, shaking—a typically shiftless junkie.

"And don't get any ideas in your poky little head," I added. "You ain't scampering anywhere on my watch."

At the cophouse I banged him through the front swingers like a hospital gurney, hoping to get to the grill rooms before I got noticed. But I'd only made it to the front desk when an old blowfly buzzed out of the shadows.

"Crusher—just come from the lost luggage office?"

I cursed the desk sergeant for letting him in. "Nipper Sweeney," I sighed. "Shouldn't you be sniffing in the gutter?"

He sniggered. "Got any scraps for me?"

"Nothing worth swallowing."

"Come on, buddy, you owe me one!"

"I owe you nothin', pal—not after the front page."

"What did I say that was wrong?"

"You bit off more than you can chew, sunshine."

A guffaw. "I ain't nothin' but a newshound, Crusher."

41

But I was already around the corner.

In the grill cubicles I found a young retriever sniffing his paw and told him to clear out. The room was made of cinder blocks and stank of urine. There was mirror-glass along one wall and a bony table in the middle. I flung Flasha into a plastic chair and shot a glance at the ticker.

"Okay, junkie, it's seven-thirty. By seven thirty-five I want a full witness report, exactly like you saw it—no gravy, no trimmings, just the meat, get me?"

He was rubbing the bump on his bobble. "I don't want no trouble."

"Shut up and start yapping."

He gulped. "Have I got your promise that—"

"Only promise you got is that I'll bite your sniffer off if you don't make with the meat."

He glanced at the two-way mirror. "But I told you what I saw . . . at Slinky Joe's, I already told you."

"An impression of movement?"

"That's right."

"And before that?"

"Before that?"

"You said you heard two gunshots, a cat squeal, and a splash—that right?"

"Maybe."

"Whaddaya mean, maybe?"

He was sweating. "I don't want no trouble."

I leaned across the table and dragged him into my face. "You want a deathshake, pal? You wanna feel your bony hide hit the tiles for the last time?"

He looked left and right, up at the ceiling—every which way—like he'd just eaten someone's homework.

"The *truth*, whippet."

He started to splutter. "It . . . it was much like you said."

"Like what?"

"Like you said, but no cat squeal."

"What's that mean? You heard no squeal?"

"No, not that. I—"

"*What?*"

He gulped. "I heard a squeal, but it wasn't no cat."

"Come again?" I barked. "No cat? You never heard a cat?"

He looked like he was sitting on a hot plate. "No," he squeaked.

"You didn't see any cats at all? Didn't hear them?"

"No."

"So two gunshots, a whirl, and a dog squeal, and then a splash? That what you're yapping?"

"Yeah."

I shook him. "Then why'd you lie?"

"I didn't lie."

"Why'd you run?"

"Run from where?"

"From here—from the station. Got something against cops?"

A whisper. "I got a nose—"

"*What?*"

"I got a nose for trouble."

"You got a nose for popping balloons, whippet. You willing to go on the record? Or do I gotta slap you around some more?"

He swallowed saliva. "Guess so."

The door creaked open and Flasha looked like he'd set eyes on a grizzly bear.

I turned, but it was only Bud Borzoi, all out of breath. "Chief wants to see you, Crusher."

"You're just in time," I said, straightening. "Our choice-cut witness is going to make it official. Get the camera cranked up. And Bud." I stopped long enough to give him a front-gate stare. "Don't ever let a suspect out of your choppers again. It don't look good. For anyone."

"Sure thing, Crusher." His head was tilted, innocentlike.

"Back in two shakes of a cocker's tail," I said.

I shot a glance at Flasha on the way out, but I could see his own tail was tight between his legs.

THE CHIEF WAS bristling. "What's going on, McNash? I've been calling you all day."

"The barkbox wasn't working, Chief."

"A fuse had blown—oh, right. Do I look like Goofy to you? That story's as old as Anubis."

"I was busy, that's the truth. I had to head back to—"

"A cat?" The chief was glaring at me. "Dr. Barnabus tells me we're dealing with a murderous cat? And you didn't think this was important enough to tell me?"

"I needed to verify it first."

"What's there to verify?" He waved at a pile of printouts. "Saliva samples. Blood samples. DNA analysis."

I shook my head. "Have you spoken to the SI boys yet? I'm telling you, it don't add up. There's no evidence of a killer cat at the murder scene."

"Are you accusing Dr. Barnabus of error?"

"He's getting old, Chief—his senses might be drooping like everything else."

"What about forensic pathology?"

"They never said anything about a cat killer. And SI's the same."

The chief frowned. "So let me get this straight. Barnabus claims a cat killed the 'weilers. SI says there's no trace of a cat at the wharf?"

45

"No, SI says there's a trace of only one cat—the victim, the lowlife who got dumped in the drink. So if there's another cat, a killer, then where'd he go—into thin air? And now I've got the word of our number-one witness—I snared him this afternoon."

"The worthless whippet?"

I ignored the worthless part. "And he backs it up, Chief. No killer cat. He saw no killer cat."

"He actually said there was no killer cat?"

"Two gunshots, a dog squeal, and a splash. But no killer cat. And no reason to call the FBI."

"That right?" The chief didn't look convinced. "Sure you're not hearing what you want to hear, McNash? You've done that before."

I bit down the instinct to get snappy. "Think about it, Chief. The 'weilers have been paid to dispose of a scumbag alley cat, probably a powder dealer. Maybe they scratch him in the Lupus, maybe before. Anyway, he leaves some DNA on them in the process. Then he gets dumped in the bay. Then some rival goons spring up, there's some gunplay, and the 'weilers get minced."

"And the killers?"

"Jump in the soup and dog-paddle away."

The chief's brow was still furrowed. "Thin as a cracker, McNash."

"I'm telling you, Chief—the killers are mutts, they gotta be."

The jangler was sounding. "You got the whippet's account on tape?"

"'Bout to."

"Then come back here when you do. I want to see the evidence. And I don't want this getting off the chain."

"Count on me," I said.

But back in the grill rooms, I found the whippet all cagey again.

"I don't know what I seen . . ."

I frowned. "Whaddaya yapping about now?"

"I'm saying it was . . . too quick . . . I ain't sure."

"What's going on?" I looked at Bud, who shrugged, and back at Flasha. "Five minutes ago you made a statement. Two gunshots, a dog cry, and a splash. Did you say that or not?"

Fleas were hopping off the whippet, he was so bloodless. "I don't remember no more . . . I really don't remember . . ."

I bared my fangs. "What's going on, Flasha? You playin' games?"

"I don't know what I seen . . ."

I thrust my muzzle into his crooked little ear. "You want me to hook you up to the slap machine? Or should I just take a bite out of you right now?"

"Crusher"—it was Bud—"the camera's on."

I pulled back, blood pumping. Bud was right. I couldn't get caught on tape ripping a chunk out of a witness—not again. "Give yourself a minute to think about it, junkie," I snapped, and went out the swingers with Bud.

We spoke under a photo of Vice President Palomine. "I don't get it," I said. "The whippet was about to howl like a wolf. Now he's clamped up like a cookie jar. Anything happen while I was gone?"

Bud shrugged. "He's a jukebox, Crusher."

"A jukebox?"

"He plays a hundred different tunes. You just gotta know what buttons to jab."

I snorted—the pup had gotten himself some good lines. "You leave the room at any stage?"

"Only to set up the camera."

"And no one got to him?"

"I woulda seen if someone did."

I thought about it. "And what happened last night? When you first brought him in?"

"We hadn't even got to my desk—I was going to clacker up a report—when he sprang off like a jackrabbit."

"Nobody spoke to him? Nobody gave him a lip curl?"

Bud shook his head. "I just think he's allergic to cop hair. He's as low as a dachshund's pecker."

At another time I might've found it funny, hearing a borzoi buttsnipe a whippet. But I didn't get much time to ponder it.

"*Crusher.*" It was Chesty White, his head around the corner. "Chief wants to see you."

"Too late—I already seen him."

"This is new, Crusher. We got another witness—someone who saw the killer just an hour ago."

"*What?*" I said. "Who?"

"A cat."

"A *cat?*" I blinked. "What sort of cat?"

"A cat in a hat."

"A cat in a *hat?*"

"Or something like that."

FIRST THING I noticed was that it wasn't exactly a cat.

Second thing I noticed was that it wasn't exactly a hat.

Third thing I noticed—it was clear from the way he was dressed, from the way he smelled—was that it was a thief.

Everyone knows that cats make the best burglars. The way they prowl across roofs, drop through skylights, slink around corners, squeeze through security bars, and when necessary just wait and wait and wait. With all that irritating catty patience. They write books about such cats. They make movies about them. They get admired like no other criminals. Because they got smarts. And class. And because they're cats.

But what was sitting now in the carpeted reception room, wearing a beret and a black skivvy, was no cat. He was a two-toned papillon with shaggy butterfly ears. He had a little black mustache and pointy beard. He was sipping from a creamy drink. He was draped in a cashmere blanket. He was speaking in a French accent. And he clearly wanted to be a cat.

". . . eet was . . . not good! *Pas bon!* Never have I seen such *horreur!*"

I looked around. The chief was keeping his distance. A secretary was taking notes. A couple of patrolhounds—probably the ones who'd netted him in the first place—were looking on with admiration. And the thief himself was sitting in the station's "special chair" (the one with unscratched upholstery), sipping his little drink, and shaking his shaggy little head, happy to be soaking up the attention. It said a lot, that a common thief could get the royal treatment in a cophouse. It said it paid to be a cat. Or at least act like a cat.

"What's going on?" I barked.

The others looked at me like I'd interrupted President Goodboy. The chief growled: "Good of you to join us, McNash. Monsieur Charrière here was just describing what he saw."

"That right?" I said. "And what did he see?"

The chief stiffened, like he didn't like repeating himself in front of a guest. "Monsieur Charrière was in the process of liberating some jewels from a storage facility in Chitterling. A burglar alarm went off and a guard—a Doberman Pinscher—went in to investigate. The guard was killed."

I looked at the papillon. "You saw it?"

The thief shivered, like a cold breeze had sneaked under his blanket. "*Quelle horreur!* Never have I seen such a thing as zis! Eet was . . . how you say?"

"An impression of movement?"

"An impression?" He shook his head. "*Mais non* . . . I saw eet most clearly! A giant feral cat—a cat like I have never seen! Eet came from nowhere!"

My pumper had started rattling. "You're saying you saw the killer—the killer of the Dobie?"

"His teeth, like razors! His claws! His greasy blue fur!"

"A panther."

"*Non, non!* A cat! *Un chat sauvage!*"

"You're lying," I said.

The papillon looked insulted. "*Porquoi?* I do not lie, monsieur!"

"You're a lying dog. And a thief."

"I am a cat burglar!"

"You're a scumlicking thief—why should I believe you?"

"Steady, boy," growled the chief.

I felt my pulse grinding in my head. "But this is gumrot, Chief—it's a setup."

"The Dobie's body is with Dr. Barnabus now," the chief said. "A cursory examination suggests he was killed by the same cat who took out the Rottweilers. And that means we've got ourselves a serial killer. A *cat* serial killer."

I shook my head. "But it don't add up. If it's a cat, how come there's no traces of him escaping the wharf?"

"The reporting officers at the storage facility"—the chief gestured to the patrolhounds—"have already discovered cat prints leading away from the Dobie's body."

"I saw eet!" the papillon insisted. "With my own two eyes. Ze feral cat! *Le chat infernal!*"

I almost lunged at him, he was such a pest. But the chief stepped forward, swelled out in front of me, and jerked his head at the door. "This way."

In the corridor outside he made sure we were alone, then gave me his best killstare.

"You really wanna be patrolling fences again, McNash? Never speak to a witness like that."

"Chief, he's a gem-lifter."

"He's our best witness so far."

"He's as crooked as my hind legs."

"He turned himself in voluntarily. He wanted to help."

"That don't mean we gotta clip his nails, does it?"

"It means he deserves some respect. If he didn't come forward, where would we be? Did you get a statement from that whippet?"

Now my eyes flickered. "I'm working on it."

"You didn't get a thing, did you?" The chief's compost-heap breath was wafting over me.

"Chief, these things take time."

"It's too late, McNash. We've got a positive sighting now. From a reliable witness. And you—"

"A reliable witness? Why should we believe a burglar? He *wants* to believe a cat could kill a Dobie. He *wants* to. Because *he wants to be a cat himself.*"

The chief was shaking his head. "You're all out of cookies, McNash. We've got ourselves a killer cat. And that means the FBI."

A wave of revulsion prickled my hair. "Just one more day, Chief—that's all I need! We don't need the FBI!"

"It's too late, McNash. I—"

"I can work it out, trust me! Together, all of us, we can do it!"

"I said it's too late. I've already made the call. An agent is on his way from Kathattan right now."

"Humphrey MacFluff?"

The chief took on a stiff-tailed look. "Not him. A new agent. Someone we've never dealt with before."

"Who?"

"Special Agent Cassius Lap."

"*Lap?*" I said. "What sort of name is Lap?"

The chief got even stiffer. "He's Siamese, they say."

"*Siamese?*" I repeated in a horrified whisper. "Did you say *Siamese?*"

The wishbone that had been caught in my gizzards suddenly jarred loose and headed for the dogflap.

WE DIDN'T KNOW any different, Spike and me. We were just a couple of young wags from the 'Loin. On weekends we played catch, raided trash cans, dug up flower gardens, and danced through wet cement. If we had enough meat tickets, we headed north for some deer hunting.

But then a letter landed in the fencepot from the Department of Vigorous Defense. We were to report immediately to the local recruiting office. From there we'd be assigned to the appropriate attack-dog squadron. We were to be stripped of all our hearth-rug comforts and softpaw inclinations. We were to eat rice and oatmeal. We were to flop on cold cement. We were to snooze just twelve hours a day. We were to be poked, slapped, roared at, and dogwhipped. They were going to make us killing machines. They were going to make us dogs of war.

And we *were* at war. We didn't know why. It didn't matter. President Willy Patton, a bullie like Spike and me, had assured us the North Siamese were threatening the free world. He had the support of half the United Breeds, mutts and moggies alike. And that was enough for us. What did us woofers know about such complicated things? For us, all that was important was knowing what to kill, and how to kill it.

I did eight weeks of seize-and-shake training under the feisty little Sergeant Barkman. In no time I could cock a gun faster than I could cock my leg. I could burst through walls. I could bite through tin. You only had to shake a pajama leg at me and I'd smell cat. I'd charge over broken glass, hot tar, even fried chicken waste, just to get a taste of feline.

I got noticed. There was a top-secret mission needing a gundog. A cat commander had gone rabid in the jungles near the source of the Shorthair River. He'd clustered around him a shaggy-coated army of filthy curs and impractical cats—grass chewers, the lot of them—and turned their brains to marrow-bone jelly. They sniffed jungle blossoms. They flopped flank to flank. They believed in everything and nothing. They obeyed no orders, answered to no commands, didn't even get them-selves registered.

I considered it a great honor to take out the leader of such garbage.

But things didn't go well. I plowed up the Shorthair in a sput-tering patrol boat with a crew of snarling sea dogs. The jungle closed around us like an invalid's backyard. The fleas were the size of leeches, and the leeches the size of lawyers. One by one my crew died off—claimed by poison baits, dog traps, distemper.

Near Seal Point I was dozing on the deck of the floater, alone and exhausted, when a clowder of North Siamese dropped out of a ban-ban tree, ripped off my dog tags, and snapped a collar around me before I had a chance to bite. They pinned me down and fanged a needle through my hide. The last thing I saw was a burlap bag closing around my bobble, so for a second I thought I'd been put down.

I woke in a bamboo cage, like some sort of common animal. Through the bars a Siamese in a knitted jacket was prodding me with a sharpened stick. Others were standing around giggling. I thrashed and snarled, but I was chained tight. The kitties purred with delight.

"You snappy snappy," the green jacket laughed. "Snappy puppy, puppy snappy!"

I vowed right then that one day I'd rip the smile from his sleek little Siamese face.

They hosed me with ice-cold water, smashed me across the muzzle with a rolled-up newspaper, taunted me with live chickens and mouthwatering roast mutton. They fed me corks, toasted bones, and bubble gum, so that my insides clogged and swelled. They tortured me with a tennis ball on a rubber band. At night they clustered behind a fence and caterwauled like a thousand alley cats.

They thought they could break me. But bullies never break—they only explode.

I got my chance six months in.

My best buddy, Spike from the 'Loin, got carted in one day, trussed up like a Thanksgiving turkey. At first we pretended not to know each other—we didn't talk, didn't sniff, didn't even look at each other. But then one night, when the kitties were setting off fireworks for some local feast, we hatched a plan in low growls like distant thunder.

A week later we were leashed and muzzled and herded into the biggest of the straw huts. There was a deep pit in the middle with rows of cash-waving kitties crowded around the sides. They forced us to the edge, ripped off our restraints, and shoved us into the hole, thinking we'd go at each other's throats at once.

But we did no such thing. We circled each other. We snarled a little. Maybe we even gave a little nip or two. We were like two gray-whiskered Labs in the local park. And the kitties were getting itchy.

They hurled fish skeletons down at us. Chicken claws. They hissed. They spat furballs. Anything to fire us up. But Spike and I weren't biting. We were only waiting. Waiting with the patience of a cat.

It didn't take long.

There was a hush, a gasp, and into the hole they tossed a third soldier, a huge pitbull covered in scars.

It was exactly what we'd been waiting for.

With the pittie's head between us we immediately clanged our chests together. The pittie dropped like a sack of kitchen refuse. Spike jumped on his back and hunched himself—two dogs one atop the other like a stepladder, a springboard.

I bounded onto Spike's back immediately and launched out of the pit, hackles waving, fangs bared. The kitties looked dumbslapped.

You don't really want to know what happened next.

But that's how I got the name Crusher.

SO THIS WAS me, late at night in the cophouse, waiting for the arrival of Cassius Lap. Thinking why does it have to be a cat? Thinking why, of all cats, does it have to be a Siamese?

When I rotated back home after the war I just couldn't deal with it—the very existence of cats. For my own good I was chained up in a hospital for mad dogs, but the tiniest scent of cat was enough to get me frothing. They put me through their detoxification program. Step-by-step they were going to suck the taste of cat blood from my brainpot. They were going to empty my gutsack and make me beg for my dinner. Then they'd make me associate food with reward. And then make me associate reward with cat-love.

That was the plan, anyway.

Six months later my doctor jumped the back gate in frustration. Desperate, they brought in a sadistic dancing-bear trainer, a husky from Siberia. By the end of his visit I was crackling with so much electricity that I wasn't allowed under the hoses in case I sizzled everyone else in the yard.

I learned to love cats at 350 v. Or at least how to pretend to love 'em. I learned to leash my impulses, which is another name for pretending.

But I knew in my pumper that something wasn't right.

I wasn't officially mad—because officially my mission hadn't even existed—so I was allowed, when I got out, to join the

Police Dog Force. I was *drawn* to the Police Dog Force. I did all the training, I passed all the exams, I swore with upraised paw to uphold the law. At the graduation ceremony the guest of honor was the mayor of Kathattan himself, a salt-and-pepper Ragdoll. I didn't even curl a lip when he stood just a few whiskerlengths away and addressed me.

"A fine-looking jaw you have there, Officer."

"Thank you, sir."

"Those slash marks on your snout—nothing sinister, I hope?"

"Just a tussle with some barbed wire, sir."

My taste for blood was gone, fried out, but in its place there was something even stronger—a secret taste for indignation. In my free time I found myself reading certain radical philosophies and underground texts: *Cat-aclysm: How Cats Took Over the World; Das Katipal; Cat o' Nine Tails: The Serfdom of the Canine World; Beware of the Dog: The Drive to Revolution.*

These were books that could have got me added to a blacklist someplace. A few might have got me arrested, even deregistered. But I needed to read them, whatever the cost. I had an appetite in me, a hunger for buried truths. For disgust. For anger. For anything that made me feel like a dog.

And I got plenty of that feeling. I read about the great feline aristocracy. The jeweled collars and mink-lined basket beds of Kathattan. The cans of pureed chicken breast and hummingbird tongues. The fancy mausoleums, bigger than most houses in the Kennels. And I learned about the shameful submission of dogs, who amazingly thought they were happier than cats—who were encouraged to buy into that propaganda—even while they were being beaten, tortured, scrap-fed, and worked to within an inch of their hides.

I read all this, and I got so riled up that for a few months I felt like I was back in that pit, that I'd broken through the dark days in the madhouse—that I was a lean mean biting machine again.

But then something strange happened. I went so far into my past that I broke through my war days, my drill-training days, my wild-running youth—I went right back to obedience school. And I got to thinking that the rules are greater than any single dog. That a mutt's life is too grubby and short to be worrying about boundaries. That you can be happy with your fences if you don't wonder too much what's on the other side. That there's no point whining or snarling or baying at the moon. Everyone knows a dog's life is a dog's life—nothing is going to make it anything more.

I didn't know if that was victory or defeat—I wasn't even sure if it wasn't a natural end in the whole brainwashing program— and I didn't care.

So this, like I say, was me that night. I still hated cats, and I loved hating them, but I didn't need to taste their blood on my licker. I'd worked with Humphrey MacFluff, a bloated Scottish Fold, and I despised every minute of it. But even when he over-ruled me, even when he tut-tutted at me, even when he treated me like a dumb dog—even when he did all those things, I didn't snap his tail off. It was enough to know that I could. But whether a Siamese would make me lose control—that was something I didn't want to think about.

I paced around the cophouse, trying to put everything in order before the cat arrived. I sat in on the Q&A with Charrière the cat burglar (you wouldn't call it an interrogation) and tried not to lose my temper when he ordered—and got—a herring sandwich. At my desk, I clackered up some paperwork, a real dog shuffle through triplicate forms. I had a yap with Bud Borzoi, working his toothpick so hard it'd worn to a splinter. I jangled my ex, Missy.

"Sorry I ain't seen the pups."

"Mother has a word for dogs like you."

"I'm tipping it's got four letters in it someplace."

She didn't laugh. "When are you going to show your snout?"

"Soon as I get a minute, lambchop."

"I've heard that before."

It was so hard to keep my mind fixed on the case. A buzz-screen in the corner of the yawn-and-stretch room was showing a late-night session of the United Breeds: the Afghan ambassador, wearing burlap robes and a dishrag hat, snarling and howling at a peke-faced Persian. But just when things started to get really tasty, they cut to an ad for Chump's Roast Lamb and Mustard Special. And an election ad for Brewster Goodboy—"STAY the course."

Then I heard an engine growling somewhere—it didn't sound like anything native—and I mushed over to the window. I looked down into the parking lot. And there, under the smoking sodium lamps, a sleek new Jaguar XJS was doing a perfect reverse park into the space next to my battered Rover.

I straightened my collar and pumped out my chest. I flared my nostrils. If dog claws were retractable, I would have popped them out.

Special Agent Cassius Lap had arrived.

HUMPHREY MACFLUFF WORE a shiny serge coat with shaggy cuffs and cream-stained lapels; what breezed through the doors now was kitted out in a superbly tailored suit of panther-black, a bone-white shirt, and a silk tie that shimmered like a crow's wing. MacFluff had tangled hair, a runny sniffer, and reeked of tuna sandwiches and Baileys; his replacement was brushed and blow-dried, bright blue-eyed, and giving off a scent that would make a civet swoon. MacFluff shuffled, waddled, and had to squeeze his great gut sideways through tight doorways; the new cat glided into the chief's office as smoothly as a serpent, curled around the desk, and in one nimble movement extracted and flipped open his ID, as if cats showed up at the station all the time and we might not know who he was.

"Special Agent Cassius Lap," he purred. "Feline Bureau of Investigation."

He was slim, above average in height—taller than me—and as finely cut as a chess piece. He had needle-straight whiskers, long pointed ears, semislanted eyes, and marshmallow cheeks. He was cinnamon point, though with slightly rounded features—not a true pedigree, it seemed, but he sure acted like one, and that made him extra gut-churning.

"A word about myself before we proceed," he said, like anyone present—me, the chief, Bud Borzoi, or Chesty White—had

61

asked for a biography. "I'm from Los Pumas originally, but I won a scholarship to the University of San Bernardo, where I earned my Ph.D. in canine-feline relations, graduating *summa cum leonine* and Phi Beta Katta, and devoting my first season at the FBI to profiling cat serial killers. I worked closely with Dr. Quentin Riossiti, the famous psychiatrist and sociologist, and later was instrumental in his conviction for murder. Since then I've been working in the Office of Interspecies Carnicide, side by side with Humphrey MacFluff, whom you know rather well in these parts. But if you have not yet heard of me personally, or read my work, it can only be because Agent MacFluff prefers, for his own reasons, to work without me."

He was speaking of MacFluff in a quiche-cutting tone, as if he, Lap, was already the leader of the pack. And as much as I didn't care for MacFluff, I cared even less for bluff-barking ama-teurs—it would be like Bud Borzoi telling them in Kathattan that I was his flankyapper.

"Very well, gentlehounds"—now he was dishing out orders— "I expect your full cooperation on this matter. As I understand it we have a bloodthirsty feral on the loose. We have three vic-tims, possibly more. We have two murder scenes five sprints apart. We have a limited amount of time before our killer strikes again. We have a large and vastly differentiated territory to explore. And no powerful scent . . . can I assume that?"

"Not until you walked in," I snarled.

Everyone looked at me like I'd just broken wind under the dinner table.

Lap himself fixed me with his cut-diamond irises. "And you might be?" he asked, cool as a spoon.

"I might be President Goodboy, but I'm not."

The chief suddenly cleared his throat. "Please forgive me for failing to introduce Max McNash, the detective in charge of the investigation. And please forgive McNash himself, for his impertinence."

I expected Lap to say something like "Think nothing of it," but he only stared at me with his icy Siamese eyes.

"Detective McNash," he said, "I've read about you, of course. I'll need you to fetch your reports on the case as soon as possible. I'll need you to fetch as many maps of the area as you can. Sewer maps also. Plans of the Katacombs. And aerial photographs. And I'd like a printout of all murders in the Kennels in the last two months, coordinated precisely to the maps."

"That's all?" I sneered.

"I'd like a transcription of all witness statements. The forensics report. Anything from ballistics would be appreciated. And I assume Sensory Investigation has made an examination of the murder scenes? I'll need to have a look at their notes. In fact, I'll need to speak to them personally. And to the witnesses if they're available. And the earliest arriving officers. It's imperative to comb the evidence for the tiniest, most innocuous clue. A pattern needs to be established. The pattern is always the key."

I snorted, like I couldn't believe it. "What—you mean you haven't already found one?"

He stared at me. "You've already arrived at a conclusion, Detective?"

"I have."

"Well, please avail us of your thoughts—that would be most helpful."

This was my big moment, but suddenly I had a tinfoil tongue. "Well, think about it," I said. "A Tom Doe is shot, and his killers are ripped to pieces. A cat burglar—a dog who wants to be a cat—is about to be caught in the act of theft, and the guard is ripped to pieces as well . . ."

He was still looking at me.

I tried desperately not to sound stupid. "Well, work it out for yourself. We got two ambushes. We got two unusually messy murders. We got some huge squirrel-munching cat, either a feral or someone made up to look like a feral, swooping in to take revenge, then taking off—into the clouds, for all we know—before anyone can get a hook on him."

Silence from Lap.

"So it's clear, ain't it? What we've got here is a cat enforcer. A cat avenger."

But Lap just kept staring at me, like I'd said the most bone-headed thing in the world. And eventually he nodded, as if he actually understood.

"Superpussy?" he said.

And that was it. Something snapped inside. I saw those sneering Siamese faces above the pit, I felt their vinegary cat spit on my snout, I tasted their blood like cod-liver oil on my tongue. And I couldn't help it—I lunged across the room, pumper thumping. "If you've got a better—"

But I hit a wall: the chief and Chesty White holding me back. I was just whiskerlengths away and—I'll give him this much—Lap didn't flinch an inch.

"Detective McNash," he said evenly—his eyes were half-lidded, like he was addressing a sloppy manicurist—"I would much prefer that we don't begin our investigation by tearing each other apart. You and I will be working very closely until we bring this killer to heel. Personal hostilities will only be a hindrance to our effectiveness." He thrust out a paw. "Shall we shake?"

I stared at his dainty little digits.

"Shake?" he said again.

Part of me wanted to crunch every bone in his scrawny frame. But another part of me wanted desperately to obey. It was like a trance.

"Shake?" he said again.

So—woozy, without any sense of control—I shook his velvety little paw. But I wasn't happy about it.

"That's a good dog," he said, and turned to the chief and Chesty White. "It's perfectly all right, gentlehounds, I can take over from here. But first of all Detective McNash and I will require a word together. In private, naturally." He looked back at me with twinkling eyes. "Shall we go for a walk, Detective?"

Shall we go for a walk?

Again there was that strange feeling inside—a real meat salad of emotions. Half of me had to stop my jaws from closing around his skull. But the other half had to fight to keep my tail from wagging.

WHEN HE LED me down the street it was still dark and our breath was rising in clouds. I was walking at Lap's heel, behind me was Bud Borzoi. When Lap noticed the uninvited company he turned.

"And your name is?"

Bud licked his chops. "Officer Borzoi."

"I'm sure you appreciate why we need to be alone, Officer Borzoi—please return to the station."

Bud looked at me. "But I—"

"But nothing." Lap pointed down the street. *"Back."*

"He can join us," I said. "Bud's no harm to anyone."

"I said *back.*" Lap wasn't fielding any arguments. "Home. *Now.*"

There was no doubting the steel in the cat's voice. And so—gulping, quivering—Bud slithered away, looking back for a second or third chance. But Lap, icy as a popsicle, was already striding down Duty Street.

"You have a regular eating place around here?" he asked. "Some place where police dogs congregate?"

"Right here," I said. "Butch's Greasy Dish Diner."

"Excellent," said Lap. "Then we know where to avoid." And he kept striding.

I caught up to him. "Got something against cops, nutmeg?"

"It's more a case of having a penchant for privacy, Detective."

66

He gestured to a bar-and-grill across the street. "What about that establishment there?"

"Pedro's? That joint's for 'wowers."

"Then we'll be needing an extra-large table," he said, without missing a beat.

The place was lit with red and green lanterns and smelled of salsa and frying plantains. There was an old mariachi record on the turntable, a gopher-sized piñata hanging from the ceiling, and everywhere candlelit paintings of St. Bernard. A couple of hairless 'wowers were huddled into their ridiculous little chairs: when we passed they looked up with snarling eyes—in this sort of place a bullie was no more welcome than a cat.

"Help you, señors?" The bartender was wearing a sombrero that almost swallowed him whole.

"A large booth, as private as possible," Lap said. "A dish of frijoles, no salsa, no cream. And a cup of soy milk, room temperature."

"We have nothing soy here, señor, 'cept the beans."

"Then a Perroquet will suffice." He turned to me. "Detective?"

"A mescal straight up," I said. "Hold the worms."

Lap raised an eyebrow—drinking tingle-water on duty was strictly off-limits—but fang regulations: I was going to show him who was boss.

We squeezed into a midget booth under a poster for Poco and the Subwoofers. "If this all seems a little theatrical," Lap began, "then I must apologize. Circumstances sometimes dictate the necessity of discretion."

"Cut the cat-speak," I snapped. "I ain't got time for it."

Lap's whiskers twitched. "Officially Chief Kessler was informed that Humphrey MacFluff is tied up with another case—a cat was murdered in the Katskills—but off the record he's not yet been told of the developments here. It's only a matter of time before he finds out, of course, and tries to insinuate himself into the investigation. But it's my hope that we can achieve significant progress before then."

I squinted. "I don't get you. You're saying you don't trust MacFluff?"

"You've worked with him, have you not? You must agree that his methods are questionable?"

"He gets the job done."

"The definition of 'job done' has many variations, Detective."

I still didn't like it—stinkmouthing a colleague was a cat hobby, not a dog's—so I sniffed. "Well, how about getting to the point, pajamas? And no pussyfooting around either. You saying MacFluff is on the take?"

"I'm saying MacFluff's methods are worthy of investigation, certainly, but there are official channels for that. And I never pussyfoot around, Detective, let me assure you. And please allow me to prove it. From now on I want you to report directly to me. No one else. Just me. I'll decide what is to be passed on to the chief, to the press, to the rest of the Slaughter Unit. In fact, it's not a request—it's an order."

"Oh yeah? And what makes you think—"

But Lap put up his paw to silence me—an old feline mind trick. "*Stop,*" he said. "*Stay.* That's a good dog."

And for all my energy I felt sapped again. I couldn't even raise a whimper.

Lap paused while the little waiter dealt out our orders—"*¡A su salud, señors!*"—before moving on.

"I've read your profile closely, Detective. And I've already witnessed your temper in action, as it were. But it's not for nothing that I majored in canine psychology. I know you're practically incapable of concealing an emotion. Equally, I know you're almost congenitally indisposed to deceit. I even know of your personal experience in the Siamese war." His eyes hadn't flickered. "So I know you don't like me. Right now, in fact, I know a good part of you wants to rip the skin from my bones. But at the same time I'm supremely confident that you are, in your heart, a good dog. And I'm willing to stake this entire investigation on the notion that, minor infractions aside"—he glanced at my mescal—"you're very conducive to following orders."

In my gutsack I felt such a bonfire of emotions—defiance, pride, anger—that I had to slam the drink down my throat, without even salt on my licker, just to snuff out the flames. "That a fact, kitty cat?" I wiped my snapper with the back of my paw. "Well, why don't you try one now—an order—and see how far you get?"

He leaned forward. "I want you to go home. *Now.* I want you to sleep. For the time being there's nothing you can do. Over the next three hours I intend to comb assiduously through the existing evidence. You'll need your energy for later."

"Oh yeah? And how is it *you* don't need sleep?"

"Through the powers of Zen I can exert total control over my circadian rhythms—my entire metabolism. I can forgo sleep, barring the occasional catnap, for up to three consecutive days. It's not a gift I expect you to share, Detective."

"Then you don't know anything about me at all, tiger testicles. I can go without sleep for a full week—just watch me. And you ain't going anyplace without my sniffer up your butt. I don't trust you. I don't trust any cat, and never will."

He sipped his parrot water and looked at me with a maddening little smirk, like the cat that swallowed the canary.

WHEN I WAS growing up in the 'Loin we believed all sorts of things about cats: that they ate their young, that they were in league with witches, that they had private torture chambers full of nine-tailed whips and moldy skeletons. Much of this I shed with age like an old coat—I no longer licked the nearest fence post when a black cat crossed my path—but even now it was too easy to believe that Lap was using magical powers on me somehow: he had a secret plan, he was up to no good. So I owed it to myself not to let him out of snaprange.

But back at the cophouse he first tried to bore me to death by sniffing over old ground: inspecting the bodies, grilling the witnesses, and with mousehole-watching patience flipping through the forensic evidence like it was the latest potboiler by John Griffon. I think I was actually snoring when Bud Borzoi poked me awake and led me outside.

"What's going on, Crusher?"

I jerked my sniffer at the office. "Puss in Boots in there thinks he can find things that us dogs are too stupid to see."

"Has he found anything so far?"

"I'm not holding my bladder."

"Anything I can do?"

"Nothing. You should be home snoozing."

"Gee, Crusher"—Bud looked nervously through the venetians at Lap—"I don't want any cat making suckers out of us."

"Relax," I said. "When's the last time a pussycat caught anything larger than a pigeon? He's just here to primp and prance, Bud—it's a cat show, it don't mean a thing."

"I don't know, Crusher."

"Trust me," I said, "we'll go in circles for a while and then—" But I stopped, because Lap was getting up from the desk and heading our way. "Later," I whispered, stiffening. "I'll tell you later."

To get to the murder scene Lap insisted we take my unmarked tooter "to avoid attention." Exactly what sort of attention he thought he'd be avoiding—a Siamese sitting muppetlike in the front seat of a Rover—seemed fizzypop to me, but I said nothing.

"Find anything in those reports, succotash?"

"My inspection was purely procedural—I didn't find anything that wasn't already apparent. But I'd be grateful if you do not discuss the investigation with others without seeking my permission, as we discussed earlier."

I looked back at the road. "I don't know what you're talking about."

"I assure you that I'm not here for 'a cat show,' Detective. Nor am I intending to 'go in circles.' And I remind you, for what it's worth, that the only creatures with more acute hearing than the cat are certain species of bat and moth."

I shifted. "That a fact?"

"A biological one, beyond all notions of hubris. So please be vigilant about what you say, and to whom you say it."

He was getting more biteable with each minute.

The storage facility—Rex's Stash & Retrieve—was a dingy acre of shuttered sheds used mainly by dogs hiding their bones for hungrier days. But occasionally there were more valuable treasures: best-of-breed trophies, gold fangs, bronzed paw

71

prints. The alarm system was rusty but reliable; the cat burglar had been chewing threw the wires with rubber teeth when the bells started clanging. Chalk lines marked the shape of the Dobie where he'd flopped in five pieces across the concrete—it looked like a beef map on a butcher's wall.

But Lap didn't say much. He minced around the joint, peering, verifying, asking questions of the manager, making sure the SI beagles were hard at work. At one point he sniffed the air.

I snorted. "Not trying to tell me cats got better noses than dogs, too?"

"Smaller noses, certainly. But the olfactory prowess of most cats equals that of many dog breeds—falling well short, of course, of the scent hounds."

"Oh yeah?" I said. "And what's your little sniffer telling you now?"

"Nothing."

"Course not."

He looked down at me. "The killer, if my suspicions are correct, has already escaped via the sewage system and the connecting branches of the Katacombs. Coincidentally, the odor of sewage serves to cloak his scent."

"Why not rooftops?" I growled. "Cats got a liking for rooftops, don't they?"

"Not second-generation ferals. Their first impulse is to go low, not high."

We drove three sprints west to the wharf at Fly's Picnic, where Slinky Joe's was belching sardine stink into the air. Here Lap spoke coolly to the cannery foreman, ignoring all the stink-eye from the floor. Someone flung a fish head at him and he didn't even blink. On the wharf outside he prowled around like he was looking for a place to flop. He must've been shocked by all the flies—in Kathattan they scrub the streets like hospital floors—but not one of them landed on him, so I guessed his insect treatments were good. But when he went to the very edge of the wharf, to survey the shoreline, I could smell it, even from a distance—the fear scent of any cat close to water.

He called me over.

"There are divers out there."

"Water dogs," I said. "Lookin' for the cat the 'weilers whacked."

"Call them off."

"Say what?"

"Order them back to the station. They're wasting their time."

"Says who?"

He pointed to a barfing sewer pipe about a hundred yards away. "The killer entered the sewage system right there. There's an egress point close to the storage facility in Chitterling."

"You're saying the killer got in there? But he'd have to jump into the water!"

"That's precisely what he did."

"But that's impossible!"

"Why?"

"Because he's a *cat*. And cats hate water."

"Not second-generation ferals. Necessity makes them more than used to it."

I struggled for a protest. "That right?"

"It's exactly right. So what we should be doing now is engaging flushing dogs to trap him in the sewage system." He pulled out his pocket jangler. "In fact, I'll order it immediately."

I gnashed my teeth. "And why shouldn't we be looking for a victim, anyway? Strays don't matter to fat-cats, I guess?"

He gave me a half-lidded look, like I'd just chewed his slippers. "There was never any victim," he said.

I tried to scoff. "*What?*"

"The cat who was shot, the cat who left his blood on the wharf, the cat who killed the Rottweilers, and the cat who plunged into the water were all the same beast. Two gunshots, a dog cry, and a splash—I believe that's how Mr. Lightning first described it. And that matches my scenario precisely."

"Flasha Lightning?" I blew out my lips. "You're basing your theories on Flasha Lightning?"

"And my own logical deductions."

"But Lightning's a scumlicker! He changed his tune a hundred million times!"

"He changed his tune because he was nervous. And that's what we should be looking for. Not bodies. Not even the killer. But what makes a whippet nervous."

"What *doesn't* make a whippet nervous?"

But Lap, plowing through flies like a border collie through sheep, was already heading back to the Rover.

I THOUGHT HE'D want to grill Flasha Lightning—but not a bit of it. In fact, for a moment he didn't even want to get into my tooter.

"Are you absolutely certain there are no bugs in this vehicle?"

"Couple of fleas, maybe—why?"

He took me aside. "I cannot overemphasize the necessity of caution. Have you ever heard the expression, 'Fish rots from the head'?"

It was an old cat proverb. "Listen, whiskers, if you don't trust the chief—"

"I don't trust anyone. And neither should you."

"—or if you're saying that this case could go higher than that—"

"Much higher."

"—then why don't you just peel open the can? What's going on in that pointy little head?"

He didn't answer directly. "Now that Cujo Potenza sleeps with the shankbones, as they say, who's the principal packland boss in the Underworld? Is it Pompey the Gross?"

"Either Pompey or Tugger Toscano."

"Is one of them approachable?"

I chortled. "Not by the likes of you."

"But by you?"

75

"Maybe—why?"

"Sometimes the fastest path to the head is through the tail," he said. "And what about the Upperworld? Who presides there? Is it still Don Gato?"

"Last I heard."

"Then please drive me to the Cradles. I'll seek an audience with the Don while you do your best with the Gross."

The Cat's Cradles was a fancy spiderweb of catwalks strung between the tallest trees, monorail pylons, towers, and monuments high over the Kennels—far out of the reach of the highest-jumping dogs. Up there in the dizzy district lived all sorts of choleric kitties—Tom Does, thrill seekers, shaggies, Goths, wordcrawlers, pillsuckers, tax dodgers, and feline fundamentalists who believed cats had a right to flop wherever they liked. They trapped birds up there with nets, harvested rats, tossed their kitty litter across the rooftops below, and every now and then risked their bony frames by coming down to ground level and "running from the Yaps." A whole subculture had risen up around it, with packs of hoondogs crouching every night near the jumping-off points and waiting for some furspitter to take them on. Many a mayor had won office promising to smoke the cats out of their nests, but one way or another nothing was ever done.

"What's the nearest access post?" Lap asked as we wrestled through a midday traffic snarl.

"The Tomb of the Unknown Dog-Soldier."

"I'd prefer not to scale a war memorial."

"Doesn't stop the rest of your lot," I said.

"I'm not a pack animal, Detective."

I pulled over at Patriot Place, right next to the WK9FM radio tower. High above, stretched like a skein of wool over the Flatear District, was the control center of the Cradles, the part where the gangster cats lived. This was the Upperworld, where Don Gato held court, safe in his cocoon of oriental rugs and feather pillows. This was where he dished out orders to his powder dealers and ratcatchers. This was where he flung the occasional stray to his messy death (from that height not even a cat could land on its feet). I told Lap I'd pick him up later and watched him straighten his raven tie, pop out his claws, and start scaling the rusty tower with that sickening second nature that, along with their conniving little minds, is all that saves cats from extinction.

They said where the Upperworld and the Underworld met it wasn't sparks that flew, but meat tickets. They said that Don Gato had "an arrangement" with Pompey the Gross that was never barked about out loud. And it was said that this arrangement was what really kept the smoke away from the Cradles—the arrangement the Don had with the Gross, the one the Gross had with the mayor, and the one the mayor had with the slinkers and shakers in Kathattan. It was all one big tangled ball of wool that the rest of us hopped through like fleas, hoping we didn't get squeezed.

In the leafy 'burb of Airedale, Pompey lived in a gaudy Roman temple full of armored-dog murals and inscriptions in Dog Latin. I didn't rightly care if he agreed to see me or not—I wasn't even sure what I was supposed to be asking—but it was just my luck that two of his whelps had just had their first rabies shots—it's a gangster tradition that no pack boss can turn away a visitor on Vaccination Day.

"What can I do for you on dis special afternoon?"

Pompey was a giant Neapolitan Mastiff with undershot teeth, a slobber problem, and a clouded left eye where he'd run into a stick. He sat in a tuxedo on the other side of a huge marble desk, his dribble spilling in strings, his great bobble waving between his lumpy shoulders. In the wine-red shadows behind him stood his caninesigliere, a Wolfspitz–Irish Setter cross, and the eldest of his pedigree whelps, a real chain-chewer. I'd already been frisked, sniffed, poked, and told to behave—all this just to get past the porch—but I wasn't going to let anybody, packland boss or not, think a bullie would ever shrink before a mastiff.

"What can you do for me?" I echoed. "Depends. How much bark you got behind that underbite?"

Pompey was known to chew the heads off goats, so he didn't need to take any lip from some flatpaw. But if he was offended he harnessed himself. "Detective," he said in his kennel-cough snarl, "in dis city power belongs to dose who open and shut de gate. And 'round here dere are all sorts of gates—not dat you'd always wanna know what's behind."

I snorted—it was the way of packland bosses to speak in riddles. "Whatever you say, pal. I'm just here to sniff the wind. You must've heard what's been going down, last couple of nights?"

"I read de rags."

"Any idea what a couple of 'weilers might be doing out on the town with a feral cat?"

"De 'weilers worked for Cujo Potenza once, never for me. Why come here?"

"Because Cujo's not giving out with much lately except earthworms. Because everyone tells me Pompey the Gross has got a sniffer over every cesspit in town. They tell me a centipede can't tickle himself without the Gross finding out. So I figure a great and powerful dog like this, he must've heard something by now. And he must be willing to pass on what he knows, in the interest of public safety."

The caninesigliere suddenly leaned out of the shadows and muttered something in Pompey's ear. The packland boss looked me up and down like I'd just asked if I could mount his daughter.

"I just been informed you been sharing your wheels wit' a member of the mewing species," he said.

"Seems it wasn't wrong, what I was told about you."

"A mewer wit' a badge and a black tie."

"Could be."

Pompey sucked in some drool and rolled his shoulders. "It makes me uncumfable," he said, "knowing my words, dey might end up in de files of the FBI."

"Nothing said here has to waft any further than these walls, if that's the way you want it."

"Why should a mastiff trust a bullie?"

"Bullies don't turn nose on anyone. Don't need to. I figure a mastiff knows that."

Pompey waved a paw at his caninesigliere, who bent forward again so the two could mumble in private. In the background his number-one whelp kept licking his flews, like he'd missed out on his own rabies shot and couldn't wait to sink his teeth into something. Pompey arrived at a verdict.

"I gotta liking for you, Detective. You don't chew on rubber bones. So here's what I'm gonna say to you now. You ask about a feral cat. You ask why a cat like dat might be getting a slug between de peepers. Well, I tell you dis—read de rags."

"I don't get it."

"'All de news dat's fit to sniff'—ain't dat what dey say? Well, Pompey asks you to tink about dat. If it ain't in de rags, did it really happen?"

"I still don't get it."

"Buy de rags, Detective. See de truth—or don't see it—for yourself."

In the shadows the caninesigliere wore a creepy little smile. The number-one whelp was giggling and slobbering.

I shrugged. "That's it? That's all you're gonna say?"

"Dat's all. Anythin' else I can do for you dis bewdiful day?"

"Not for now."

"Den my son Brutus will chase you to the gate."

"That's okay—I'll chase myself. *Canem te esse memento*."

They looked at me quizzically as I headed for the swinger.

I PARKED AROUND the corner and had a secret snooze—fang Lap if he was waiting. But when I finally got to Patriot Place I couldn't see any sight of him anyway—not at ground level, not in the steelwork of the radio tower. I did a few circuits and was about to head back to the cophouse when the passenger door flew open and a shape slid inside. I hadn't even stopped.

"Greetings," said Lap, like it was all prearranged.

"Where you been?" I snapped. "Been looking for you."

"I've been scrounging around the neighborhood—please forgive me."

"*You've* been scrounging around? Out there?"

"Don Gato is in possession of an extremely effective distillation—I believe it's called *eau de chien*. A spritz around the ears, and a little extra around more tender parts, seems to be enough to forestall canine antipathy. The master of the dog's nose is, I'm sure you'll agree, the master of his mind."

I grunted. "And what were you looking for, anyway?"

"Newspapers." Lap held up the *Daily Growl*. "Don Gato instructed me to 'read the newspapers.'"

"That's exactly what Pompey said to me—'read the rags.' What did you find?"

Lap gestured to the paper. "When did you intend to inform me about this?"

Still driving, I glanced at a front page split into two head-

shots: Rocky Cerberus, the champion boxer, and Zeus Katsopoulos, the feral-cat challenger. The headline read: LET THE FUR
FLY!

"Tonight's prizefight? What about it?"

"Did it ever occur to you that I might be interested in a cat
such as this?"

"Katsopoulos?" I said. "You're not saying he's the killer?"

"I'm saying he's a feral cat."

"So?" I said. "When you kitties put up a prizefight challenge,
you always use ferals." And wildcats, I could've added. Pumas,
ocelots, lynxes—all of them disguised as regular cats. For a while
the scandal had threatened to deck the whole industry. But boxing, like all sports, is too important to stay on the canvas.

"I'll need to see this for myself," Lap decided. "How does one
acquire tickets?"

"Never been to a fight before?"

"I admit it's not my favorite pastime."

"Figures. But all the seats have been snapped up anyway. To
get in you'd need to flash your tags."

"I'd prefer to do this unofficially. Are you certain there's no
way to obtain a seat?"

"Scalpers," I said, "but you'd have to sell your hide."

"Money is no hurdle."

"Or wait." I thought of Spike. "I can probably score a couple
of tickets. From an old pal."

"Then please do." Lap slapped the front page. "Read the
newspapers, they told us. Well, unless the packland bosses—
and my own feline instincts—are misleading us, there's something decidedly suspicious about Mr. Zeus Katsopoulos."

I stopped the car and called from the nearest public booth.
"Spike, it's me. About the fight tonight—"

"You can come?"

"I just need those tickets." I winced. "For me. And someone else."

In the silence I could almost hear his head tilting.

"I can't explain," I said. "But it's real important. There's a six-pack of Chump's in it for you, pal."

"Gee, Crusher, I don't know—"

"Remember Seal Point? Remember who it was who dragged you out of that pit?"

I didn't enjoy calling up the war, and I especially didn't enjoy swiping tickets from my oldest buddy, but the idea of seeing the prizefight for free—and as part of an investigation—was too drool-worthy to pass up.

"Crusher, you know what I owe you for that. But I already—"

"Then I'll see you in twenty small ones," I said. "You won't regret it."

Back in the tooter I turned my shame on Lap. "You'll need a half-gallon of that dog scent, Tigger, if you're going to a prize-fight."

"I'm not certain I understand."

"This ain't no symphony recital. There'll be some mean door-scratching mutts there, and they won't fancy no Zeus fan cheering in the middle of them."

"I assure you I'm completely impartial to the result."

"Yeah, just like a cat to sit on a fence, ain't it? Well, that won't help you."

I didn't say it, but I didn't much like the idea of being squeezed next to a cat at the biggest show in town—if word got out, my pals would never sniff me the same.

I left Lap in the tooter and headed down Respect Street past a plastic-dish outlet and a dry-food distributor. Spike was a small-time importer of rubber squeakmice and chewtoys—a

lot of puppy stuff that somehow sold like tripe to grown-ups—
but his storehouse, like his home, was ringed with spikes and
barbed wire, like he thought he was protecting the Declaration
of Undying Loyalty. He was alone, as always, and happy just to
have company.

"Here they are, Crusher." He took the tickets out of his safe.

"Sorry, pal, I know how much this meant to you."

"Forget about it, Crusher. I'll find a safe bar someplace, watch
it on RCN."

"I wouldn't be asking if it wasn't extra-important. I owe you
one."

"Is it a hot date, Crusher?"

"Say what?" Spike was wearing an Elizabethan collar after a
fistula operation, so it was hard to hear him.

"I said is it a hot date—is that it?"

"Yeah," I said, "a hot date."

"What's she like? Does she stink?"

After the war Spike wasn't so good with the bitches. I knew
he lived a lot of his life through me, in fact, always asking about
my love life, always giggling. "My eyes water whenever I hear
her name," I said, and sighed, thinking about it. "Anyway, you
look after yourself, pal—don't go biting any wooden chickens."

"Smell you when I sniff ya."

"Not if I sniff you first."

But despite all the nudge-and-tickle I left with a curdled feeling in my gut, like I'd just run off with his sausages.

MY PAPPY FIRST took me to Solidarity Stadium when I was just a pup, but since the war I'd never felt fully at ease there. They were extending it outward and upward—they wanted it to hold one hundred thousand howling fans in time for the Globe Games—but it was still like one giant pit, and whenever I looked into a pit these days I got queasy flashbacks to that night in Siam. It sure didn't help that I was arriving, right now, with a prissy Siamese.

He was still wearing his shimmering black suit, like he didn't see any need to blend in, but he was positively reeking of dog juice, so if I closed my eyes tight I could almost imagine I was standing in line with a common coonhound. As for me, I was buried deep in an anorak with upturned collar, paws in pockets, muzzle out like a beak, doing my best to look invisible. We breezed through the click-swingers without a word and plunged into the stadium itself, hoping desperately to avoid any snarl-and-snap.

We were lucky. The opening bout on the card—a rasher-weight clash between Australian champion Deefa Dingo and local contender Leroy Spitz—was already in its tenth round, and every peeper in the place was fixed tight on the ring. We shuffled and squeezed down the twenty-second row as Spitz gave Dingo a real workout, ducking and dodging like a cheeky terrier. The crowd was loving it.

"Give him a jab in the chops!"

"Let that baby-muncher have a taste of his own medicine!"

I tried to ease into the spirit but all I could think about was that someone might see me. All sorts of dogs were crammed into the joint, whisker to whisker: sporting dogs, working dogs, toy dogs, setters, terriers, mutts, and pooches. Not to mention big-biscuit celebrities: Brad Pitbull, Mutt Damon, Benji Affleck. I could even see fat-cat superstar Tom Manx, in town to shoot a marrowbrained cop-buddy flick, *The Unscratchables*, with Jack Russell Crowe.

Lap surveyed the pit slowly.

"See anything, Lap-lap?"

"Frisbees and biscuits . . ."

"What's that?"

"Nothing," he purred. "I find it . . . fascinating . . . in an atavistic way."

I almost bit him just for using big words. But then there was a huge howl from the crowd, because Deefa Dingo, like a cornered dog, had burst off the ropes to score a few rib-crunching blows to Leroy's brisket. The contender staggered and swooned and had to be carried back to the stool when the bell rang. His Boston Terrier trainer immediately bow-wowed with the ref and decided to toss in the flearag. Dingo was declared champion for the third time and did a circuit of the ring holding his studded collar high in the air. The crowd growled and snarled.

But soon a crest-tingling sense of excitement took over, because now it was time for the main bout. A hush ran through the stadium, then a chorus of panting lungs, then the pounding of thousands of paws. Above the ring, the buzzscreens were flashing replays of Rocky Cerberus pounding his challengers senseless—real pumper-stirring stuff. Then there was an ad for Chump's new Turkey & Jerky flavor sensation: Doofus Rufus, the company frontbarker, personally roasting a meal in his up-country oven—"Melts in your gobbler or I ain't a doofus!"

Then there was a profile of Zeus Katsopoulos, a moon-faced moggie with spiky black hair and a permanently flapping licker, jogging through the streets of Athens in a sweatshirt, chasing chickens, juggling balls of wool. There was no footage from his fights, but the stats were impressive enough—six bouts, seven knockouts (he got the ref once as well).

"Katsopoulos is new to the sport?" Lap asked.

"First time in the stadium. First time as a championship contender."

"So you'd never heard of him before this year?"

"Never heard of him before this fight."

"How very interesting."

I grunted. "Rocky will make cat mince out of him—you watch."

But suddenly a familiar rock song began pumping through the loudsquawkers: "Eye of the Tiger." And then, surrounded by a posse of trainers, managers, and parasites (including his American Wirehair manager Linus "Lion" King), Zeus Katsopoulos entered the pit, wearing silk boxer shorts and a tiger-striped robe. As he waddled down the stairs, looking like he'd just woken from a dream, I could actually hear the dog hair bristle.

When he climbed into the ring—empty tingle cans and fatburger cartons went sailing through the air—it was a wonder half the crowd didn't jump the ropes and rip him apart. But Katsopoulos didn't turn, didn't blink, didn't even seem to notice. And for the first time I saw that he was wearing headphones, big ones clamped tightly around his bobble to keep him from getting the jeebies. And when we got an even closer look at him—the screens had him twenty feet high—we saw that he wasn't nearly as big or hateable as he should've been. For a start, he looked smaller than he'd seemed in the footage—not much bigger than a Kathattan stockbroker—and about as scary as Doofus Rufus. He had a snagtooth, a couple of scars, and a few patches of missing fur, but all in all he wasn't much different from your average alley cat.

So a new hush settled over the crowd as everyone struggled to stay angry, couldn't, and fizzled into silence.

"Hear it?" asked Lap.

"Hear what?"

But he didn't answer.

I was about to growl but suddenly another song cranked up—"Bad to the Bone." Then the swingers blew open and the champion himself strutted in, surrounded by his own pack of trainers and support staff. A thousand flash-and-clinks popped, the music pounded, the floors shook. And there was no doubting Rocky Cerberus was a superbly cut boxer, with a rod-straight back, bulging muscles, and a sleek shiny coat. When he sprang into the ring and did a few air jabs—Katsopoulos was watching dumbly—there were so many tails wagging that a gust of wind rushed through the joint and nearly cracked the back windows.

On the screens meanwhile they were showing an electoral ad for Brewster Goodboy—a montage of cats and dogs united in battle, at work, at play, as Collie Clarkson warbled "Simple Gifts," the old folk song that had somehow replaced "The Spots and Stripes" as the national howl:

'Tis a gift to be simple, 'tis a gift to obey
'Tis a gift to accept that there is no better way,
And when we find ourselves in that place just right
It will be in the backyard of endless delight.

When true simplicity is gained,
To beg and to roll we shan't be ashamed,
To heed and to heel will be our delight,
Till by heeding and heeling we turn out right.

"See it?"

"See what?"

"At least," said Lap, "you won't need to worry about being noticed anymore."

I had no idea what he was mewing about until I saw that the giant buzzscreens were showing faces in the crowd. And there, five times larger than life—televised right around the stadium, right around San Bernardo, right around the whole country— was me, yours truly, sitting all chummy with my "hot date"—a suit-wearing Siamese.

If there'd been a rabbit hole nearby I would've stuck my bobble down it and never come up for air.

THE FIGHT WAS over in seconds.

First the ring announcer introduced the combatants: Zeus Katsopoulos, the Cat from the Acropolis, and Rocky "Slaughterhouse" Cerberus, the Hound from the Pound. The crowd went fizzypop.

The fighters retreated to their corners. They shed their coats. They mumbled with their trainers. They slotted in their mouth guards.

The ref took his position. The whole crowd hushed as one. Someone quietly slipped off Katsopoulos's headphones.

The bell rang. The fight began.

And suddenly—without any warning at all—an amazing change came over Katsopoulos.

His fur rose up like needles. His tail shot up like a flagpole. His ears swiveled. His back arched. His pupils dilated. He swelled to twice his size—maybe three times.

Even Rocky didn't know what to make of it. He came out making his usual dodge moves but seemed unsure if he should get any closer—Katsopoulos was pressed back into his corner and looked like he was about to explode. The crowd held its breath—not a pant, not a heartbeat, not even a whisper. I'm a bull terrier, and for a moment even I was scared.

Then Rocky inched forward, dukes up.

Katsopoulos got even bigger.

Rocky paused, looked for somewhere to land his first clonk.

Katsopoulos hissed a warning.

Rocky got even closer. A few whiskerlengths away.

And he risked one little jab.

That's it. Just one little jab.

He didn't even get a chance to yelp.

Katsopoulos rose up—there was "an impression of movement"—and suddenly Rocky was blown clean out of the ring. He flipped end over end like a toy bone. He landed twenty rows back, just in front of us, right in the middle of some business-suited Pomeranians. He was bleeding, drooling, and as limp as a tug-rope. The Pomeranians couldn't even wake him. He was zonked.

Back in the ring the Katsopoulos team wasn't waiting for any official announcement. They wrapped their boy in his tiger-striped robe—all of a sudden he'd shrunk in size again—and clamped his headphones back on and bundled him up the stairs to safety. But the crowd wasn't moving a hair anyway—everyone was nailed in place, dumbslapped. From the loudsquawkers a sound was pulsing—I couldn't quite make it out.

"This," Lap said to me, "is what I'd call suspicious."

"Maybe." But I was frozen stiff.

"Come with me," Lap said. And when I couldn't budge: "*Come.*"

So I wrenched myself from my seat—it was real difficult for some reason—and followed the Siamese up the stairs. But he was so quick, so slithery, that I had trouble keeping pace. In the tunnels I caught a glimpse of Katsopoulos and his crew oozing around a corner. Lap moved even faster. But now a few spectators were spilling out of the pit, vendors were asking what was going on, and some latecomers were still rushing in. Lap was threading between them all like weaveposts. I saw Nipper Sweeney in the middle of the blur.

"Crusher—speak to you a moment?"

"Not now, Nip."

I didn't even get time to take in his reaction. I reached the click-swingers just in time to see Katsopoulos sliding into a stretch limo with his trainers. Lap was already there, flashing his badge.

"—we gotta skedaddle!" Linus King was saying.

"I'm afraid this is not a matter of choice," Lap responded smoothly.

"I know the governor!"

"I'm sure you do."

I arrived at the scene, panting. "What's going on?"

"Detective McNash," said Lap, "you're just in time. Mr. King here was about to give me five minutes with his client."

"Just five minutes?" I said.

"It's the very least he can do. He doesn't really wish to obstruct the law."

King looked cornered, and not happy about it. "Okay—five minutes!" he spat. "Thaz all. Five minutes! Den we gotta ske-daddle! We gotta scat!"

We slipped into the trailer-sized limo and the door slammed like a refrigerator. The double-glazed windows shot up. The engine was already throbbing.

Katsopoulos was lounging on a deer-hide seat as big as a sofa. He was still in his robe, gloves, and headphones. On a plate in front of him was something that smelled like possum meat. Beside him, tickling his cheek, was a spangled Bengal queen wearing hot pants and not much else.

"What's dis?" Katsopoulos's oldboy trainer—Gus Bowser, the

Raging Bulldog—was chewing on a cigar as big as a shinbone.

"This won't take more than a few moments," Lap assured him. "I'm from the Feline Bureau of Investigation. My partner is from the San Bernardo Slaughter Unit. We have some questions for Mr. Katsopoulos here."

"'Bout what?"

"'Bout time you put a zip on it, pal," I snarled, but Lap raised a silencing paw.

"You must surely have heard by now of the unfortunate killings in recent days," he said. "We simply need to establish Mr. Katsopoulos's movements at correlating times."

"Why?" Bowser spat a gob of cigar juice into a pot. "What's Zeus got to do with anythin'?"

"Nothing at all, I'm sure. Which is why we seek to rule him out officially." Lap turned to the slugger. "Mr. Katsopoulos, may I assume you've been training all week?"

But Katsopoulos didn't answer, didn't even seem to have heard. He was eyeing me the whole time, like he was scared I might take a chunk out of him.

"Mr. Katsopoulos?" Lap tried again.

"Zeus spent da whole week in da gym and da hotel," Bowser chipped in. "I was wit' him da whole time."

"Can you verify this?"

"Don't need to. A newshound from da *Dog Whistle* was wit' us all week—read da rags."

"Read the newspapers?"

"I reckon dat's what I said."

Lap glanced at the boxer. "May I ask this of Mr. Katsopoulos personally?"

"Why? I ain't no liar."

"I'd just like his own opinion. In fact, I insist upon it."

Bowser looked uncomfortable. Outside a presspack was

forming. Linus King was trying to hold them back, but the flash-and-clinks were popping madly. Zeus kept flinching, like he thought it was lightning.

"You heard him, pal," I snapped.

"Orright, orright." The trainer shifted his cigar. "But make it zippy—Zeus don't like noises."

He unclamped the headphones—Zeus looked wasp-stung—and Lap leaned over, asking no questions of the cat at all.

"Do you mind?" he said to Bowser, taking up the phones and putting them to his right ear. He listened, frowning, then he picked up the tape player, started pressing buttons, forwarding and rewinding, still asking no questions. He popped the cassette out and held it up.

"May I keep this?"

"Why?" asked Bowser. "Dis is crazy."

"I can insist, if you like."

"It's just music."

"Then you have no objection?"

"Orright, orright."

"And one last thing, please forgive me," said Lap. "I have a young nephew who's something of a boxing aficionado. I'm sure he'd be overjoyed to receive an autograph of—"

"Zeus don't do signatures," Bowser said.

"Yes, but—"

"Zeus don't write."

"I see," said Lap. "Then perhaps I can settle for a lock of his hair?"

"A lock—?"

"Never mind, there's one right here." Lap plucked a blue-gray bristle off the rug. "Much appreciated—my nephew will be overjoyed."

The swinger suddenly opened. "Your five minutes is up," snapped Linus King. "We gotta vamoose!"

I curled a lip. "We'll leave when we wanna—"

But Lap put up a paw. "It's perfectly all right, Detective, we've finished now."

We slipped out of the limo into the middle of the rabid press-pack. The door slammed and Katsopoulos and company roared away down the street, pursued by the newshounds with their flash-and-clinks.

In the lingering cloud of exhaust Lap pulled out a little snap-tooth bag and carefully slid the cat hair inside.

"What you should do," I said, "is get a DNA analysis of that hair."

"What a splendid idea," said Lap.

IT STARTED DRIZZLING as we headed back to the cop-house. Lap had the cassette in the Rover's tape box and kept running through it, stopping every now and then, listening for a few seconds, and moving on.

"Looking for something?" I said.

"I'd be happy if I could just identify this music."

"What"—I sniggered—"you really don't know what it is?"

Lap looked at me. "Are you saying that you do?"

"It's *Kat and the Kream*."

"A popular album?"

"Everything by Puss Galore is popular. Why?"

"Then can you identify these lyrics?" He rewinded. "Can you tell me what she's singing here?"

I felt ashamed that I knew. But I did my best:

"'Thump me in the back, Jack/Slap me in the face, Jase/Kick me in the spleen, Dean/Knock me off my feet, Pete/Uh-huh, uh-huh/You da bomb, Tom.'"

"You da bomb, Tom?"

"Muttslang. She's telling her pimp-cat he's got it all."

"While offering herself up for a beating in the process?"

"She's supposed to be a dog. Puss Galore sings doggie-style, everyone knows that."

"So the lyrics are essentially about dog domination?"

"What of it?"

96

"And dogs don't mind?"

"It's a good tune."

"How fascinating," Lap said, slipping the tape into his pocket.

I grunted. "What were you looking for, anyway?"

"I was hoping to identify something on the tape that might account for Katsopoulos's transformation in the ring—his engorgement as soon as the headphones were removed. A few veiled instructions, perhaps."

"Instructions?"

"'Knock me off my feet, Pete'—things like that. And yet he was listening to the very same lyrics in the back of the limousine without effect. So perhaps there's something else—something hidden."

"Like what?"

"I'm not certain. Cats are traditionally harder to command than dogs."

I drew up at a stop sign. "That a fact, puddy-tat?"

"Regrettably so. You might not have been aware of it—the messages were delivered fractionally beyond a dog's conscious recognition—but when the fight ended, the stadium loudspeakers were pumping the command words 'STAY' and 'SIT' repeatedly. Without them there could well have been chaos."

"That so?" I eased into Contentment Street, irritated. "We're just all dumb dogs to you, I guess."

"I make the observation not as a personal opinion but as a psychological fact. You must have noticed by now that the electoral campaign of Brewster Goodboy employs just such command words? 'STAY the course.' 'WALK the distance.'"

I hadn't noticed, but I was hardly going to admit it. "So what?"

"And you must have noticed that when I first arrived at the

97

station I purposely incorporated key command words into my introduction? Fetch. Heel. Shake. Walk. It's the very first lesson in canine-domination techniques. Establish authority. It doesn't even matter if it's obvious—beyond a certain age, resignation overrides resistance."

I ran a red light, just to show him I didn't obey everything. But as much as I didn't like it, the sniffy way he was talking about dogs, I was amazed he was admitting it—cats usually buried their secrets like their doodah. "It's all tied up with some sort of boxing scandal," I said, "is that what you're saying?"

He looked at me. "Would it be fair to assume that in the Kennels the sport has attracted some controversy recently? Betting syndicates? Packland bosses? Massive media investments?"

"Does the pope squat in the park?"

"Then what would you say to this scenario? An 'interested party' with a great deal at stake wants the fight canceled. Zeus Katsopoulos is catnapped by some hired goons and taken to the wharves to be executed. But before he can be disposed of he rises up in self-defense. In making his way back to his hotel he also kills a security guard. And then he's spirited in and out of the stadium by an understandably protective entourage. What would you say to that, Detective?"

He sounded like he was really sounding me out. Like my opinion was actually important to him. But I only shrugged. "I don't do theories anymore. What do you think?"

"I admit there are some fundamental flaws. I can't see a logical pattern, for a start. Because ferals, unlike fully domesticated cats, kill only for sustenance—not amusement. So why would Katsopoulos kill the guard at the storage facility?"

"Maybe for self-defense."

"I can't see why. Besides, I smell something considerably more sinister here than a garden-variety boxing scandal."

He sounded like he was baiting me—begging me to ask more questions—but I didn't swallow. "That hair in your pocket will say a lot."

"And the tape, hopefully. I'll have it analyzed for hidden frequencies. As soon as we get the opportunity, of course."

But when we got back to Duty Street we found a herd of squad tooters already pulling out of the station and racing into the rain, lights spinning and flaring. The chief, seeing them off, looked grim as a furnace wall.

"Another murder," he said. "A top dog this time. Chopped up like a meatloaf."

"Where?" Lap asked.

"The Museum of Reigning Cats and Dogs."

"At what time?"

"Eight-thirty."

"Eight-thirty," echoed Lap, and I could see the disappointment on his mug.

One hour ago—the same time as the fight began.

Part of me had to slap down a sense of satisfaction.

BY THE TIME we arrived it was raining rats and mice. The museum, a huge Corgian building full of pillars and gargoyles, was on the east side of Barkley Park about three sprints west of the last murder scene. I'd never liked the joint. I'd taken the pups once—it was free—but I always got the impression that they gave too much space to cat rulers over dogs: that Catterine the Great and Moggie Thatcher got twice the space of Napoleon Boneaparte and Josef Snarlin. Not long ago they'd put up a panorama of wall paintings unearthed by archaeologists in the Katacombs—pictures supposedly proving that cats settled in the area long before St. Bernard arrived to convert the 'wowers—and some shaggy-haired mutts from the PPU had picketed in protest. But I knew the place was still popular with school groups and tourists, even the occasional kitty who wandered across the river to purr approvingly at the displays.

The body of the latest victim, diced like a cheese platter, lay on a side street halfway between the parking lot and the entrance swingers. The first cops on the scene had put up a tarp to shield it from the rain. The SI boys were there, already having a sniff. Bud Borzoi was directing things from under an umbrella so small it could've been sitting in a piña colada.

"A purebred, Crusher." He spoke to me as if Lap didn't exist. "A curly-coated retriever, name of Corky Farr-Fetch."

"From Kathattan?" I asked—most double-barreled surnames came from the island.

"Uh-huh. A marketing manager at Chump's Incorporated."

"What was he doing here?"

"There's some new exhibit opening tonight—the Glory of the Pharaohs or sumthin'. Chump's is one of the sponsors."

I looked back at the parking lot. In front of some fancy foreign tooters a few knitted-jacket pooches, poodles and Pekingese mainly, were huddled under fat umbrellas getting grilled by an officer. I looked back at the body—the head was at least ten leashlengths from the torso, like someone had gone bowling with it.

"No statement from the victim, I'm tipping?"

Bud giggled. "Wouldn't've seen a thing, Crusher. *Whack!* The bobble's off like a cork."

"Did anyone witness the attack?" Lap interrupted. He was standing nearby, under the museum eaves, trying not to get wet.

"The curator saw something." Bud spoke like I'd asked the question.

"And this was at precisely eight-thirty P.M.?"

"At eight twenty-five—five minutes to closing time."

"Did he see the killer?"

"Just a gray blur."

"Where'd he go, the killer?"

"Jumped back on the roof and ran away."

"The roof?" Lap said. "Did you say the roof?"

And now Bud turned. "Ask the curator, pal, if you don't believe me."

Lap simply nodded, looking so pathetic—with his wet hair and his dripping whiskers and his dog juice all washed off—that I almost felt sorry for him.

"Then please excuse me," he said. "I'll need to have a little prowl."

We watched him slither off, glistening with rain, like a common stray streaking across a backyard on a stormy night.

Bud shook his head. "Where d'you think they dug him up, Crusher?"

"Beats me. We've been chasing our tails all day."

"You found nothing? Nothing at all?"

"Not even a punch-drunk flea."

Bud sniggered. "You wanna take over again?"

"In a hamster's heartbeat."

But Bud's tail suddenly stiffened. "Not sure you'd get the chance. There's some curly things going on back at the cop-house."

"You heard something?"

"Maybe. The chief was—"

"Wait a tick." I couldn't see Lap anymore—it was like he'd vanished into the rain—and I didn't much like the idea he might overhear us again. So I found a side door and slipped into the darkness of the museum.

We ducked down a few empty passageways past a reception room crowded with mouthwatering treats. The Great Hall was full of Egyptian knickknacks: statues of the cat pharaohs, wall paintings showing cats whipping dogs, rows and rows of cat mummies. I dragged Bud into a little mock-up tomb full of wicker baskets and toy mice—the burial chamber of King Tutenkitten.

"You said you'd heard something?"

Bud nodded. "The chief was on the jangler to Kathattan. Sounds like they're gonna send in reinforcements if nothing happens quickly."

"The CAT Squad?"

"Could be."

I shuddered. The CAT Squad was a tactical response team, the elites of crime fighting—highly trained, flak jacket–wearing moggies who tumbled across roofs like acrobats and always landed on their feet. But they were usually only called in to combat terrorists and political troublemakers. To have them take over now would be like some public admission that the case was too much for dogs. Too much for Crusher McNash.

"More likely it's Humphrey MacFluff," Bud went on. "He's flying back from the Katskills right now."

"MacFluff knows about the case now?"

"He ain't happy. He should've been involved from the start. It's real strange. The way the Siamese scored the gig in the first place. The way he took charge. The way he's leading you up the garden path." Bud shifted his toothpick. "You shouldn't trust him, Crusher—he's one strange cat. And he's using up his nine lives real fast."

I could barely see Bud's face—the only light was a flickering lamp—but I could smell his hatred, even stronger than mine. And it didn't make me feel right. Strangely, I felt almost defensive of Lap, like he was my sidepaw and Bud was the upwoofer. Maybe those command words really had messed with my brainpot.

"What's that?"

There'd been a sound, halfway between a whistle and a hiss.

"I didn't hear nothing, Crusher."

But I sidled out of the tomb, hearing the noise again—someone tapping on glass. I looked up, scoped around the gloomy hall, and finally saw him—there, high above the sphinxes, high above the pharaoh statues, standing on an outside ledge, his paw scratching the windowpane: Lap himself, all white and bright against the night sky.

"Detective," he hissed. "Up here."

Immediately I wondered if he'd found something—I was real curious—but at the same time I didn't want Bud thinking I was Lap's lapdog, or anyone else's. So I stayed still.

"Here," Lap said again.

I trembled.

"Here, boy."

And again came that terrible need to obey. And again I couldn't fight it.

I took a guilty glance at Bud, who had a look in his peepers that would fry bacon, and tried to find a solid staircase.

WITH HIS BACK to the museum dome, Lap was standing on a ledge between the crouching lion and wolf statues, well protected from the slanting rain. He was staring out across the jagged sea of rooftops, chimneys, cooling units, and water tanks of the Kennels. Beyond was the shiny ribbon of the Old Yeller, Amity Bridge with its sweeping searchlights, and the Christmas-tree glitter of Kathattan.

I edged my way toward him, trying hard not to shiver—nothing in the Kennels is higher than three stories—and hoping like hell it was worth it.

"'A dog may catch the worm that infesteth the cat,'" he muttered. "'The worm may infesteth the dog, but doth the dog ever infesteth the cat?'"

"Say again?"

He glanced at me. "It's Shakespaw, Detective—act 2, scene 3, *The Great Dane*. I was wondering how you felt down there."

"Down where?"

"In the museum. With the eyes of ancient cats staring over you disdainfully. Did it make you feel humbled? Awed? Or just irritated?"

I wondered what this had to do anything. "Irritated," I said.

"But why?"

"'Coz I'm sick of kitties acting like kings."

He smiled faintly. "So you recognize, at least, that the exhi-

105

bition serves a larger purpose? That it's part of a systematic and highly organized domination agenda?"

"Course."

"And you choose not to fight it?"

"What's there to fight?"

He looked at me strangely, and I wondered what his game was, talking to me like this—was Bud right? Was he off his pills?

"And over there, Detective." He pointed to an illuminated Chump's sign. "Did you know that Doofus Rufus was the brain-child of a Kathattan advertising executive who later became an adviser to President Brewster Goodboy? That the whole aim of the Doofus campaign is to manufacture around Chump's an air of harmless naïveté? An absence of cynicism? So that the consumer equates innocence with trustworthiness?"

He sounded like one of those spectacle-wearing idealists who wrote some of the radical texts I read after the war. I didn't think they bred them anymore. "What of it?" I said.

"Do you eat canned meat, Detective?"

"I ain't got time to catch my own."

"And it doesn't bother you that the food is ninety percent offal? That it's processed by dog workers paid two biscuits an hour? That Chump's is just one leg of a multinational conglomerate that owns a full quarter of Kathattan and nearly half of the Kennels, including quite possibly the building you live in?"

"So what?" He was treating me like a schoolhound.

"Can I show you something?"

He went nimbly along the ledge. I shuffled after him, not looking down.

"There," he said, pointing across the river, "the tall building shaped like a ziggurat. Imperial Heights. That's where I live. As many as nine hundred other cats also reside in its apartments.

Most live alone. They dine well. They dress well. They earn exceptional money. They travel widely. They drive vehicles three times too large for them. They primp and preen themselves obsessively. But would you care to guess how many have ever met a dog? And by dog I don't mean a top dog, a servant, or a maintenance worker. I mean a regular dog, a Yap. Because that's what they call them in my building—Yaps."

I shrugged. "About the same number of Yaps who've met a Mog."

He smirked. "A solid answer, Detective. You know, I myself had never sustained a long conversation with a dog until I went to university. And it was this—my blatant ignorance—that impelled me to seek enlightenment. I studied canine history. Canine psychology. I acquainted myself intimately with canine societies. I hunted with the Malamutes in the wilds of Canada. I lived with Elkhounds in the forests of Norway. I herded goats with Kuvaszes in the Alps of Hungary. If it had not been against the law I might even have married a dog. But I did the next best thing. I wed a highly progressive Abyssinian. A legal adviser, a specialist in canine dialects. Cuddles was her name."

"You're married?" I said—I thought all cats were loners.

"I *was* married, Detective." Lap was looking into the sheets of rain like he was staring into the past. "Two years ago Cuddles was doing some pro bono legal work in the Kennels. Late one night she was trying to hail a cab when she was ambushed by a pack of hoondogs. They chased her into a Laundromat and drowned her in a washing machine."

"That's too bad," I said, meaning to sound honest, but it didn't quite come out that way.

Lap glanced at me. "You're wondering if I blame your species. Not at all. Such acts are reprehensible, even inexcusable, but sociologically not unexpected. The tragedy, indeed, only deepened my resolve to continue her work—to further bridge the chasm between dogs and cats. But it changed me in less constructive ways, too. For a start, you can surely appreciate how it made me feel about water."

I looked out at the rain. "We can go inside, if you want."

"It's all right—one cannot overcome one's fears without confronting them," he said. "But what about you, Detective? Are you yourself comfortable up here?"

"I've been higher before."

"Comfortable with me, I mean? Do you have confidence in my abilities?"

"I'll let you know when I see your abilities."

He smiled. "And now you're wondering if the CAT Squad will be summoned, am I right?"

I grunted. "What I'm wondering is how a mutt gets a private conversation around here."

"Never mind," Lap said. "I do believe the CAT Squad will be brought in at some stage. But only as a last resort."

"I don't get you."

"They're too good at their work. They're capable of capturing a feral without killing him."

"I still don't get you."

"I mean there are many 'interested parties' out there who don't want to see the feral alive."

"What parties?"

"That's what I intend to find out. But you'll recall that I said I was looking for a pattern? Well, tonight I believe I might have found one. Here." He handed me the brochure for the Pharaohs Exhibition. "The corporate sponsors—please read them out."

I squinted—even a seeing-eye dog would've struggled in the gloom—and did my best: "Chump's, Inc. . . . RCN . . . Cleopatra Flea Treatments . . . Piñero and Valdez Limited of Venezuela . . .

the *Dog Whistle* . . . *Whine Magazine* . . . Dogma Records . . ."
I shrugged. "What about it?"

"Three of the major sponsors are branches of the Reynard
Media Network."

"So?"

"So do you not think it curious that we have been repeatedly
advised to 'read the newspapers'? By Don Gato, by Pompey the
Gross? Even by Gus Bowser?"

"We're not going to catch a killer by reading what's in the
newsrags."

"No," said Lap, folding the brochure into his pocket. "But
perhaps we can find where he's hiding—or *why*—by reading
what's not."

"You ain't making sense."

" 'Let Hercules do what he may, the dog will bark and the cat
will have his day.' That's Shakespaw again, Detective. Shall we
go?" He brushed past me on the way to the staircase. "It's cruel,
is it not, to leave a dog and a cat out in the cold?"

I thought about giving him a nip on the way through, but I
bit my tongue instead.

I STILL DIDN'T get Lap. His patience, his prissy movements, his silky tongue, his failure to get angry or frustrated or even to explain himself properly. It was like we were hunting a bunny rabbit, not a mad killer. He was a pussy, sure, and therefore with an entirely different brainpot, but not even Humphrey Mac-Fluff was as cool and curly as this.

"We need to consult with the press," he decided.

"Nipper Sweeney's probably outside right now—I saw him at Solidarity Stadium."

"I was thinking of something higher than a simple news-hound."

"The *Daily Growl*? It's just a couple of blocks away."

"Higher still."

"I don't get you."

And I still didn't. We were pulling up to a jetty in a bend of the Old Yeller River. Through the wagging wipers I could just make out the Isle of Tartare, halfway between the Kennels and Kathattan. Many centuries ago they said cat witches were burned there. Then it'd been used as a prison for a while. More recently it had been the San Bernardo residence of Lassie, the first transsexual movie star. And now it was the city base of Phineas Reynard, the world-famous media magnate.

"What's Reynard got to do with all this?"

"Phineas Reynard has a financial interest in both the United Boxing Federation and the Pharaohs Exhibition. And the reportage of the murders in his newspapers has been, to say the least, interesting. So what does the fox himself have to do with all this? That's exactly what I'd like to find out."

I gestured back at the Kennels. "There's a murderer loose out there, case you forgot."

"A loose feral is one matter. Why he's killing is another. And why the Rottweilers were hired to kill him in the first place is yet another. In any case, when spearing a fish you aim not at the image of the fish—because that's just a refraction in the water—but slightly askew, at the real fish. Any heron will tell you that."

"Herons can talk now, can they?"

"The point, Detective, is that sometimes the best way to catch a quarry is to come at them from an angle."

But I was a bull terrier—an attacker, not a stalker. I sniffed out my quarry and when I saw it I charged for it. The only thing standing between me and blood was a straight line. But now, with this Siamese trickster, I felt like I was back on the obstacle course, still earning my dog tags.

To get to Tartare we needed to take Reynard's private barge, but there was a toffee-nosed dachshund at the guard post trying to act tough.

"Mr. Reynard requires advance appointments for all visitors to Tartare."

"We're officers of the law," said Lap. "We require no appointments."

"Mr. Reynard is a longtime supporter of our law enforcement agencies and a contributor to its related charities. But he still requires—"

"Listen, sausage." I forced my way forward and thumped him

with my chest. "Either you get on the jangler and tell him we're on our way or I'll dunk you in the water and hold you down like a biscuit."

He shrank to the size of a party frankfurt. But within minutes we were on the barge, in the open cabin, plowing across the water. Soon Tartare was looming up in front of us, with rain-swept Kathattan behind it—the closest I'd ever got to the island, and the smell of furballs and fishmeat was so strong I nearly barfed.

At the docking point were a couple of uniformed Dobies. They led us wordlessly through the pine trees and down a gravel path to the elaborate door of Reynard Manor. The place was dressed up like a hunting lodge, with tethering posts, a water trough, and staghead statuary. I jabbed the door-dinger and there was a sound like a hunter's bugle.

"I'll do the talking," said Lap.

"And I'll do the biting."

"I trust it won't come to that."

The timbered door creaked open and a mallet-headed Scottish Terrier stared down at us over his muzzle.

"We're here to see Phineas Reynard," said Lap.

"As we've been notified," sniffed the butler, stepping aside.

We entered a paneled vestibule four times the size of my apartment. There were mounted trophies all over the walls: rabbit heads, weasel heads, piglet heads. There were paintings of squirrel hunts in heavy frames smoky with age. The ceiling was ribbed like a palate. The carpet was grass green and plush as a meadow.

"Cozy little burrow," I muttered.

The butler coughed. "Mr. Reynard will join you imminently," he said, and headed off, sniffer in the air, to fetch his master.

I cast an eye over the framed photographs on the walls:

Reynard as a cub reporter in his breakthrough interview with Fido Castro; Reynard with dogfood emperor Ronald Chump; Reynard with General Snowy Wolfenson, the lupine Secretary of Vigorous Defense; Reynard at the inauguration ceremony of Brewster Goodboy; Reynard on the links with Tiger Woods.

I knew there'd been a popular biography, *The Quick Brown Fox*, covering Reynard's rise to the big time. I'd never read it but I knew the rundown. How he grew up in a quiet little hole a hundred sprints north of Edinburrow. How he'd stolen geese and poached eggs. How there was an ancient clan of foxhounds living on a nearby farm—the fourth estate from the river—who made life hell for young Phineas. How they chased him for sport. Flooded his family's burrow. Ripped apart his brothers and sisters. And how they left the little fox with one gutburning ambition—that one day he was going to *own* the fourth estate.

"Wet outside?"

I turned. It was Reynard's vixen—his fifth, I think—all coiffed and dolled up and wearing a chiffon number that plunged half-way down her furry brisket.

"The rain has not yet eased, ma'am," Lap said, with a mincey little bow.

"I like it when it's wet," she breathed. "Makes you want to snuggle up inside."

"It can do that, ma'am."

The vixen swayed across the hall, eyeing us up and down like we were for sale in a pet store. "Are you from the war cabinet?"

"Not us, ma'am," said Lap.

"From the campaign office?"

"Not us."

"From that South American place?"

"South American—?"

But I butted in. "We're from the law," I said. "I'm from the Dog Force. He's from the FBI."

I could tell Lap wasn't happy with me. But the vixen, pausing at the bottom of the stairs, gave a crafty little smile.

"Has Phineas parked his helicopter illegally again?"

"Nothing like that, ma'am," Lap said.

"I hope one of his rabbit warrens hasn't collapsed?"

"Not that I'm aware of, ma'am."

"Then it's nothing to do with me, is it? I like to keep my tail clean."

"I'm sure you do, ma'am."

As if to prove it she swiveled around to show her shiny red tail, as bushy as a feather duster. "Until we meet again," she hummed. "Perhaps some dark night . . . at some dark hour . . . in some dark forest glade?"

Lap bowed again. "It would be our pleasure, ma'am."

And with one last pointy smile—she was staring straight at me—she sashayed slowly up the stairs, steamy as a husky's turd.

"Wouldn't mind getting that on a chain," I muttered when she was out of sight.

"I very much doubt you'll get the opportunity."

I was about to reply but Lap held up a silencing paw. I followed his gaze and saw a glinty-eyed figure standing at a side door.

"Greetings," the figure said, with a lamb-snatching little smile.

It was Phineas Reynard.

HE WAS A stylish old fox, rusty red with a few streaks of gray, sharp-nosed, finely whiskered, pointy-toothed, with a firm white-tipped tail that some said was fake. He was kitted out in a ruffled cravat, leather foxgloves, and a silken dressing grown the color of sheep's-liver. Putting aside a champagne glass brimming with sparkling springwater, he lured us into a little room filled with cluck-cluck clocks—I knew they were a passion of his—and started winding them with a bent little tool.

"Please forgive me, officers—I'm leaving for my up-country estate tomorrow and I need to wind my clocks. How long will this take?"

"No more than a few minutes," Lap assured him. "But we come with grave tidings, Mr. Reynard, I regret to say. Mr. Corky Farr-Fetch, the well-known marketing manager, has just been viciously murdered."

"Who?" Reynard hadn't even turned from his clocks.

"Corky Farr-Fetch—I assumed you knew him."

"Why would I?"

"He worked for Chump's Incorporated, which has an intimate relationship with the Reynard Media Network. And both companies are principal sponsors of the Glory of the Pharaohs Exhibition, where Mr. Farr-Fetch was killed earlier this evening."

"Such sponsorships have little to do with me personally."

Reynard was still working the winding mechanisms. "Nor do marketing managers from companies in which I have no financial stake."

"So his death doesn't trouble you at all?"

"Of course it does. I'll have a wreath of dogwood sent to the widow."

"So you do know him after all?"

"What do you mean?"

"I never mentioned he was married."

"I assumed, of course." Reynard turned briefly, with a cunning smile. "And in truth something came back to me as we've been talking. A vague image of his features. A retriever, was he not? With a startled look on his face?"

"You could say that."

"Yes, I remember him." Twisting his clocks again. "I do hope he didn't suffer."

"Only he can know that for sure. But would you not care to know how he died?"

"I have a delicate stomach."

"He was torn into several pieces—murdered, we believe, by the same culprit responsible for the earlier killings in Fly's Picnic and Chitterling."

"Truly? How terrible."

"And we'd like to seek your cooperation, if we may."

"How so?"

Lap cleared his throat. "What I'm about to say is highly confidential, Mr. Reynard, and extremely explosive." He actually shifted on his feet. "But there is a high probability that the murderer in all three cases is a cat."

"A *cat*?" Reynard glanced at us with ginger eyebrows arched. "A cat is responsible for murders like that? Whoever heard of such a thing?"

"So you didn't already know about all this? The news hasn't leaked out?"

"Of course not."

"And yet you knew of the other murders—the details?"

"I read my newspapers."

"Then I'm sure you'll agree that this makes for a very volatile situation? A cat murdering dogs in the Kennels? With an election imminent? And a possible call to arms? Not to mention the sheer panic and antipathy such a crime would arouse at the very best of times?"

"Undoubtedly."

"Then we were wondering if you'd be willing to suppress the coverage of the incident in your newspapers, at least until we feel closer to apprehending the killer."

Reynard was already shaking his head. "I approve of the sentiment in principle, of course, but in reality it's my editors that make all decisions relating to newspaper content."

"You're saying you have no direct editorial control?"

Reynard gave a sad smile. "Such heavy-handed influences exist only in media mythology, I'm afraid. It's not the fox that controls the hounds."

Lap nodded. "Then to whom do we owe the exceptional discretion displayed this morning?"

"Discretion?"

"The first murder—two nights ago—occupied the front pages of the *Growl*, the *Dog Whistle*, and featured prominently in the *Scratching Post* and the *Caterwaul Street Journal*. The second murder—when it became clear we were looking for a cat killer—occupied just one column on page seven of both the *Growl* and the *Whistle*. Though it retained some prominence in the *Post*, which is not officially distributed in the Kennels."

Reynard turned back to his clocks. "Perfectly understandable," he said. Twist twist twist. "There was an important sporting contest in town tonight. To focus on such a newsworthy event in the dogsheets, at the expense of an unpalatable crime, is simply to acknowledge the dominant interest of our readership."

"So a contrived clash between a dog and a cat is of greater interest than a murderous one on our streets?"

"I'm not the master of our culture," Reynard said. "And in any case I don't recall seventy thousand attending the crime." Twist twist twist. "Besides, I was rather unhappy with the report of the first murder. I detected an unacceptable degree of hypothesis in it. The sort of speculation that should never have been allowed."

"So you *do* exert some control?"

Reynard glanced at Lap with narrowed eyes. "Did I say that? I was merely informed of a rather reckless report. By a rather reckless reporter. Sweeney, I believe his name was."

"*Nipper* Sweeney?" I said.

Reynard looked at me. "A friend of yours?"

"Maybe."

Reynard sniffed. "Then perhaps he'll be calling upon you soon for scraps. I had him fired this afternoon."

I started to reply, but Lap cut me off:

"Or perhaps he fired himself? Since you, of course, exert no direct editorial control?"

Reynard pocketed his little winder and turned with a mocking snort. "You're a very interesting agent—what did you say your name was again?"

"I didn't. But it's Lap, Cassius Lap."

"I'll be sure to remember that name. You know, I had a very productive relationship with Special Agent Humphrey Mac-Fluff. A very shrewd and pragmatic cat. I must say I'm surprised he's not been assigned to this case already."

"He may yet be."

"Then I hope he finds your preliminary work satisfactory. And you, Officer"—he turned to me—"may I ask your name?"

Lap answered for me: "His name is McNash, Max McNash. Also known as Crusher."

"Of course. The strong, silent dog. My wife is very fond of such types. But I'm sure you've already guessed that."

"You'll be pleased to hear we make no hypotheses."

Reynard surveyed the two of us critically. "You know," he said, "this might sound strange, but I'm convinced I've seen you two together somewhere."

"Did you happen to watch this evening's prizefight?"

"Such barbaric spectacles are not to my personal taste— why?"

"My partner and I were featured in the crowd."

"You were at Solidarity Stadium? You don't say? Well, then, you could have saved yourself a lot of trouble—and considerable expense—by watching it at home on RCN. Single-round knockouts offer such little value for money, do they not?"

"I suspect there's more value than meets the eye in most single-round knockouts," said Lap. "But I take it you *did* overcome your distaste for barbaric spectacles, at least for tonight?"

"I was informed about the outcome, if that's what you mean."

"Or perhaps your confidence in the outcome meant you didn't need to be informed?"

Reynard smirked. "Clairvoyance is not a weapon in my arsenal, Mr. Lap, though you can be certain my arsenal is rather well stocked." He stifled a foxy yawn. "Will that be all, or should I fluff the spare beds?"

"That will certainly be all. But can we take it you're willing to cooperate, at least for the present?"

119

"To instruct my papers to be discreet about the attacks? I'll do everything I can."

"Then we thank you for your hospitality, Mr. Reynard. We hope your trip to the up-country estate is restful, and your sleep productive."

Reynard's eyes slitted and twinkled at the same time. "A fox counts chickens in his dreams, Mr. Lap," he said, and just then his clocks struck midnight and a hundred spring-loaded roosters popped out and cock-a-doodle-dooed—a deafening chorus of windup chickens.

And that was the way we left the old magnate—as sly as a fox in a henhouse.

DRIVING BACK TO the cophouse I was so angry I almost took a bite out of the steering wheel.

"I can still smell him," I said. "That weedy fox scent. I still got it in my nostrils."

"That's your imagination," said Lap.

"How would you know?"

"Reynard had his scent glands surgically removed several years ago. He uses cat shampoo. He bathes in bottled cat saliva. All this to neutralize his natural vulpine odor."

"Know a lot about him, don't you, Deuteronomy?"

"I know a thing or two."

"Sure." I twisted the tooter around a corner. "Pity you didn't have the heart for a catfight, though, ain't it?"

"I'm not certain I understand."

"The fox was lying. It was as plain as the leg on a ham. If it'd been up to me, I would've shaken him like a Ragdoll."

"Aggression is rarely the most productive option."

"Better than pussyfooting."

"And besides, I believe I was too aggressive to start with."

"Call that aggression do you, Simba?"

"Intemperate, perhaps. I made some rash claims. He was rightfully insulted."

"Rightfully? You had him pinned against the fence—he didn't know which way to run."

"If he appeared evasive it was because he can't *help* appearing evasive. He's a fox after all. But I believe he was speaking the truth. And I don't believe he has anything significant to offer us. You might say we were—what's the expression?—barking up the wrong tree."

I snorted, barely believing it. "Seems to me we've been barking up the wrong tree from the start. This don't look good. For my reputation."

"You'll have to trust me."

"I had more trust in Humphrey MacFluff," I snapped, and for the rest of the trip I drove with my bobble out the window, not even listening to him.

But when we reached Duty Street he tapped me on my shoulder. I pulled my head in. "What now?"

"I'd like you to stop here."

"Why?"

"Because I have something important to say to you."

"Say it now."

"*Stop,*" he said. "*Now.*"

He didn't raise his voice, but somehow his tone worked on me like a whip snap. So I pulled obediently to the curb. I followed him into Pedro's. It was like I was in a daze.

The 'wower behind the bar looked pleased to recognize us. "We got soy milk now, señor."

"Excellent," said Lap. "Half a glass with a sprinkle of chives, if you please."

"And two half glasses for me," I said. "With chili."

At the back of the room we squeezed into the same booth as before. "Flap your licker," I said. "I'm starting to get snappy."

"First of all," said Lap evenly, "I want you to disregard everything I just said in the vehicle."

"I don't get you."

"Phineas Reynard knows a lot more than he is willing to divulge. Just what that is still needs to be ascertained. But it's safe to assume he knows the identity of our killer, and wishes to conceal it."

"*What?*" I snorted. "But that's exactly what I said in the tooter. And you turned up your little cat nose."

"I disagreed, Detective, because your car is bugged."

"*What?* How do you know?"

"Because it's only logical."

"I didn't smell anything."

"Your vehicle was empty and idle at the jetty for over thirty minutes. Reynard had plenty of time to give the order. And he would certainly be curious about our response to the interview."

I was getting more and more ruffled. "Listen, doughnut, I'm getting mighty sick of your ways. You're holding out on me, and I don't got a lot of patience. So why don't you just open up for a change, or I might make a little sharp with the fangs."

Lap sighed. "May I ask if there's anyone at the station you trust implicitly?"

"There's a lot of mutts I trust at the station."

"Who?"

"Bud Borzoi . . . Chesty White."

"Chief Kessler?"

"Maybe."

"Why 'maybe'?"

"He's always giving me lip."

"That sounds like a reason to trust him more than anything—your own inexhaustible snipes are one of the reasons I trust you. It's important, in any case, that we identify someone with whom we can liaise with complete confidence."

"You liaise with *me*," I said. "That's what I'm here for."

"You don't seem to understand. Certain processes have been set in motion. Certain parties are shifting behind the scenes. And the bottom line is we have at most twenty-four hours before we are reassigned. More likely it's much less. If I personally have been protected thus far it's only thanks to my commanding officer at the FBI, along with his opposite number in the Cat Intelligence Agency—two cats of peerless integrity. But even so, we have a limited amount of time to poke around a fiercely guarded rockpool and stir up some very big fish. And you, Detective, have a very important decision to make. You must decide if you're willing to see it through. Or if you'd prefer to bow out gracefully."

"Giving orders again, are you, Lionheart?"

"I'm saying it might well get very dangerous. And we'll need to trust each other unconditionally. But I'm not asking you to deny your instincts. It's completely up to you."

The waiter arrived with our drinks. I picked up the first glass and tossed it down my gutchute like a shot of drain water. But I got a taste of it on the way down anyway—there wasn't a trace of animal product in it—and I coughed and spluttered.

"You drink this stuff?" I said, wiping my snapper with the back of my paw.

"I'm lactose-intolerant, Detective, if you must know. And yes, my markings are cinnamon. And yes, I can trace my lineage back to the lords of the jungle. And yes, I wear pajamas. And yes, I comb my whiskers." He stiffened. "I floss nightly, I play the harp, I practice tai chi, I read novels by French philosophers, I sleep in a cot, I have quarterly flea injections, I eat free-range fish, and I decorate my rooms with indigenous paw paintings. But no," he said, "I don't make love in alleyways, I don't sit on fences, I don't consort with witches, I don't sing in Broadway musicals, and if you touch me"—he looked at me steadily—"you'll *never* understand what happiness is."

He drained his soy milk—one gulp, most uncatlike—and licked his chops.

"That's all there is to know about me. And now it's up to you to look into my eyes and decide if you're willing to trust me."

I tried to look into those sea-blue peepers—by Our Lord and Master I tried—but all I saw was a couple of marbles I wanted to rip out and roll down the gutter.

WHEN I PUSHED open the front door of my flopdown the answering machine was woofing aggressively. Four woofs— four messages.

I was meant to hit the rugs. I desperately needed a snooze. I'd left Lap at the station still talking to everyone—the beat cops first to the museum murder scene, the forensics team who'd analyzed the DNA in the Katsopoulos hair (similar but not the same as the killer), the audio mutt who'd had done a check on the cassette tape (no hidden frequencies), and the flushing dogs who'd gone into the Katacombs (nothing down there but squeakers). He wanted beefed-up patrols. He wanted armed cops in the alleyways. Sighthounds and pointers at high-vantage points. Snifferdogs on every corner. He wanted a hotline so he could get constant updates. And he wanted the feral alive—he'd made that plain.

"Under no circumstances is that cat to be killed," he'd said. "I don't care where the order comes from. Any dog that shoots him will be answerable to me."

I'll give him this much: He had nerve, staring down a pack of San Bernardo's finest—any one of whom could've chomped him for breakfast—and never letting a tremble into his creamy cat voice. And I'll give him this much, too: He'd done his homework on the Kennels, and was happy to prove it.

"The locations of the murders so far," he said, pointing at a survey map like a military commander, "indicate that the killer is gravitating in a southwesterly direction at approximately three and a half sprints a day, possibly heading toward the wilds at the western end of San Bernardo. By now, if my estimates are correct, he is most likely somewhere between Barkley Park and the east end of Pugkeepsie. To be even more specific, here"— he pointed—"in a fifteen-block radius between Yield Street and Blissful Way. I believe he will soon pass through the Flatear District, here, which is riddled with abandoned tenements, but he might pause here, at Lake Docile, to replenish himself on water, or here, near the Felicity Street Dump, to feed on the resident rodents. But there are no guarantees."

There were no guarantees, all right, just like there were no guarantees I wouldn't go frothy from frustration, or take a bite out of something, if we didn't get back on the trail. My bobble was throbbing.

"Detective." Lap took me aside and peeled open a can. "Nonprescription stimulants, perfectly legal, straight from Kathattan's finest veterinarian. Please take one—it will keep you on your feet."

"I don't eat pills."

"I can use a pill gun, if you wish."

"Keep your guns away from me, Tex. I don't need any cat medicine. When I get wound up I buzz all night like a mosquito."

But the truth was I was legless. My brainpot was steaming. My eyelids felt like bricks. So I took the first chance I could find to cut loose. Flasha Lightning, the worthless scrumlicker who'd been held in custody for supplying misleading evidence, had squeezed between the bars of his cell (I'd told them a million times, whippets need to be chained) and wormed his stringbean frame through a ventilation duct. I said I had an idea where he might be hiding. I said I'd bring him back.

If Lap didn't believe me, he didn't let on.

So here I was, back home, pressing the button on my answering machine. And ignoring a strange feeling in my gutsack that I'd regret it.

"The pups can't even remember what you smell like."

That was it—a typical snarl-message from my ex. If the bitch wanted reliability, I thought, she should have married a sheepdog.

Second message: "Crusher—it's me, Spike. Just wondering how you enjoyed the fight . . ."

He was using a wound-licking voice, as Spike usually did when he was trying to be angry. Obviously he'd seen me on the buzzscreen and was wondering what the hell I was doing at Solidarity Stadium with a cat. And I couldn't imagine what I was going to tell him.

Third message: "Crusher—it's Nipper Sweeney." A whispered voice, like he was speaking under a fence. "I need to speak to you. Back of the Stunted Muzzle, first thing tomorrow?"

The Stunted Muzzle was a downtown bar much favored by newshounds. But I didn't read much into it—I figured Nipper just wanted to whine about Phineas Reynard, not knowing I'd already yapped with the old fox myself.

Then the last message clicked in. And my hair immediately pricked up.

"Detective Max McNash?" She made my name sizzle like a sausage. "I hope this doesn't sound untoward . . . I hope you'll understand . . . but I just can't get you out of my mind." The same husky voice, the same trap-me-if-you-want-me tone. "I'm here, alone, at the In-Season Hotel. Room one-oh-one, booked under the name of Ruby Fox. Can you meet me tonight? To discuss a few things? It's entirely up to you."

And that was it—a dangling bait, nothing more. I stood in place for a full minute, staring blankly at the box.

I should've been laying my bobble on a blanket. Or I should've been reporting this new development to Lap. But suddenly all I could think about was those jeweled eyes. That flaming red tail. Those curves. Those points. The way she glided across that lobby, smooth as butter.

I checked my reflection in the side of a toaster. Broad shoulders, trim coat, a jaw that was made for chewing. I still had my charms. I could look after myself. And I was unchained, free—nobody had any hold over me anymore.

Fang caution, I thought. Fang Spike, fang Lap, and fang the investigation. And fang sleep.

I seized some smelling salts from behind the bathroom mirror and sucked in half a can. I squirted some Buffalo Juice on my neck. I poured some gravy down my gutchute to freshen my licker. When I slid into the Rover I was tingling like a freshly shorn sheep. Nothing was going to stop me now.

I'd heard the call of the wild.

THE IN-SEASON WAS on Ecstasy Street midway between Perky and Pliant. It was a real sleazy part of town, full of sniff shows, heavy petting saloons, and all-fours clubs, and thick with staghounds, carpet chewers, and shaved poodles. But it was also popular with well-at-heel whelps from Airedale and Baskerville, who crowded the bars, swaggered down the streets, and picked fights with the locals, like you couldn't really call yourself a mutt till you'd tasted slime. Sometimes thrill-seeking kitties even slinked in from across the river to play chicken in the gambling houses—often the fire brigade had to be called out to rescue one of them chased up a tree or flushed down a drain.

I parked my tooter under the monorail and locked the doors tight. Next to the hotel entrance a mangy fleabag with untrimmed whiskers was lounging against a wall, sucking rusty water from a flask.

"Whatcha looking at, buddy?" he sniped.

"I ain't your buddy and I ain't looking, pal."

I breezed into the lobby feeling full of coyote juice. There was a droopy little mongrel behind the front desk leafing through some dog-eared comic book—he didn't even glance up when I bounded up the stairs. But I knew the In-Season well enough by now. A lot of notorious things had happened within its Kleenex walls. In Room 403, the archbishop of San Bernardo had been caught licking brown sugar off the floor. In 612, a bucket of water had to be thrown over the governor of Newfoundland and three silky terriers. In 101, the very room whose door I was now rapping on, an untold number of Dalmatians had been skinned alive.

"Who is it?" The voice was so sultry it'd put mildew on a wall.

"It ain't room service."

"The door's open—come right in."

I paused, wondering for just one moment if I should've brought along my Schnauzer .44—if the whole thing was some sort of setup. But this was no time for shuffleback. I nudged my way inside.

She was standing in front of the window, wearing a steamy off-the-shoulder number and a sable so freshly dead its eyes hadn't stopped rolling. Behind her a pink neon sign blinked on and off, on and off, lighting up her flowing tail and furry profile. In a ceramic holder she held a smoldering smokestick that stank of moss, birchwood, and moor. The only thing thicker than her lashes were her flews.

"I want you to know what this means to me," she breathed.

"Can it, meatcheeks, I didn't come here for a head-pat." I closed the swinger and mushed across the room, glancing left and right.

"There's only you and me," she said, "I promise."

"You, me, and just two dozen ghosts if we're lucky. Know the history of this room?"

"Do I need to?"

"It'd only scare you."

"I don't like being scared."

I edged toward her, my chest out like a barrel. "You're safe with me, titbits."

I was so close now I could see the beads of saliva on her lipstick. Her tongue was out like a red carpet. I shook myself.

"First things first," I said. "How'd you get my name?"

"I overheard you talking to my husband—I was crouching outside."

"Then how'd you get my number?"

"My husband ran a check on both of you as soon as you left. I sneaked into his study and checked his notes."

"They don't give Dog Force details to just anyone."

"My husband has very high contacts."

"How high?"

"How high does it go?"

She was staring at me the whole time with her beady yellow eyes. Half of me wanted to sink into those urine-colored pools and frolic across the hills and dales for eternity. The other half didn't want to show any chink of weakness.

"You sound scared of your husband."

Finally she looked away, blowing out a plume of smoke that dissolved around her in a pink-lighted mist. "I'm scared of him . . . and I'm scared *for* him."

"I don't get you."

"You'd have to know my husband—it's very complicated."

"I ain't going anywhere."

She took another drag of her mulchy smokestick. "As a cub, my husband was humiliated by his lack of power. He was determined never again to be in such a position. It became his obsession. And yes, he did a lot of dubious things to gain his sense of control, but nothing ever illegal. But lately . . . lately he's got mixed up with some very strange types . . . shady cats . . . financial wolves . . . political animals . . . and he's changed . . . he's changed dramatically. He doesn't even seem to realize it. And me . . . I don't know what to think."

"You want to know if you should leave him?"

"Should I?" She stared into my eyes and I felt a jolt run from the end of my tail to the tip of my snout. My mind reeled back to my days as a whelp, when I'd spent half my playtime drooling over vixens in smelly sniffrags. And I wondered how it might be, just me and this fox snuggled up in some burrow together.

"You do what you think is best, porkchop."

She edged forward. "But do you know something? Does the cat know something?"

"That cat thinks he knows everything."

"But does he really think my husband is involved in those murders? Those terrible murders? I don't want to believe it . . . I'm terrified."

I wanted to tell her everything. I wanted to protect her. Trouble was, I hardly knew anything—Lap kept his cards close to his brisket. "The cat doesn't trust your husband," I admitted.

"But has he found anything incriminating? Has he mentioned someone called Riossiti?"

"Riossiti?"

"Does he have any evidence—the Siamese?"

"He's got theories."

"So he knows something for certain?"

It sounded like she was willing me to say something. Like she really wanted to believe the worst. So she could leave her husband. And run away into the woods with me. Everything in her peepers seemed to be begging me for bad news, and everything in my gutsack was itching to deliver it.

"I don't know what he knows," I said. "He's as tight as a church warden's mousehole."

Her eyes dropped. "I see."

"But why not come and ask him for yourself?" I said. "He'll set you straight."

She turned her head. "I don't trust cats."

"You don't have to trust him."

"I don't like the way they move. The way they smell. They're not like us."

"You can work your charm on him—he'll bend like a rubber hose."

She was still looking away. "You're thinking of someone else."

"You worked your charm on me, didn't you? Why the red face?" I reached out and touched her elbow. "It's not too late, sweetbread. You can still make a move. For your own safety."

"No." Very suddenly—it didn't smell right—she was as cold as a kitchen floor. "You don't seem to understand. I need time."

"You don't have much time. If—"

"No." She stared at the neon sign. "I have to sort things out."

"I can put you in a safe house if—"

"I'm not going anywhere."

I frowned at her. "But you're not going back home now, giblets? It's too late for regrets." I reached out to touch her again but she jerked her body away.

"Please don't touch me. Please."

She had her bushy tail between us like a police baton. And I didn't like it at all. One second she was terrified of her husband, the next she didn't want to know me. Was it really something to do with Lap? Or was she playing me for a sucker? So I tried again: "Listen, foxy lady, if you don't want Lap to—"

"Leave me alone—*please*." She blew smoke at the window. Outside, the No Vacancy sign winked on.

My instincts were fighting like terriers. I didn't know what to do. I looked at her.

"Fine—if that's really the way you want it."

Nothing but her bushy tail.

I nodded, struggling to stay polite. "Your choice, ma'am."

I backed across the room, listening hard for a sniff, a whimper, a tone of regret. But nothing. At the door I paused. "You never told me your real name."

"Read it in the newspapers," she said.

I should've arrested her right then, but too much of me still wanted to believe she'd really wanted me. So I just slammed the door and headed downstairs, drained and confused. When I entered Pliant Street the tramp slurred a question:

"Know where the nearest boneyard is?"

"What's it to you, pal?"

"I need to bury my hopes and dreams."

"You and me both, pal." I headed for my tooter—I was going to wait for the vixen to come out, then tail her—but the tramp had one last snipe:

"Catch ya later, investigator."

And I stopped in my tracks, blinking. *Investigator?*

I swung around, prepared for anything, but the tramp was already on his feet and scampering away.

Quick as a flash I bolted after him. He turned down a scummy alleyway. I chased madly, tossing aside old crates and cardboard boxes. There was a brick wall at the end, but the tramp was a spring-heeled jack—he hurdled it in one jump. I sprang too, but only got my forelegs over the top. I tried to haul myself over— my back paws were scratching for leverage—but I could already see it was too late: The tramp was whisking around the corner with one last backward smirk. And suddenly I knew it:

I'd swallowed the bait—again.

I dropped back to the ground and raced back to the In-Season, but the vixen was already sliding into a luxury Fuchswagen

—license plate OUTFOX—and snuggling up to a figure who looked like Reynard himself. Then they were launching off down the street.

I tried to chase but the chauffeur put paw to the floor and they rocketed under the monorail and disappeared into the Flagwag Expressway. I pulled up in the middle of the street, panting, sweat rolling off my licker, feeling dumbslapped. A giant billboard was glaring at me from the top of a nearby building.

WHEN IT COMES TO MEAT, I SURE AM A CHUMP.

Doofus Rufus said it all.

THE NEXT MORNING I said nothing to Lap about the In-Season, and he never asked why I didn't have Flasha Lightning with me anyway. He was camped in my office—it was like he owned the joint—with more newspapers around him than you'd find on the floor of a kindergarten.

"Look at this," he said, with his furry little smile.

It was the morning's *Growl*. The front page was all about the STUNNING KO at Solidarity Stadium, a series of snaps showing Rocky spinning out of the ring. On pages two and three there was an interview with the humble champion, Zeus Katsopoulos. "I'm just a simple kitty," he said. "I hope Rocky recovers." On page four there was another exposé of the Party of the Perpetual Underdog, with one of the leaders secretly recorded saying sympathetic things about the Persians. On page five there was an update on the war itself, with Brewster Goodboy pictured in consultation with General Wolfenson ("Instability in this region poses a grave threat to the globe," said the prez). Only on page nine was there any mention of the murder at the museum ("Police are still looking for suspects").

I grunted. "At least the old fox cooperated."

"Our request had nothing to do with the suppression," Lap said. "That order would have been issued, or implied, long before our visit. The plot isn't thickening, exactly—it's merely running to course."

"Worked out anything yet?"

137

"I sense I'm getting close. But now we must advance to a new phase. Might you have the time to join me for a little trip, Detective? No last-minute assignations?"

"No"—I coughed—"why?"

"You'll need all your wits about you. The cat I intend to visit is exceptional in many ways."

"Sure," I said, too embarrassed to ask questions, "then let's mush."

But Lap, to my surprise, stopped halfway across the room to examine the prints on my wall.

"Interesting paintings, Detective. Your choice?"

"Dogs not allowed to like art?"

"They can like whatever they choose. But I could not help noticing the marks of previous paintings underneath. May I ask what they were?"

I shrugged. "Old pictures of dogs playing cards, shooting pool—why?"

"So you replaced the original prints with these cat cubists?"

"What of it?"

"So some intruding voice, some sense of fashion, told you not to trust your original preferences?"

"They just seemed . . . wrong."

"How fascinating," Lap said, but in his irritating way he didn't explain.

Outside we squeezed into his fancy Jaguar. The seats were covered in imitation badger fur. The dashboard had a fancy fish-scale pattern. There was a tinkle toy hanging from the mirror and harp music playing in the tape box. The smell of mint and sandalwood was almost sickening. I would've stuck my head out the window but I couldn't work out how to wind the thing down.

"The vehicle itself runs on camel urine and cod-liver oil," Lap said. "Very environmentally friendly."

"I'll keep it in mind."

"You seem angry, Detective."

"I'm always angry."

"But especially irritable. Is something bothering you?"

"You wanna tell me where we're taking me to?" I asked—we seemed to be heading for the rump end of town.

"To Cattica Correctional Facility," said Lap.

"To *Cattica?*" I blinked. "The clanger?"

"If that's what you'd prefer to call it."

I didn't like it: Cattica was the hardest feline prison in the country, home of the worst of the worst, the really bad cats. Covering four acres in the middle of Chuckside, it was wedged between a dog pen on one side and a mad-dog house on the other. Only three cats had ever escaped from Cattica, and all three had immediately tried to "escape" back in.

"And who's at Cattica, anyway, that we—"

But suddenly Lap ran the Jaguar through some wild course changes down side streets and screwtail alleys—throwing pursuers off our scent.

"We being followed?" I asked, glancing behind.

"Not anymore."

I turned back to the road. "And who's at Cattica, anyway, to make all this worth it?"

"Perhaps you've heard of a cat called Riossiti?"

"Riossiti?" I asked—the name seemed familiar.

Lap glanced at me. "I assumed he was well known around here. Quentin Riossiti—the convicted murderer."

"*Quentin* Riossiti?" Suddenly it all rushed back to me. "The psychocat?"

"If that's what you'd prefer to call him."

Quentin Riossiti. I'd heard the name all right. The case should've been ours—there were dog victims as well—but somehow it never got near us. Humphrey MacFluff took complete control—no consultation at all. The story disappeared from the newsrags. The name drifted into nightmares.

"I don't like it," I breathed, shuddering. "I got no time for moggie murderers."

Lap shifted gears as we headed into Chuckside. "What do you know about Riossiti?"

"What's there to know? Made giant rat-traps for his victims, didn't he? Put their kidneys in a blender? Ate their brains with cottage cheese? Something like that."

Lap grunted. "The details seem to grow more extravagant each year—not that anyone, least of all Riossiti, has done much to challenge them. But the precise details remain frustratingly vague. One can only take a guess, for instance, at the exact number of his victims—perhaps as many as fifty."

I felt a chill in my gutsack. "Any cat with that number of kills should've been put to sleep a long time ago."

"Riossiti began the trial proclaiming his innocence—he insisted he'd been framed—but when the evidence became overwhelming he claimed insanity—the diminished-responsibility defense. The plea failed—in part due to my own testimony—but not without many strange antics in court. The death sentence, however, has been continually commuted. It's very curious. Almost as if Riossiti made a deal with the DA."

"He knows something?"

"It's difficult to say. When I first met him Riossiti was a brilliant psychiatrist and sociologist—Dr. Quentin Ledgewarmer, he was called then—with a special interest in hierarchical structures and social engineering. He wrote a few brilliant and highly influential academic texts, some of which were integral to my own studies. Have you ever have heard of *The Mighty Lamb*?"

"Only lamb I know comes in a Chump's can."

"It was Riossiti's most controversial work. In it he claimed that in any society, but in democracies especially, the most powerful force is neither dog nor cat but the highly impressionable public consciousness, which he compared to a mighty lamb that everyone—literally everyone—is attempting to shepherd in some direction."

Again I remembered the longhairs who'd infected me in my youth. But I only shook my head. "The lamb isn't in charge if it's being shepherded," I said. "The sheepdog is."

"Ostensibly the sheepdog shepherds the lamb, yes, but if the sheepdog owes its very existence to the lamb, and devotes the bulk of its time controlling the lamb, could it not be said that the lamb is really shepherding the sheepdog?"

"He wrote this before or after he lost his mind?"

"Riossiti's point was that there comes a time when, through our unrelenting attention, we allow the lamb to take control of us. It was his intention to examine the worlds of politics, media, and marketing to identify the precise moment of surrender. Part of this involved a close study of feral cats and dogs, whose minds he regarded as the closest we have to the primeval consciousness—untainted by societal conditioning, aspirations of status, or the laws of fashion. But then he was recruited by a secret think tank, part governmental and part private enterprise—Phineas Reynard himself was involved—and something very strange happened. He changed his surname to Riossiti. He ceased writing. He denounced his former work. He withdrew from society. And for some inexplicable reason he became a mass murderer."

I snorted. "That's what happens if you think too much."

"Indeed." Lap seemed amused. "Indeed."

We arrived at Cattica.

"DO NOT TOUCH the cage. Do not approach the cage." The prison warden, a fussy Welsh Terrier with crimped hair, was leading us downstairs through a series of wire security doors. "Do not listen to his taunts—he is a consummate trickster. Do not stare into his eyes—he will try to mesmerize you. Do not allow him to whisper—it's a ploy for drawing you close. And whatever you do, *never* reach in and stroke him if he purrs—you might not live to regret it."

I did my best to laugh it off. "What's he gonna do, hiss at me?"

The Welshie looked at me like I couldn't possibly understand. "Do you see these?" He gestured to three claw marks on his throat. "There are six more of these under my shirt. And more on my hindquarters. And I was one of the lucky ones—I only required stitches."

He led us past a command center full of armed Dobies and closed-circuit buzzscreens. There was a door like something you'd find on a bank vault. The Welshie spun the dial but paused before opening it. "I'll have the security buzzer ring after exactly five minutes," he said, grave as a headstone.

"We might need more than five," I said.

The Welshie shook his head. "That's all Riossiti is allowed. Besides, more than five minutes would be dangerous to your mental health. I'm sure Special Agent Lap will concur."

Lap gave a nod.

"Then I wish you a safe journey," said the Welshie, like he was sending us into a war zone.

We stepped into a gloomy dungeon and the door clanged behind us. I blinked, adjusting my eyes. There was a row of cages curling up the left wall. There were strange hisses and purrs. Licking sounds. The nauseating stink of unemptied litterboxes. Somewhere a generator was pounding like an elephant's heart.

BOOM BOOM BOOM.

Lap straightened his tie. "Ready, Detective?"

"I ain't never been less scared."

Then the cat was moving ahead of me into the dark. I wrenched myself forward and hugged his heel.

A mad Burmese chuckled at us from the first cage. In the second cage a long-haired mackerel tabby in an orange jumpsuit—I think it was the terrorist Muezza al-Qit—was doing prostrations. In the third cage a half-bald Birman—he looked like he'd bitten off his own fur—was fighting madly with his blanket.

We pulled up in front of the last cage. It was half in darkness. There were tiny bones on the floor. Artworks of fences, fireplaces, and cozy hearth rugs. A carrion smell of decay and sour milk. And at the back, reflecting the light from behind us, two glowing, blinking, grass-green eyes.

BOOM BOOM BOOM.

"Quentin—may I still call you that?—I have no need to introduce myself."

Not a whisper from Riossiti—just those evil staring eyes.

"Come now, Quentin," said Lap. "Your *tapetum lucidum* is showing."

A few blinks, but still not a word.

"We have a limited amount of time, Quentin—less than four minutes left."

Nothing.

So I coughed. "Open your snapper and start mewing," I snapped—partly to steady my nerves, partly to hide them.

For a few seconds, just his unblinking eyes, narrowing slowly.

Then a voice that would curdle cream.

"Well, well, well. Look what the cat dragged in."

Then the eyes were moving forward—there was the jingle of a collar bell—as he glided out of the darkness. He was coming straight at me. I held my ground.

BOOM BOOM BOOM.

He stopped like a streetcar about half a leashlength from the bars. And stared at me.

BOOM BOOM BOOM.

He was a common tabby, striped like a tiger, his head tilted up like royalty, but his eyes were sunken and his coat greasy, like he'd been locked in a garden shed for a month.

"'Here comes a pair of strange beasts,'" he hissed, "'which would drool in any tongue.'"

Lap nodded. "*As You Lick It*—act 5, scene 4."

But Riossiti never removed his green eyes from me.

"Who are you, sir—please tell me your name."

I swallowed. "I'm Detective Max—"

"His name is irrelevant, Quentin," Lap interrupted. "We're not here to socialize."

Riossiti smiled, and I noticed for the first time his filed-down fangs. "My Shakespaw-loving apprentice says that you're irrelevant, Detective Max. How does that make you feel?"

Lap didn't give me the time to answer. "We're here to seek your assistance, Quentin. Perhaps you've read of the recent murders in the Kennels?"

Riossiti sneered. "Your friend asks me about some murders, Detective Max. Does he really believe they give me access to newspapers here?"

He was still piercing me with his peepers, daring me to be sucked into his evil spell. I tensed myself and stared back.

"Three separate murder scenes," Lap went on. "One killer— an unidentified feral, still on the loose."

"A feral, your partner says. He clearly remembers my exhaustive study of ferals. Of the lower intelligences in general."

He was baiting me, I knew it, but I made sure I didn't twitch. BOOM BOOM BOOM.

"Four confirmed victims so far—two hoodlums, one guard dog, and a marketing manager from Chump's Incorporated."

"From Chump's, your partner says." Now Riossiti actually glanced at Lap, as if something finally clicked, and for the first time I noticed he was holding a little white mouse in his right paw, stroking it madly. "Good riddance to bad meat," he said, chuckling. "Or is that the company's motto?" Then he looked back at me with the killstare.

"But do you see any connection?" Lap asked. "Does it mean anything to you? Do you know something about Chump's?"

"Your partner calls me by my first name, Detective Max, as though we share an agreeable past. But does he really expect answers from me now, when he was so instrumental in my conviction?"

"I was merely asked for my opinion in court, Quentin."

"He played a role, that's what your partner really means."

"I played no role. I told the truth."

"He played his role in telling the truth—in testifying at all."

"I know you initially alluded to some great conspiracy, but—"

"Tell your friend it doesn't really matter," Riossiti said to me. "Nothing really does. 'All the world's a pound, and all the cats and dogs merely pets.'"

Someone in one of the other cages giggled madly.

"There's a connection to Phineas Reynard as well," Lap went on, "whom you know personally. And perhaps with a certain boxer—a feral cat by the name of Zeus Katsopoulos. He destroyed the reigning dog champion, Rocky Cerberus, in a first-round knockout."

But Riossiti no longer seemed to be taking it in. He stroked his little mouse and stared at me. "Tell me, Detective Max, does your back leg twitch if you get tickled under the ribs? Does the jingle of keys make you expect a walk? Did your daddy train you to cock your leg or did it come naturally? Will you vote for Brewster Goodboy even though you must know he's a corporate stooge?"

"What's that got to do with anything?" I snarled.

Riossiti smiled his stunted fangs, happy enough to rile me. "'Roses are black, violets are white, the cat doesn't purr and the dog doesn't bite.' Have you ever had your scruples so scrambled that you no longer trust your most fundamental principles, Detective Max?"

"No games," Lap insisted. "Quentin, I ask you. If you know something about ferals or Phineas Reynard—about anything—please, say it plainly."

"Act 3, scene 1—"

"What?"

"Act 3, scene 1, line 106, *Much to Mew About Nothing*. Ask your friend if he remembers it."

Lap didn't hesitate. "'Some rats are killed with snares, others with sounds.' What does that mean, Quentin? Something to do with subliminal messages, is that it?"

Riossiti grinned at me. "Tell your friend I no longer have anything left but my games. Some sell their souls, I sold my sanity. And now the only thing saving me from execution is my unpredictability—the very possibility that I might divulge something explosive. But I would hardly expect you to understand, Detective Max." He sniggered. "'As a dog returneth to his vomit, so a cat returneth to his toys.'"

I was about to give him some jawback but there was a ringing sound—our five minutes were up. And I'd sure had a gutful of Riossiti anyway. He was like a tick who'd dug into my brainpot and sucked out the sense.

"One last time, Quentin," Lap tried. "Will you play ball? For my sake? For the sake of society?"

But Riossiti didn't give a damn. "Your friend would condemn me to everlasting shame, Detective. But Quentin Riossiti might already be beyond that."

The bell rang again.

And Riossiti did a strange thing. He lifted the little white mouse and—*snap!*—he bit off its bobble. One bite of his stunted teeth, one swallow, and the head was gone. Then he tossed the body onto the floor as blood dribbled down his furry chin. And he chuckled.

"Ding dong dill,
Pussy likes to kill.

Who made him so?
That's for you to know."

And like one of Phineas Reynard's clockwork roosters he drew back into the darkness, and all that was left were his evil green peepers.

"Come with me, Detective," Lap said, disgusted. "We've wasted our time. Dr. Riossiti is no longer interested in contributing to justice."

As we went past the other cages—the other inmates were shrieking like chimps—I could feel Riossiti's peepers burning holes in the back of my bobble. I took one last backward glance but there was no sight of him, nothing at all—the darkness was as black as his murderous cat soul.

"THAT WAS ONE sick kitty."

Now that we were back in the Jaguar I couldn't believe I hadn't just rammed my fangs against his cage and scared the living worms out of him.

"You would be unwise to take Riossiti too seriously," said Lap.

"Defending him now, are you?"

"I'm merely suggesting that he might not be quite as mad as he seems."

"He's a killer, ain't he? That don't count for madness in the cat world these days?"

"You would have to had met him in his academic days. He was brilliant and charming back then. He remains charming, in a curious way."

"Charming like a rectal thermometer."

"But there's a certain method to his madness—you'll admit that?"

"Madness is madness. You put a needle in it. You don't give it a smack on the ribs."

Lap shook his head. "Riossiti's insanity, I assure you, is not somatic. If he lost control of his mind—and if he continues to promote that impression—it's merely as a by-product of his brilliance."

"You gotta be kidding."

"I'm entirely serious." We were weaving in and out of traffic on the Liberty Expressway. "Social engineering has a habit of throwing up challenging ethical dilemmas. It's more than likely that Riossiti faced a score of them during his secretive work for the think tank. Enough, in any case, to unbalance his whole ethical framework, with devastating consequences."

"Everything's the government's fault, ain't it?"

Lap glanced at me, probably guessing that I didn't like the government any more than he did. "Did you know, Detective, that some years ago a secret government laboratory formulated a completely safe and inexpensive formula for flea control? Something that would have negated the need for flea collars, flea powders, flea treatments—and all the associated discomforts? And yet before the formula could be properly medicated, presented to the appropriate authorities, and run through the necessary tests, it fell victim to a highly influential focus group of social engineers. And suddenly a dangerous new society was envisaged—a world in which dogs were not distracted, aggravated, and belittled by their fleas. In which they might suddenly be free to become bored, jealous, resentful, and rebellious. So it was decided, after much confidential debate, that it would be best to suppress the magical formula in order to preserve the stability of society. The fact that numerous senators had their campaigns funded by existing flea-treatment companies had, it goes without saying, no official influence on the decision."

"You're telling me you cats had a foolproof flea killer?" I gnashed. "And you buried it?"

"I'm afraid so."

I shook my head. "Typical conniving cats."

"You think so?"

"What—you defending them now?"

"I merely suggest that there is often more to social dilemmas than meets the eye. In his books Riossiti suggested that a dog's psychology makes him happiest with a rigid hierarchical structure, a firm master, a strict routine, and carefully defined limitations. Unbalanced, bored, or spiteful, the dog can easily become depressed and angry. Is that good for society? Of course not. But is it good for the dog? Equally not, one could argue."

"So dogs need fleas, is that what you're saying?"

"Personally I would find the argument unsustainable. But then I was not privy to the full details. Perhaps the data was compelling. And perhaps it's not really so outrageous to suggest that we all have an appetite for aggravations, and the dog divested of his fleas is a dog who instinctively looks elsewhere for indignation. Anger management, as Riossiti himself used to say, is one of the staples of social engineering."

For a second I remembered my own appetite for radical texts. "Well, I'm getting angry right now," I said. "Maybe we should go back to Riossiti and argue the point jaw to jaw."

Lap took the sweeping off-ramp into Compliance Avenue. "Whatever you make of Riossiti now—and regardless of how many he killed—I assure you he did not begin as a dog baiter. That verse of Scripture he quoted—'As a dog returneth to his vomit, so a cat returneth to his toys'—is equally disparaging of both canines and felines. Is a dog that swallows its own filth any more objectionable than a cat obsessed with trinkets and manipulations? Or is it all part of a natural order, too ossified to break down? Riossiti always argued that the one psychological characteristic more developed in the cat than the dog is inquisitiveness—a pathological need to seek answers. But really, is life any more fulfilling when one is trying to find a path through a maze of unanswerable questions? Might it not be best to refrain from poking one's nose into every room and every mysterious crevice? And stay within one's own boundaries? It's

significant, in any case, that he changed his name to Q. Riossiti—'Curiosity'—before he was caught by the police. Clearly
he was trying to make a statement of some sort."

"With another catty little game."

"Virtually everything Riossiti says begs a deeper interpre-
tation. The Shakespaw, the Scripture, the link of instinctive
behavior to voting habits, the poetry . . . everything he said and
everything he did."

"Snapping the head off a mouse is poetry now, is it?"

"Who can say what he really meant by that? Did he kill for
food or amusement? Riossiti always argued that the cat that
kills for sustenance—as ferals do—is exercising a responsibility
to himself. The cat that hunts for pleasure—as fat-cats do—is
beneath contempt."

I didn't mention my pig-hunting with Spike.

"One thing's for certain, though," said Lap, "we've not yet
heard the last of Q. Riossiti—I can promise you that."

"I thought you said he didn't want to help?"

"Riossiti was acting and so was I. It's not for nothing that I left
my contact details with the Cattica warden. Mark my words—
Riossiti will attempt to contact us. My only hope is that it's not
too late when he does."

I shuddered. "Well, don't expect me to hold back next time.
There's only so much stirring a bullie can bear."

"I'll warn Riossiti to be cautious," Lap said, but I could tell
he had his licker lodged in his furry little cheek. I unleashed a
whopper, just to irritate him, but he pressed a little button and
the windows purred down.

BACK IN MY office Lap was fussing over his patterns, still try-ing to find the thread that made everything plain. His survey map of the Kennels now had colored pins all over it showing the murder scenes and all the places the killer had been sighted. Looped around these pins he had lines of red and yellow wool, crossing the map, intersecting, turning at sharp angles, so that altogether it looked like some modern art tapestry. He had cards, too, each holding scraps of information he was trying to piece together: the riddles of Quentin Riossiti, the responses of Phineas Reynard, the clues of Don Gato and Pompey the Gross. And meanwhile he was getting up-to-the minute reports on everything from the employment record of Corky Farr-Fetch (once with the United Boxing Federation), to the movements of Zeus Katsopoulos (on his way back to Greece by private jet), to the latest from SI and Dr. Barnabus (a new report on the Katso-poulos hair Lap had picked up in the limousine).

"A chemical analysis shows trace elements of somatotropin and sildenafil citrate," Lap said, looking pleased with himself.

"Bark like a dog."

"Somatotropin is a common growth hormone. Sildenafil cit-rate is injected into feline erector muscles to make them engorge when under threat. Both have been known to be exploited in combat sports. You'll recall the way Mr. Katsopoulos doubled in size when the fight began?"

"So Katsopoulos is a hypohero?"

"That's an issue for other authorities," said Lap, "but it seems highly probable that he's been groomed in the same way. But by whom, exactly? And to what ultimate end?"

Working three janglers at once—his pocket unit, his hotline, and my bone-colored dialer, so old you had to shout into it—he peeled open a sardine can and dropped a little fish down his gutchute, so pressed for time he didn't even have time to chew.

"Mr. Lightning," he said to me between conversations.

"Say what?"

"I believe you said you were hunting Flasha Lightning."

I spluttered. "That's right . . . last night . . . that's exactly what I left to do. To chase Lightning. Why?"

"I'd very much like to speak to him again."

"Good luck. I couldn't pick up his trail."

"I thought you said you had a good lead?"

"Seemed like a good lead. Turned into a frayed string. But I'm still gonna round him up—you can bet your whiskers on it."

He got distracted for a few seconds, talking to someone on the jangler, but before I could sneak away he put a paw over the squawker.

"Detective," he whispered, "if you're heading outside then I insist you wear a bulletproof vest."

"You gotta be kidding?"

"I wish I were. But all my instincts—and all my logical faculties—are urging caution."

"I ain't never needed a bulletproof vest," I said. "Never have and never will. Slugs just bounce off my hide."

And it was true. I could've ripped off my shirt and shown him the divots. I could've told him about the time at the police academy when I chased a wayward Frisbee across the firing range. I could've mentioned that night in Siam when I'd sprung out of the pit with guns woofing at me—they might as well have been using peashooters. I could've done all that, but I didn't want him using command words on me again. So I just left, finding Bud in the corridor, chewing his toothpick.

"Where you goin', Crusher?"

"Out to find Flasha Lightning, that's where."

"Too late, Crusher—ain't you heard? The whippet was found dead this morning."

"*What?*" I said. "Murdered?"

Bud shook his head. "The mutt put a leash around his neck and threw himself off a porch."

I remembered Flasha's quivering flanks and curled tail, his dodgy eyes and dry nose, but I couldn't quite match it with a suicide. Flasha was the sort who'd do backflips around the world before he'd top himself. Unless, of course, he was under more stress than I'd ever guessed. Or unless he'd been given no choice.

"This ain't good," I breathed.

"Talk about it with the chief, Crusher?"

"That what the chief wants?"

"He's been waitin' to get you alone."

"Sure thing." I grunted, making the best of it. "It's about time we had a bowwow, anyway."

But in his office the chief was looking out-of-sorts: un-groomed, watery-eyed, and his ten o'clock shadow was hitting midnight. He ordered Bud to shut the door and spoke in a low growl. "I need you to make a judgment call, McNash."

"'Bout what?"

"About the course of this investigation. About Special Agent Lap." The chief glanced at Bud and lowered his voice even further. "Is he making progress? Any progress at all?"

"Depends what you'd call progress, Chief. I couldn't tell you if we were going forward or backward. Mainly seems sideways, though."

"Then you're officially registering dissent?"

"I'm registering confusion, if there's a difference."

The chief squeezed the words from the side of his snapper. "Bud here tells me you think Lap should be taken off the case."

A buzz ran through me. "That possible?"

The chief sighed. "Already I've submitted a report to Commissioner Gordon Setter. I've told him how Lap is performing. Very authoritative. Very thorough. But at the same time I've had to admit that nothing's happening—would it be fair to say that?"

"You could say it." I felt my pumper throbbing.

"So we've got a mad killer on the loose and an investigator more interested in insulting Phineas Reynard?"

"You heard about that?"

The chief shifted. "Reynard jangled the governor. The governor jangled the commissioner. The commissioner jangled me. And the bottom line is they're gunning for a change, and sooner rather than later. But I don't want to do anything until I know for sure. I'm not delegating responsibility here, McNash, but I want your opinion. Should we show the cat the door?"

I thought of everything Lap had hinted about—great conspiracies, higher forces wanting the truth suppressed, corporate and government interference. And I wondered if I could be the one who'd flush him down the gurgler. But at the same time I was sick of all his hints, sick of running in circles, sick of not being in charge. At the side of the room, meantime, Bud Borzoi was nodding like a dashboard toy, so keen to get back on the case he was practically slobbering.

"How long will it take?" I asked.

"Give me the word and I'll jangle the commissioner. Humphrey MacFluff will be here in an hour."

"MacFluff?"

The chief squinted at me. "MacFluff will assume complete control, of course. I expect he'll engage you as second-in-command as usual. Why? Does that rub your fur the wrong way?"

In a flash I sized them up together, seeing Lap's tapestry map and fussy notes, seeing MacFluff throwing around his full cream gut. I heard Lap's mind-twisting philosophies, I heard Mac-Fluff gobbling a custard doughnut. I smelled Lap's high-price colognes, I smelled MacFluff's fishy cat scent. And I wondered if a change, now, would just be robbing Rover to feed Ralph.

But before I could answer the jangler sounded. The chief answered, spoke for a second, and hung up looking like he'd just swallowed a Christmas decoration.

"What's the meat?" I asked.

The chief was toneless. "Reynard Studios . . . just an hour ago . . . on the set of *The Unscratchables*." He shook his head in disbelief. "Jack Russell Crowe was bitten in half by a giant feral cat."

I DIDN'T MUCH care for the flickers anymore. In the good old days they were lean and mean and as hard as a concrete slab. *Where Beagles Dare; Dirty Harrier; The Good, the Bad, and the Mexican Hairless*. Movies where mutts were mutts, pussies were pussies, and everyone knew what you scraped off the sidewalk. But nowadays they were all bark-and-flash, bark-and-flash, born in yap rooms, manufactured in buzz-boxes, and rolled off the churn belt like Chump's.

Lap didn't seem to care for them either.

"Riossiti himself wrote of popular entertainment—the 'catnip of the masses' he called it. Tranquilizing fantasies essential to the pacification of volatile populations. Yet nowhere will you find the Mighty Lamb more conspicuous. An obsequiousness to the mass consciousness justified by the profit motive and the need to recoup enormous costs by enormous consumption. A world where the most successful flavor is the spiciest and most attractively packaged, regardless of nutritional value; where the lowest common denominator, like a lobby group of stupidity, wields a truly exorbitant power; where success feeds upon itself and the Mighty Lamb becomes ever more powerful and voracious—until it crosses the line where the sheep begins to control the sheepdog."

"All part of the great conspiracy, is it?"

"Not if the phenomenon is purely market driven. But what if

high-ranking social engineers, at a governmental level, decided that it's in the interest of the ruling elite—or indeed the greater organism itself—to keep the public intelligence at a pliant and highly impressionable level? To celebrate the undemanding? To promote the inane? And simultaneously encourage the higher arts to mutate into irrelevancy? Why, if that were the case, fully grown hounds might be playing with toys meant for pups, reading books meant for whelps, and listening to music snarled by junkyard dogs."

We were speeding through traffic in the Jaguar and I could tell Lap was excited in his quiet catlike way—not with the new murder, exactly, but with the chance to see a pattern: something he could pin on his wacky map and fit into his messy puzzle. Of course, I didn't mention that I'd been a second away from turning nose on him, but it gave me a good feeling anyway, knowing he was at my mercy whether he knew it or not. I had dominance. Now all I needed was the excuse to use it.

Reynard Studios was on the riverside of Ribeye next to the disused Wagtail Park with its sagging roller-coaster tracks. We flashed our tags and got ushered through some half-built fairy-tale sets to the scene of the crime—an elaborate mock-up of a disused fun park. At the rear was a painted backdrop of some sagging roller-coaster tracks. Wind machines stood ready to blow away the fog so they could pump in the dry ice. There was a crumbling ticket booth, an old sheep carousel, and a House of Horrors made up to look like a veterinary surgery.

"It was like nothing I've ever seen—in real life or the movies," said Brian DePuma, the film's chief leash-puller.

"What happened precisely?" Lap asked.

"I was directing a scene in which Tom and Jack are about to kick open the House of Horrors to arrest a powder dealer. Suddenly there was an almighty squeal and this huge . . . *presence* . . .

sprang out of the building into the middle of the street, staring left and right."

"Did you get a good look at him?"

"It was all over in a flash . . . a feral, I think . . . monstrous . . . he looked directly at me, he looked at Tom, then he looked at Jack . . . and it was almost as if he recognized him, Jack . . . and he opened his jaws like a steel trap . . . and, forgive me." DePuma shivered. "I've never seen so much blood anywhere, even on the screen."

"He targeted Jack Russell Crowe, you say?"

"He seemed to pick him out."

"Because he was a star, or because he was a dog?"

"I can't say, Inspector."

"And you were about to shoot a scene, you said?"

"That's right."

"Then did you happen to catch any of the attack on film?"

"If only we had," DePuma moaned, like he'd missed out on a money shot. "But it all happened so unexpectedly . . . just between the alarm for silence and the roll of the cameras . . . seconds before I was about to shout 'Action!'"

We wandered over to have a look-see at the body. Lying in two neat pieces in the middle of a pool of blood, the actor looked a whole lot smaller and less fearsome than he did on the big screen. I knew Crowe was popular in the Kennels. He'd played poodles and huskies and blue heelers and Labradors— even a bull terrier in *S.B. Confidential*—and always got the wags and twitches just right. Even I'd paid to see him in his famous role, as the bullmastiff gladiator who takes on the tigers of the Coliseum, and I joined in the howling when he died at the end. He'd won a Best in Show for that.

"I know something about ferals, of course," said the actor Tom Manx—he'd played one in *Forest Runt*. "But I've never seen

160

anything like this. If I didn't know better I'd say he was less cat than special effect, but special effects don't kill your costars. Not after the guild got its act together, anyway."

"Did you notice which way he went?"

"He bounded over the green screen and disappeared into the amusement park. Do you have any idea who he is?"

"We're trying to ascertain that," said Lap.

"Is he in the trade?"

"Not that we know of."

"Does he have an agent?"

I was never sure about Manx—whether he was on the level or just a trickster. He'd once played buddy to a dog in a mut-tonheaded cop comedy, but the woofer was such a slobbering imbecile that even the critic in the *Daily Growl* had snarled for blood and the picture got virtually chased out of the Kennels. Since then Manx had fallen over himself getting photographed with high-profile pooches—even playing packhounds and gun-dogs, heavily fluffed up and padded out, in a movie or two. And now he'd agreed to share the screen, if not the billing, with a famous dog star in a big-biscuit gangster flick. And his partner was getting loaded into the back of a meat wagon.

"He was so . . . sociable," said Manx, making with the watery eyes. "I know he had a reputation as a feisty little fellow, but to me he seemed so . . . well behaved . . . happy . . . such a friendly dog." He shook his head. "He didn't deserve to go like this."

"A quick death is a good one," I said.

For the first time Manx seemed to notice me. "Are you assigned to this case, Detective . . . with the inspector?"

"We're assigned together."

"How about that?" Manx grinned. "Dog and cat together . . . just like in *The Unscratchables*."

I was about to ask if he wanted my paw print but Lap called

us over to a video monitor. By great good luck a documentary crew had left its camera on long enough to record the murder. So for the first time we actually saw our killer in all his glory: a bearlike forest cat wearing nothing but a natural doublecoat, bigger even than Zeus Katsopoulos and twice as scary. In a mad whirl of movement—even in slo-mo it was a blur—he snapped Jack Russell Crowe like a breadstick and tossed him aside much as Quentin Riossiti had done to the mouse. Then he looked directly into the lens—eyes bulging, irises like slits, fangs dripping, hair waving—like he was staring straight at Lap and me, like he was challenging us.

Then static as he bowled everything over on his way past.

Brian DePuma shook his head. "He looked at the camera . . ."

"He'd need to be trained," muttered Manx.

"Perhaps he already has been," said Lap, though he didn't explain himself.

"WHAT'S THAT MEAN?" I asked. We were out of the studios, slipping away from a presspack and some buzzing publicists, and heading down Festive Street to Wagtail Park. "He's 'already been trained'?"

"Did you not notice on that video footage," said Lap, "how the feral made a quick check of the cast and crew before settling on Jack Russell Crowe? Before identifying a recognizable dog? Almost as if he'd been *trained* to kill dogs and dogs alone?"

"By who?"

"Most likely by the same facility that trained Zeus Katsopoulos."

"Zeus didn't *kill*."

"Given enough time, and bared claws, I've no doubt he would have come close. But even so, it's possibly because our killer was *too* good at his work that he needed to be put down in the first place."

My head was spinning like a circus-ring spaniel. "You're saying these two cats were groomed to take out dogs?"

"The efficacy of their work suggests a highly trained regime, requiring subjects with untainted instincts. Ferals would suit the need perfectly."

"The UBF?"

"Much higher. Which is why none of us—you, me, even the

killer himself—is safe. And why it's imperative to unearth the full truth before it's completely buried."

The gate of Wagtail Park was chained shut, but Lap squeezed himself under the fence and then popped up at the top, paw down, to help me over. I didn't much care to be seen in such a pose—being assisted over a fence by a Mog—but there didn't seem to be anyone around, thank the Master. I landed inside near the old ticket booth and took a quick scope.

The joint was riddled with weeds, cracked asphalt, and scattered garbage. The roller coaster looked like a half-eaten rib-cage. The whole place stank of rotting wood, peeling paint, and stagnant rainwater. I'd been here a few times in better days. On weekends you could hardly move, the concourse was so jam-packed, dogs nose-to-tail like slaughterhouse bulls. But there'd been too many scandals for the place to survive—mutts on the Big Dipper getting brained by the support posts, mating couples getting locked in the Tunnel of Love, dirty old mongrels using the Great Slide to clean out their scent-sacs. When the health inspectors gave the food stalls the official stiff-tail—the candy apples weren't the only things that had worms—the whole place buckled under the bad publicity. They should've chopped it up and tossed it in the furnace years ago. But the rumor was the government wanted an even bigger fun park in its place.

"Frisbees and biscuits," Lap muttered.

"What?"

"Nothing."

I had my Schnauzer .44 drawn and was too distracted for yapping. We were taking tight deer-stalking steps into the misty grounds, eyes shifting, sniffers twitching, ears swiveling—ready for the slightest sign of movement. Near the back fence there was a clump of gray-blue hair. Lap picked it up with tweezers and gave it a sniff.

"Feral," he said. "Probably got snagged on the barbed wire. Let's follow the trail before the Sensory Investigation team arrives."

"Not in on the conspiracy, too, are they?"

Lap sealed the hair in a snaptooth bag. "It only takes one."

But suddenly there was a yelp and a crashing sound from the side.

I froze, fur tingling. I looked at Lap and jerked my head. We fanned out and closed in.

The sound had come from between the fence and the old Freak Show, tattered canvas rolls still advertising the Three-Legged Dog, the Bearded Collie, the Forty-Pound Cat. I crept along the side of the building, stepping over a dead squirrel. I counted to twenty, steeled myself for action, and was just about to swing round the corner when there was a yowl and a flurry of movement—Lap, fang him, had got there first.

But the critter was too fast for him.

Something shot out right in front of me—a brindle blur, smaller than I expected—and I didn't wait. I pounced, grabbed fabric between my front teeth, and snapped him back, hurling him against the tin wall and ramming my Schnauzer into his snout.

"Freeze, maggot!"

"Don't shoot, Crusher!"

It was Nipper Sweeney.

But my pumper was still pounding, my hair was still standing on end. So I thumped him with my chest, just to teach him a lesson.

"What're you doing here, you son of a bitch!"

"I needed to see you, Crusher!" He looked sapped and dry-tongued, like he'd been running all day. "To speak to you!"

"About your job? I heard all about that, scumlicker!"

He was panting. "What—what've you heard?"

I lowered my gun. "What's there to say? Phineas Reynard showed you the door for bad reporting."

"There's more to it than that, Crusher, much more!" But now Nipper gulped and looked sideways, because Lap had arrived.

"You can speak in front of him," I said.

"Gee, Crusher, I don't—"

"Quit whimpering and start yapping!" I said—I almost chested him again.

He swallowed drool, caught his breath. "It's like this—"

"I'm listening."

"There was a story I was covering—two years ago, it was—about a couple of ferals living on the outskirts of San Bernardo, half in the woods, half in the 'burbs—"

"On the streets?" Lap asked, stepping forward.

Nipper still looked like he didn't trust the cat, so I shook him again. "Keep it coming!"

"They were roof dancing," he said. "Leaping from warehouse to warehouse—catching birds—jumping down to snatch things, then scampering away."

"Urbanized ferals," Lap said, nodding. "That explains our killer's adeptness."

"I went out to interview the locals . . . the cats were making a lot of trouble, and a vigilante pack was forming to catch them . . . but suddenly they just disappeared—no sign of them anywhere—and my report disappeared, too, never published or seen again!"

I felt something sting the back of my skull—I couldn't explain it.

"Phineas Reynard ordered the story suppressed?" Lap asked.

Nipper looked at him hopefully. "All I know is I went looking for those files yesterday, when I heard the killer might be a feral . . . but I found nothing, no trace—then I got whistled into the editor's office, and I got told I was no longer required—*me*, an award-winning newshound!"

"No explanation?" I asked.

"Not a thing!"

"Then you still might be able to help us," Lap said. "The names of the ferals—did you find out what they were called?"

Nipper nodded. "The locals called the smaller one 'Kitty.' The bigger one they called 'the Cat.'"

"But their real names, did you ever discover their real names?"

"Their real names were—"

But at just that moment a bullet hole the size of a kebab opened up in the side of the newshound's skull. His eyes spun, his tongue rolled out like a party favor, and he keeled over like a top-heavy trash can.

Nipper Sweeney had been nipped.

"DUCK!" HISSED LAP, and Nipper rolled over, dead, as another bullet whanged off the steel wall.

I looked up as I hit the ground, fixing eyes on a shadowy figure high up on the roof of the Stink Palace. I saw an assassin's rifle, a huge silencer, and the dark shape of the shooter himself. Then another puff of smoke as he fired again.

But I wasn't going to be picked off like a sideshow duck— bullies never die without a fight. So I launched from the ground and started plowing through mist. I ran over broken glass. I ripped up broken cement. I was moving so fast that when I reached the palace I had no time to pull up—I bounced off the wall like a medicine ball. I found a rickety old staircase and bounded up three steps at a time.

But when I got to the roof the assassin had already disappeared. There were only spent cartridges, a doormat to rest on, and the smell of something—deserts, prairies, carrion. I looked back into the park, where Lap was bending over Nipper, then the other way, into a vacant riverside lot, where there was a cloud of dust as something tawny and bushy-tailed blurred through the tangled weeds and tooter wrecks.

It was a twenty-foot drop. With no blankets to soften the fall. But I didn't hesitate. I was a dog-soldier again.

As soon as I hit the ground I did a commando roll and was on my feet before I had a chance to register pain. The assassin was loping through the mist. I dragged my Schnauzer out and woofed off a couple of shots. There was a blast of bristle at his shoulder—I think I hit him—but then he curled around a shed and disappeared.

I ran to the corner and did a quick scope and sniff. The place was a maze of deserted storehouses and cinder-block offices. Thistles. Rusty machinery. Broken windows. It was like I was back in the bombed-out cities of Siam. Only now I was chasing, not fleeing.

I rolled into open space and sprang to my feet with gun drawn. Nothing anywhere. I rolled for cover, sharpening my ears, but all I could hear was a barge horn from the river. Hugging a brick wall, I ran with my snout close to the ground, trying to pick up a scent, a blood trail—anything.

Behind an old boiler a couple of no-good whelps were chewing some grass—I nearly scared the ticks off them.

"See anybody run past?" I cried.

"Dunno, you haven't run past yet," they said, higher than a Soviet spacedog.

I poked my sniffer under every sheet of tin and every wall crack but all I got was spiderwebs in my nostrils. I crept along the side of an empty warehouse, shooting glances in every direction, and finally got a glimpse of something.

Distorted in a bent windowpane was the reflection of someone aiming something from a tripod. He was on the east side of the warehouse and seemed to be waiting for me. But I was too quick for him.

I ducked behind the building and circled it from the west, picking my way over rusty metal and old nails. My gun was cocked and loaded. My teeth were clenched. I reached the corner.

I sprang into open space.

"Freeze, cockroach!"

It was a pointy-eared Laika. He started to shrink away so I leapt forward, hurling him behind an old generator and pinning him in place.

"Who are you?" I barked, ramming my Schnauzer under his chin.

"I've done nothing wrong!" he squealed. "This is police intimidation!"

"Just answer the question!"

"I'm from the PPU!"

"The PPU?"

"The Party of the Perpet—"

"I know what it is! Why'd you shoot at me?"

"I didn't shoot at anyone! I'm only taking photographs!"

"Photographs?" I looked back at the tripod, saw he had a camera mounted on it—not a rifle at all.

"Haven't you heard?" he said. "They're gonna raze this whole area. They're gonna—"

"*Who's* gonna?"

"The Reynard Corporation. And the government. They're gonna build a giant casino here—Babylon Towers—a hundred and fifty stories high. The top floors connected to Kathattan by closed bridges and—"

I shook him again. "You seen anyone else pass through here, someone wounded maybe—"

But even as I said it there was a splash somewhere—the river. I flung the Laika away and raced through the mist, gun drawn. There were footprints in the mud. Droplets of blood on the reeds. I squinted and saw a rusty barge churning through the muddy waters. I looked back to the surface, waiting for something to pop up. But I didn't see him until it was too late.

In the blink of an eye he was dragged aboard the barge, dripping and smiling, still clutching his assassin's rifle. He flopped onto the deck and got to his feet, ducking into the cabin at once.

But not before he'd looked my way with those sparkling peepers. Not before I recognized him—those donkey ears, that pointy snout—from the newsrag headlines.

The most famous assassin in the world.

Carlos the Jackal.

Then the barge was throbbing down the Old Yeller to safety, melting like dogbreath into the mist.

I LIMPED BACK to Wagtail Park. The gates were open and the SI boys had flooded in. Nipper Sweeney was getting a chalk outline like a cheap cartoon. Lap was conferring with the chief.

"What's that on your collar?" the chief asked.

I put a paw to my neck and it came away red. "A wound."

Lap examined the back of my head. "Bullet strike. It bounced off your skull."

"The first shot," I said, suddenly remembering the sting. "I must've got in the way of Nipper."

"Or perhaps not," Lap said. "More likely you're lucky to be alive." He held up a compacted slug. "One of the assassin's bullets—possibly the very one that struck you. You'll need to verify this with ballistics, but I feel confident in identifying this as a modified .338 Lapua case—a 'wildcat.' And there's only one assassin in the world who uses such ammunition."

I nodded, remembering the look he gave me from the barge. "The Jackal," I said. "He slipped away from me . . . just."

Lap nodded grimly. "Carlos the Jackal is good at that. But his mere presence here is proof that our foes are getting extremely serious." He looked at the chief. "Can we discuss this privately?"

A couple of cops were circling around. Bud Borzoi kept glancing our way like he was waiting for a morsel.

"In here," said the chief, and the three of us shifted deep into the half-collapsed Hall of Mirrors. "What's on your mind?"

Lap rolled his shoulders and spoke in an undertone. "Unless I'm terribly mistaken Carlos the Jackal's principal mission is to take out the Cat—the rogue feral that Mr. Sweeney told us about. The report of Jack Russell Crowe's death would have alerted him to the killer's whereabouts. But at the same time those shots at Sweeney and at us were no accidents. This is simultaneously a sinister and a very encouraging development."

"I don't follow," the chief said, frowning. "You're happy to be shot at?"

"Someone must know we're getting close. And they'll stop at nothing—certainly not lives—to conceal their secrets. But at least one of those secrets is now becoming clear. The feral has been specifically trained to attack dogs. As a means of showing dogs just who's in charge."

"You show dogs who's in charge by killing them?"

"By thumping them. In the boxing ring. Part of a much larger tapestry of social engineering, all carefully timed and calibrated to coincide with President Goodboy's election campaign."

"To make dogs vote for Goodboy?"

"The proxy cat candidate, yes."

The chief still didn't look convinced. "Got any evidence of this?"

Lap's whiskers tightened. "You'll have to trust me, Chief— and I take no pleasure in revealing this—but such conspiracies have been common currency in Kathattan for some time now. The efforts of many, including Humphrey MacFluff, to conceal the truth have been extremely effective. But now we might be on the cusp of something truly explosive. The commissioning of Carlos the Jackal only confirms my suspicions. This goes right up the chain."

"To where?"

But suddenly there was a burst of harp music as Lap's pocket jangler played a little tune. He flipped it open, looked at us apologetically, and slunk off to the side, deep into the maze of broken mirrors, to answer in private. The chief took the opportunity to speak to me in a whisper.

"Are you willing to stick with him?"

"How's that, Chief?"

"Now that your life's in serious danger?"

"Takes more than bullets to put down Crusher McNash," I said. "But I don't get you. Two hours ago you wanted me to throw him to the wolves."

The chief shifted, put his back to the cat, and spoke without moving his lips. "Just before I left I got some more information. Seems this Lap"—he nodded backward—"has a very shady past. Case tampering. Fabricating evidence. Cooking up conspiracy theories. Not to mention a lot of bad blood at the FBI."

"But he spoke of some top cat there . . . and somebody else at the CIA . . . said he'd trust them with his life."

"Both those cats are as bent as a T-bone."

"Says who?"

"Says the governor himself—he was the one who jangled me."

I looked at Lap, reflected back at me in a hundred busted and distorted reflections—a whole clowder of Laps. He was muttering into his jangler but he was looking straight at me, two hundred unblinking cat eyes—and then one of his ears turned, like he was listening in as well.

I swallowed. "So this whole investigation—?"

"Could be a means of leading everybody astray. So certain parties can be captured and silenced. Did you see any of the assassin's bullets go near him?"

"You're not saying he's tied up with Carlos the Jackal?"

"I don't know what I'm saying, McNash. I honestly don't know what to believe."

It seemed like this might be exactly what Lap had been warning about—a spiderweb of lies fanning out to wrap him up like a fly. Or, then again, maybe I was the one who was being wrapped up—by Lap himself. I felt the blood wet and sticky on my collar.

"What about MacFluff?" I whispered.

"Already on his way."

"You opened the door?"

"It's the only thing I could do. But I don't want Lap to know just yet. So are you willing to keep an eye on him until I get a better idea of what's going on? Even at risk of your life?"

I was about to answer when Lap returned, snapping his jangler shut. "That was Cattica Correctional Facility. Quentin Riossiti has agreed to talk, just as I predicted. This could be exactly the break we've been hoping for. Chief," he said, "may I borrow an impounding wagon?"

The chief stiffened. "Of course."

"And Detective McNash"—he looked at me—"are you ready to come with me again? 'Once more into the pit'?"

I glanced at the chief and I glanced at Lap—his icy blue eyes, daring me to run and hide.

Once more into the pit . . .

"Course," I said hoarsely. "I'm in this to the end."

But whose end that was I suddenly wasn't sure.

175

"THIS IS MOST undignified."

"Can it, chipmunk."

"There's not enough room to swing a leg in this thing."

"Be even less room if I get my jaw in there."

"Would you really care to join me, Detective?"

I felt a cold shudder. "Just can it."

We were in the impounding wagon, me at the wheel with Lap in the passenger seat. In the back, behind the security bars, was the carry-box containing Quentin Riossiti, mass murderer, his evil mug all that was showing behind the little grille. He kept running his pink licker over his filed-down fangs—I was watching him in the mirror—but whether this was because he was hungry or because he had something else in mind I didn't care to guess.

It was mid-evening. We were heading into Kathattan. To a fancy French muncherie, La Plume du Poisson—"The Feather of the Fish." It was a trade-off—fancy meal for info—but I didn't feel waggy about it. I still wasn't sure about Lap. I couldn't even be sure, after what the chief had told me, that the Siamese wasn't in cahoots with Riossiti—that the two of them weren't planning to team up on me, cut out my pumper, fry it like a trout, and gobble it down with a twist of lemon. Just the thought made me feel like I'd swallowed a canful of maggots. So I just kept driving, into the night, into the fog.

176

"I was hoping for a more civilized evening," Riossiti said. "This could well be my last meal."

"Why last, Quentin?" Lap asked.

Riossiti looked at me in the mirror. "Surely I don't need to tell your partner why?"

"We're not doing this for personal amusement," Lap told him. "You'll need to tell us eventually."

"Ask your friend if he remembers *Oldfellow*, act 2, scene 2, line 376."

Lap didn't even miss a beat. "'How pained are those that have not patience! What wound was ever licked but by degrees?' What does that mean, Quentin?"

"I reveal no explanations on an empty stomach."

"Just shut your maw," I snapped, tilting the mirror so I couldn't even see him by accident.

At Amity Bridge the traffic was snailcrawling. Searchlights were swinging through the mist, up into the crisscrossing girders, around the rail tracks, down into the murky river. At the first checkpoint there were six stiffbacked mastiffs in black-and-tan uniforms. They sniffed the impounding wagon, looked under it, shone flashlights inside at Riossiti—who hissed at them—and barked for our ID.

"Police business," said Lap.

The mastiffs waved us through. We were lucky. To the side a couple of Chows were getting probed against a guardrail. We joined the cat lane and whisked past the backed-up line of dog tooters. But then, at the far end of the bridge, there was an even bigger checkpoint, this one staffed by uniformed cougars. More sniffs, stares, and ID checks.

"Duration of visit?" one of the cougars snarled at Lap.

"No more than ninety minutes."

"We're tagging the vehicle," the guard said, stamping something electronic on the roof.

"One can never be too cautious," Lap said drily.

A boom gate rose and we rolled into Kathattan. And now my gutsack really started heaving, because now I was truly out of my territory.

"Have you ever been to the island before?" Lap asked.

"Why would I?"

And why would any ordinary mutt, except to feel bad about himself? Five hundred years ago the whole place had been bought from the local 'wowers for a smelly blanket and a knotted rope. In the centuries since then the pussies had done everything to preserve the place as an exclusive cat enclave, where dogs did nothing but water the trees, deliver newspapers, and eat the trash off the streets. Two years ago they agreed to open up the gates for the San Bernardo marathon—it was good for the buzzscreen—but so many dog runners piled up on one another staring up at the skyscratchers, and so many cats crowded the upper floors getting as far away as possible, that the whole thing was a bulldog's breakfast. As for me, I'd only seen the joint from a thwucker—a tourist flight—but even those had got snipped recently for security reasons.

And yet here I was now, gliding up the tree-lined avenues. Glancing at the spotless sidewalks. The Egyptian obelisks. The statues of sphinxes. The lion-headed door knockers. The sparkling windows of jewelry stores and perfume vendors and carpet emporiums. The opera houses. The theaters as big as temples. The flower boxes. The cast-iron lacework. The cemeteries with house-sized mausoleums. And everywhere the gardens—clipped and shaved and pruned and combed and watered with hidden sprinklers. In the Kennels, we had overgrown parks, where dogs ranged over hills and rolled down slopes and wallowed in mud pits. In Kathattan, they had finicky little gardens with fountains and hedges and gazebos, where the kitties curled onto little benches and leafed through their feel-good guides while sipping herbal teas.

It was about as much as a bullie could bear. Everything out there was virtually begging me to leap out the window and start ripping. Slinking, slithering, prancing felines drifting in and out of the fog like ghosts. Fat-cats in svelte pinstripe suits, waist-coats, and gloves, carrying camel-hide briefcases and rolled umbrellas and legal documents. Glamourpusses in furs and feathers and sparkling tomfoolery sashaying down the street with troutskin handbags and ribboned gift boxes. Upnosed gri-malkins with drumtight faces and horn-rimmed glasses leading pet lizards on jeweled leashes. Not to mention the occasional turncoat pooch—stuffy Pekingese and King Charles spaniels, mainly—mincing down the sidewalks like they'd never rolled in their own stink, never eaten their own vomit, never cocked a leg on a mailbox. The stench alone was enough to make me giddy.

I was so distracted that I only heard snatches of the madly rambling Riossiti:

". . . conspicuous consumption . . . artistic coprophagia . . . systematic domestication . . . the illusion of self-determination . . . the world as a theme park . . . infatuation with bodily functions . . . the worship of kittenish females and puppylike males . . ."

"Put a lid on it," I said.

"Actually," said Lap, "what he's saying is very interesting."

"Oh yeah?" I remembered the Cattica warden warning us not to listen to him for more than a few minutes at a time. "Got an ear for dribble, have you?"

Riossiti interrupted. "Do I really seem mad to you, Detec-tive?"

"Mad as a ferret."

"Then I've done my job well. But in truth you have nothing to fear from me. My only madness was—and continues to be—my curiosity. If that makes me mad, then you may call me barking."

"I'll call you whatever I want, gummy."

"Next corner," said Lap.

We passed a billboard showing President Goodboy wearing a leash and collar—not an image we'd seen in the Kennels—and finally I spotted the gilded awnings of La Plume du Poisson, wedged between a luxury hotel and an art gallery. I parked the impounding wagon in a vacant space in front of the joint. They were expecting us.

THE WHOLE PLACE had been closed on police orders. All bookings had been canceled and some high-society kitties were being turned away at the door. We had an armed cop at each exit and a Malamute playing watchdog in the corner. We had three chains hooked to Riossiti's collar—one attached to the floor, one to his velvet chair, one held tight in my paw. And under the table I had my Schnauzer cocked and loaded, ready to blow a hole through his catguts if he dared give me so much as a dirty look.

But Riossiti was acting like it was all just a lazy evening with old pals. He shared a gag with the maître d'. He chatted with the headwaiter. He waved to the chef. And he made his order without even checking the menu.

"I dare say we don't have sufficient time for the entrée so I'll go straight to the *plat principal,* if that's acceptable."

"Certainly, monsieur," chimed the waiter, a stuck-up Chartreux with curled whiskers.

"The swordspine snook, how fresh is that?"

"Netted last Friday in the Orinoco River, monsieur."

"Excellent. And what's the parrot of the day?"

"*Ara chloropterus,* monsieur—the red and green macaw, with a most exquisite undertaste of Brazil nuts and Jabillo nectar."

"May I see it?"

"One second, monsieur."

The waiter selected one of the bamboo cages that ringed the room and returned to show us the terrified-looking flapper inside. Riossiti put his mug right up to the bars and made sucking sounds, so the parrot looked like its pumper might explode.

"Yes, yes, very tasty," he hissed, eyes sparkling. "I'll take it braised and roasted very lightly—please make sure I can taste the blood."

"Naturally, monsieur."

"And please leave the beak and claws. I'll have a side order of *pommes parisiennes* with sour cream. And Pont l'Évêque cheese. And, Jean-Charles"—he hailed the milk steward—"what's the house goat milk?"

Jean-Charles produced a bottle of Château Chevrette.

"Vintage?" asked Riossiti.

"Squeezed this morning."

"Excellent. I'll take it skimmed and lightly dusted with cinnamon."

"Certainly, monsieur."

"That all?" I barked, losing patience.

"Oh dear, please forgive me," Riossiti said, "I've completely neglected my guests." He offered me the menu. "Would you care to order now, Detective? I highly recommend the mousse au chocolat."

"Snip it, nutsack. We ain't your guests and we ain't here for munchies. So shut your clamhole and start mewing."

"What my partner said is correct, Quentin," Lap said. "Your request was exceptional. Our indulgence to this point has been equally exceptional. We can only hope your revelations will be accordingly exceptional."

"Tell your partner he'll need to make his own verdict on that," smirked Riossiti. "But really, are secrets not best left to *après-dîner* conversations, when everyone is sated and comfortable?"

"We're comfortable now," I snapped. "So get on with it."

"Do you promise I'll be able to complete my meal before departure?"

"We promise," said Lap.

"Very well," said Riossiti, waving away the waiters. "Curiosity is a cat's most ravenous appetite, is it not? So why should I expect your partner to be any different?" He unfurled his napkin and nodded at Lap. "Please ask him where he'd like to begin."

"With the truth," said Lap.

"With the truth, the cat says." Riossiti smiled his blunted choppers at me. "And yet there are so many different varieties of truth, are there not? As many varieties, one might say, as there are South American parrots in this room."

"The trigger of my Schnauzer is sweating right now," I said.

Riossiti ran his licker across his fangs. "Ah well, Detective, if that's the way it has to be. 'Let them obey that hold not the can opener,' as they say." He sighed. "You can start by asking your partner if he's familiar with the word 'neoteny.'"

"*What?*"

Lap interrupted. "He means the retention of juvenile characteristics into so-called maturity. Go on, Quentin."

"Your partner is very cultured, Detective. But then he knows my work well, and neoteny was one of my areas of specialty. Not the physical aspects as such—though they themselves are fascinating—but the psychological ones. It was the subject of one of my best, though sadly unpublished, works."

"And what's this got to do with anything?" I said.

"It has everything to do with the pursuit of your investigation, let me assure you. For it was through this book, suppressed as it was, that I was recruited to a secret government organization."

"The Office of Enforced Perspectives," said Lap. "This is well known, Quentin."

"Your partner thinks he knows it all. But can he really appreciate how seductive it was for me, a doctor of psychiatry and sociology, to be consulted by some of the most influential figures in the nation? Political strategists, press barons, advertising executives, financial wolves, military tigers . . . figures with tendrils extending into media, entertainment, education, health, fashion, law and order, organized religion . . . anything with an influence on the Mighty Lamb?"

"Please, Quentin—this was all covered in the first stage of your trial."

Riossiti smiled at me. "Your partner is becoming impatient. Or perhaps just insensitive. Perhaps he doesn't want to hear the full story. Perhaps it discomforts him. The idea of a humble intellectual being corrupted by the company of big cats, foxes, and pooches. And all of them without exception living with contempt for dogs in their very marrow. Scornful of their intelligence, mocking of their pastimes and aspirations, disgusted by their uncultured taste, and yet inherently fearful of their numbers and potential for savagery."

I heard something sizzle in the kitchen and smelled something chickenlike. I swallowed my own slobber.

"The organization that made me feel so special was dedicated to manipulating and controlling the canine consciousness. They achieved this—or imagined they did—through a highly sophisticated combination of browbeating, brainwashing, and beneficence. 'Petting and bloodletting' they called it. They worked to some extremely complex mathematical formulae. They read the population like climactic conditions. They forecast mood shifts like meteorologists. They harnessed the pack mentality by exaggerating and encouraging foreign threats. They channeled unwieldy aggression into sporting contests. They pacified and intoxicated with frivolous entertainments and vicarious celebrity existences. They sustained futile hopes with endless lotteries and gambling opportunities. They riddled the populace with phobias about physical imperfections. They encouraged short attention spans and constantly reinforced powerlessness. They kept the population puppylike, in short, in order to keep it obedient and emotionally dependent."

Lap tried to interject—"This is nothing new, Quentin"—but Riossiti cut him off:

"Manufactured neoteny, they called it. Because neoteny's natural selection—the morose don't find partners and the cynical don't breed—was deemed too unreliable. Because they wanted to leash and muzzle an entire lower demographic with swift and measurable results. And why? For some noble purpose? For the greater good of society? For progress and stability?" Riossiti gave a hairball-coughing cackle. "Of course not. It was all so they could sustain their own form of neoteny. Furs and feathers. Crème liqueurs and fishcakes. Whispering galleries and back-alley gossip. Epaulettes and plunging gowns. Territorial show business. International catfights. Teasing and tormenting. Basking in the sun. Stroking each other and stroking themselves."

"Do a bit of that yourself, do you, kitty?" I asked, but Riossiti wasn't fazed.

"I became tremendously disillusioned, naturally, but I remained curious—too curious. I asked too many questions. I went into too many forbidden rooms. I looked under too much furniture. Because I wanted to know exactly what they were doing with my research. And for my sins I was framed. There was no point fighting it. They had immeasurable power. The only way to keep myself alive was to play their little game. To accept my own insanity. But that—"

"Quentin, you've claimed before that you're innocent and—"

But Riossiti whipped around—his chains jangled, his collar tinkled—and he stared Lap in the face.

"And do you really believe I was lying?" he hissed.

There was a furry second or two when the two of them glared at each other with tin-cutting glares, like two alley cats in a backyard dispute.

"Easy, tigers," I said.

But then the parrot arrived.

"DING DONG DEET"—RIOSSITI smiled—"Pussy likes to eat."

All knives, forks, spoons, and toothpicks had been removed, so he was left to dig in with his stunted claws. He flipped some macaw flesh onto his paw, tossed it into his gobbler, and chewed like he'd never tasted anything so sweet. He made lip-smacking sounds. He shuddered with pleasure. But when it came to getting the beak down his gutchute he seemed to have some trouble.

"Would you mind, Detective, loosening this collar a notch or two?"

"I'll loosen your ribs before I loosen that collar."

"I can do it myself if you'd prefer."

"Put a digit near that collar and I'll blow you and your nine lives through the back wall."

Riossiti swallowed lumpily and took a sip of his Château Chevrette. "Detective, I was rather hoping you'd be sympathetic even if your partner stubbornly refuses to be. But then again I can hardly blame you for being suspicious. It's true that one can quickly become what one pretends to be. By which I mean that I've now played the psychopath so long that I fear I've lost touch with my real identity. It's not something that makes me proud. Was I mad when I was seduced by the Office of Enforced Perspectives? I think I was, in part. Was I mad when I tried to claim

187

the insanity plea? Not at all—it was my only logical escape. But am I mad now? Of that, even I'm no longer sure."

"This is self-indulgence, Quentin," Lap said. "Are you prepared to name names or not?"

Riossiti smirked at me. "Your partner thinks I've shortchanged him. He believes I'm yet to live up to my part of the bargain. Alas, he might still be disappointed."

"Why disappointed?" Lap asked.

"Because he might not appreciate my rather perilous position—that I'm still in no position to say anything directly."

"What does that mean, Quentin?"

Riossiti stripped skin from the parrot wing. "Delicious," he said. "If I'm not mistaken I can detect a residue of Venezuelan clay."

"I said what does that mean, Quentin?"

"Answer the cat," I said, flashing my choppers.

Riossiti dabbed his maw with a napkin. "I mean that I've spent a good deal of my incarceration examining legal texts—those that I'm allowed to read, of course. And I know that whatever I say now can be attributed to me in court. And that, accordingly, it is not in my best interests to speak unequivocally, especially with an election imminent. So I find myself compelled to speak metaphors that can easily be dismissed as mad ramblings. Anything else and my life might end in a matter of days."

I leaned forward, shifting my gun. "It'll end in seconds if you don't make good with the meat."

Riossiti hissed at me—his licker vibrated like a snake's—so that for a second I thought he really wanted to be blown away, that this whole meal was about killing himself.

But then he cackled. "You seek information about murderous feral cats, Detective. About two cats, specifically, who have been programmed to kill dogs alone. You wonder how—and

188

why, and *where*—it was done. Well, I simply ask you to compliment the chef on this outstanding meal."

"That ain't an answer, fungus."

"Isn't it?"

Lap said, "You can still be punished, Quentin—privileges can be removed from you."

"Does your partner really believe I have any privileges worth preserving?" Riossiti sniggered. "Tell him to ask, when he compliments the chef, exactly how much the fish costs."

"What's the price of fish got to do with anything?" I growled.

"Tell him to ask specifically about the swordspine snook. And the red and green macaw. Ask the chef where the delicacies were obtained. And I don't mean the country."

"No more games, Quentin."

"When spearing a fish," Riossiti said, "the heron aims not at the image of the fish, but slightly askew, at the actual fish—is that not so? That's what I used to tell my students anyway. So why does your partner not simply follow my advice? There's no harm in trying."

Lap looked at Riossiti and then to me. "Can you handle him yourself, Detective, if he tries anything foolish?"

"I'll be all over him like flea-rash if he does."

"Then please give me a minute."

Lap nodded to the Malamute and went through the swingers into the kitchen. I saw him mewing with the chef as Riossiti returned to the meal, cleaning up everything—claws, ribcage, fish bones—like he might never eat again.

"Scared of water and yet not scared of me," he said between swallows.

"What's that, nutball?"

"Your partner thinks I don't like him."

"Like he gives a gopher's gizzards what you think."

"Do you like him?"

"He's a cat—what do you think?"

Riossiti smiled. "I think he's an extraordinary detective. With an intractable, impractical, infuriating code of ethics. And that's the real reason I can't bear to look at him, Detective. Because he puts me completely to shame. Because he would never allow himself to be led down any dark and twisted alleys. But don't be fooled by my acts of indignation—I like him about as much as a cat can. Just, for that matter, as I like you."

"I'm all warm and tingly inside."

Riossiti took a sip of his drink. "May I ask how you got that wound on the back of your head?"

"A mosquito bit me."

"Was the mosquito fired from an assassin's rifle, by any chance?"

"Who are you all of a sudden, that you're asking all these questions?"

"I'm Q. Riossiti. It's my curse. It's my destiny. But please let me assure you of something." He leaned forward to whisper, breathing goat milk over me. "I will do everything in my power to save you—both you and Agent Lap. Because it's so terribly important to protect honesty and integrity wherever they bloom."

"You're gonna save *me*?" I snorted. "You're off your saucer."

Riossiti leaned back and his bell tinkled. "It's all I have left, Detective—the possibility of public redemption. For what I got myself tangled in. For the unspeakable corruption I served. Please don't take that possibility away from me."

I was about to answer when Lap returned, looking like he'd swallowed a firecracker. "Detective, it's time to go."

"Were you satisfied with the information?" Riossiti asked, smiling his cut-tooth smile.

"Let's go. There's not much time."

"Time enough to finish my Château Chevrette?"

"If you hurry."

Riossiti read it as a victory. In one gulp he tossed down the rest of the milk and put down the glass, wearing a milk mustache and a Cheshire grin.

"PIÑERO AND VALDEZ Limited of Venezuela."

"What?"

"They have a warehouse on Loyalty Street in Fly's Picnic, just three sprints from the first murder scene. Can you take me there immediately?"

"Why?"

"It's an importer of exotic birds and fish. They supply the kitchens of La Plume du Poisson."

"This is Riossiti's big lead?"

"It is."

"So what is this—a murder investigation or a shopping trip?"

I was getting sleepier and angrier. My collar was biting my neck and I had a flea loose in my groin. And there was still no sign that was all going to end. We'd dropped Riossiti back at his Cattica cage—he'd said, "Au revoir," and melted back into the darkness—and now we were in the impounding wagon again. And all I could think of was Lap's face multiplied a hundred times in the mirrors of Wagtail Park.

"Piñero and Valdez Limited of Venezuela, as you might recall, was one of the listed sponsors of the Glory of the Pharaohs Exhibition. Not only that, but you'll remember that Reynard's vixen confused us initially with visitors from 'that South American place.'"

"So?"

"Does it not seem unusual to you that a boutique importer of exotic cuisine is sharing the stage with multinational corporations like Chump's and Reynard Media?" Lap shook his head. "It's a front."

"For what?"

"Why don't we stir up the feathers and fish, and find out?"

We glided into Fly's Picnic past a roaming pack of hoondogs in Hellhounds jackets tagging their territory with spray cans of urine. High above, a blazing billboard of President Goodboy urged them to "CATCH the spirit." As I swung into Loyalty Street the fog was lifting and dispersing.

"That's it," said Lap, gesturing to a warehouse ringed with gravel and barbed wire. Lit by soupy white light, a sign over the doors read PAVLOV. "An excellent place to train boxers, wouldn't you say?"

"You think the two ferals were kept there?"

"There's only one way to find out," Lap said, already opening the door. "But are you ready to put on a show again, Detective? Good cat/bad dog?"

"I was bred ready."

Circling the joint were at least three guards, each as big as a baby rhino. When we headed for the front door a nasty-looking Ridgeback, a steroid gobbler by the look of him, swelled out to stop us.

"Goin' someplace?" he snarled in his Afrikaans accent.

I swelled out, too. "Any business of yours, is it, pal?"

But Lap already had his ID out. "We'd prefer not to call in reinforcements," he said icily. "Or indeed, to check if your own registration is up to date. Or your work visa. Or your medical records, for that matter. The pounds are already so terribly overcrowded, are they not?" He gave a meat-slicing smile.

The Ridgeback wavered. "Hey . . ."

"Hey what?" I snarled.

"Hey"—the Ridgeback was already stepping away—"I don't need trouble."

I poked him in the chest. "Then back to your humping cushion, muscles."

When we blew through the front swingers I was full of ginger. The walls of the front office were covered with pictures of parrots and piranhas. There was a dopey-looking Labradoodle behind the desk.

"May I help you?" he asked, his tail jittering.

"For your sake I hope so."

Lap flashed his ID again. "We're investigating the theft of a prized and extremely expensive parrot. It was the property of a very high-profile sporting figure—I assume you've heard of Zeus Katsopoulos?"

The 'doodle blinked. "No . . . I mean yes, yes."

"You *have* heard of him?"

"Of course. The . . . the boxer."

"Then you must know how Mr. Katsopoulos came to form such an affection for brightly plumaged birds?"

The 'doodle gulped. "I don't think I . . ."

"He grew up next to the parrot market in Thessalonika. The birds, he says, remind him of home. Last night one his favorite birds was stolen from his Kathattan apartment. Mr. Katsopoulos—currently overseas—was distraught when he heard. May we inspect your stocks?"

"I don't . . . I'll have to call . . . this isn't—"

I thrust my muzzle across the desk. "Get those keys jingling, doodah."

The 'doodle looked like he didn't know whether to bark or

barf, as 'doodles usually do. But he fumbled for his keys and led us down a corridor.

"May I ask why there are so many guards outside?" Lap asked.

The 'doodle's tail was still shaking. "Noise restrictions," he said. "We're not allowed to use alarm bells."

"But the nearest property is a hundred leashlengths away."

"I . . . I don't make the rules."

We entered a back room and the fluorescent lights flickered on.

It was as big as a gymnasium. On one side there were a few fish tanks—maybe ten of them, holding sawfish, snooks, puffers, and pikes. On the other side—a long way distant—were about the same number of birdcages, each holding a different type of South American parrot. The air reeked of disinfectant.

"Why is there only one specimen in each container?" Lap asked, doing an inspection tour of the birds with paws behind his back.

"We like to keep them apart . . . no fighting."

Lap admired the flappers. "Beautiful birds," he said. "I can certainly see how Mr. Katsopoulos gained such an affection."

"What sort of parrot was stolen?" The 'doodle was trying to sound annoyed.

"*Ara chloropterus*," Lap said. "A red and green macaw."

"We have no *ara chloropterus* here."

"What about these?" At the end of the room there were two massive cages, each holding a bird with a huge beak.

"Amazon kingfishers," said the 'doodle.

"Of course," said Lap. "*Chloroceryle amazona*. But are they particularly active specimens? There are scratch marks all over the floor."

195

"Very active."

"And chew marks on the bars."

"They chew from habit."

"Not good for their teeth," Lap said.

"No . . ."

"And what about the cans of cat food?"

The 'doodle frowned. "Cat food?"

Lap looked at him. "The water vessels in these cages are cut from old Slinky Joe's cans. So cat food has been stored here recently. To feed the catfish, perhaps?"

The 'doodle coughed. "We have visitors . . . from Pavlov . . . they come here sometimes . . . we feed them in the dining room."

"Señors Piñero and Valdez of Venezuela?"

The 'doodle's ears dropped. "That's right."

"You feed the company owners from a can?"

"It's . . . it's a very cost-effective organization."

"No doubt."

The 'doodle tried to huff. "Would . . . would you care to speak to my superiors in Kathattan?"

"Not at all. I'm sure you'll do that as soon as we leave." Lap extracted a card. "But please be sure to mention my name. And please be sure to tell them we found you an unusually accommodating and enlightening guide dog."

The 'doodle looked trapped between a steel fence and a brick wall, as 'doodles usually do.

IN THE IMPOUNDING wagon Lap mewed openly about the big cages at Pavlov, the arrangement of cages and fish tanks, the scratch and chew marks—it could only be evidence that ferals had been imprisoned there, he claimed. I didn't say anything, but I couldn't help wondering why he was talking about all this out loud, when the tooter was probably bugged, and why he'd thrown himself among the pigeons in the first place, by being so hissy with the 'doodle.

"I drew a line in the sandbox tonight," he said, as if he'd already read my mind. "It's time to bare claws and flush them out once and for all. We're clearly beyond the need for smoke screens now."

All of a sudden he had a burr in his voice, like he'd been chewing on thistles, and I wasn't sure I liked it—it made him sound mad. "What's your plan?"

"Not yet," he said, as we pulled into the station parking lot. "Special Agent MacFluff has arrived, just as I predicted."

I looked at the cophouse. "You can smell him?"

"Not quite. But I can certainly recognize his car." He pointed to a Cadillac Sabertooth in the parking lot. "Ah well," he sighed, "shall I meet you over a soy milk, Detective, in, say, twenty minutes?"

"You're not coming in?"

"There's no point at this stage. I might be apprehended, even locked up. But that doesn't mean you can't sniff out the latest developments. If you're willing, of course."

I coughed. "Course."

"One caution, though. You'll hear all manner of lies about me, I can promise you that. So I ask you to remember one thing. Never forget the bullet strike in the back of your head. Never forget what they're capable of."

In my office I found MacFluff already having a bowwow with the chief. The fat cat looked even bigger than ever, his nylon shirt straining to harness his stuffed-cushion gut, his tie splayed down his brisket like a show ribbon. He had a sharkburger in one paw and mayonnaise on his chops. Sniffing, chewing, scratching his tail with a free claw, he fixed his squinty eyes on me.

"Crusher McNash—how goes it, pal?"

"I still smell and so does my nose."

"Agent Lap with you?"

"Don't know where he got to. Slunk off someplace."

MacFluff burped. "Makes sense. Cat's off his tree, you know that, don't you?"

"Fill me in."

"What do I gotta say?" MacFluff waved his burger at Lap's tapestry maps. "He's as nutty as a squirrel."

"Maybe." I shot a glance at the chief, who had his muzzle lowered.

"I'm tellin' you, McNash. The cat's been under surveillance for a while now. Just how he got assigned to this case, and how I got diverted to another one, is an all-you-can-eat scandal. It's being looked into right now." He gobbled another chunk of sharkmeat.

"Got evidence, have you?"

"Evidence of what?"

"That he's off his skull."

MacFluff squinted at me. "What's the matter with you, McNash? He's rabid—ain't that plain? Few years ago he was part of some secret government outfit—a population control squad or something. There were foxes up-country running amok. Thieving. Terrorizing. Breeding like rabbits. Lap and his hero Quentin Riossiti got sent into the field to study them— behavioral patterns or something. Both got bitten. Both went fizzypop. Riossiti was completely frothy. Lap recovered, or that's what we thought. Ever heard of a place called Pavlov?"

I made sure I didn't blink. "Pavlov?"

"A secret quarantine facility, an isolation ward. Runs out the back of a fish importer. Riossiti and Lap were there, caged up for months. Injections. Medications. Strict diets. Electroshock therapy. The works. Riossiti chewed through the bars and got out, started murdering. Lap pulled through and we took him back into the bureau—everyone likes a happy ending. Seems we were a bit hasty, though. Seems while he was chained up he'd developed a pathological hatred for foxes—they were the ones who'd sent him mad. Started to think up all sorts of wacky theories about Phineas Reynard, for a start. Sent him bags of anonymous hate mail—we've only just pinned it on him. Reynard and his vixen are very worried about it all, and who can blame them?"

I remembered Reynard's wife at the In-Season. And I couldn't help wondering, in the back of my bobble, if she might really be a victim after all.

"There were a couple of others—ferals—who Riossiti and Lap were using in the field. Tracking foxes for 'em. Got bitten as well. And now one of them's off rampaging—'the Cat.' And Lap's doing everything to save him. Throwing everyone off the scent"—MacFluff jerked his head at the maps—"so the Cat can get away. His old buddy. There's even a rumor he's got Quentin Riossiti in on the job—heard of that?"

I glanced at the chief—who was still looking at the floor—and shrugged. "Why would he do that?"

"Who knows? Maybe to jerk a few chains. Maybe it's all some sorta sick game—that's what he and Riossiti are into. Maybe it's worse than that. Got life insurance, McNash?"

"Me?"

"You've been at his heel these last few days. Maybe you ain't seen it yet, but he's ruthless, Lap. He'll turn you into mincemeat in an ear twitch. Hey." All of a sudden MacFluff was looking at me with a tilted face. "You tellin' us everything, boy?"

"What's there to tell?"

"Just the truth. There could be lives in danger here. Is it about Lap? You know something about Lap, is that it?"

I shifted. "Why would I?"

"Hey, boy"—MacFluff's eyes narrowed further—"if you've got something rotten on your tongue now's the time to spit it out. So come on, boy. Drop it. Drop it."

I felt a sting right through my brainpot. MacFluff was using command words, just like Lap.

"Drop it."

So I felt an almost overpowering urge to get a bad taste off my licker, to sell Lap to the skinner's (fang him—what had he ever done for me?).

"Drrrropppp iiiiittttttt."

But at the same time something inside was holding back. Something small but angry as a bullant. Something that went back to the war. To those radical texts. To the very idea of being manipulated. I didn't know if it was my bobble or my gutsack, and I didn't care.

"Drop it, boy . . ."

But I didn't drop it. I held on tight. MacFluff's peepers were burning holes but I didn't blink. I was as good as telling him—

telling the whole world—that things had changed. That I was my own dog now.

Bells saved me—the chief's jangler.

The chief answered with a look of relief, but almost immediately his ears flattened. I heard a few growls—"When? How? I see"—and he hung up. He looked at the two of us and spoke in a whisper.

"That was Cattica Correctional Facility. Quentin Riossiti has just escaped from his cage. He's stray on the streets right now."

HE'D COUGHED UP his fish and parrot meal, used the bones to pick the lock, the beak to snip the alarm wires, and the claws to hook onto the electrical cable linking the prison to Justice Street. Like a commando he'd sailed across the yards of the dog pen—where the inmates had started barking all too late—and dropped into the darkness beyond the south wall, where he'd hurdled a few fences and melted quickly into the back alleys of Chuckside, his collar bell tinkling and fading.

The chief didn't mention that me and Lap had taken Riossiti to a fancy dinner just a couple of hours earlier, and I was grateful for that. But it didn't seem to make much difference anyway, because I got the feeling MacFluff already knew exactly what I'd been up to, and was happy to make me feel like a sap.

"Got a place where you can lie low, Detective? Then I'd go there now if I was you. Lap's probably out to get you, if Riossiti don't get you first. And no bulletproof jacket's gonna save you now, pal—those two kitties wrote the book on assassinations."

When I got out of the cophouse my head was reeling. I didn't want to believe anything MacFluff had just told me, but I couldn't help remembering the shivering look of fear on the 'doodle's face. Did he recognize Lap from his days in quarantine? And what about the byplay between Lap and "his hero" Riossiti—was it all some sort of catty game? Not to mention the Jackal's bullet whanging off my skull—had the assassin been

202

hired by Lap himself? Was I meant to be blood-and-bone on some rose bed right now?

It was getting to the stage that I couldn't even trust my own instincts, and for a mutt there's no greater mind-frazzler than that.

Approaching my Rover I saw Bud Borzoi squirming out of the parking lot, looking like he'd just killed the family hamster.

"What gives, Bud?"

He pulled up. "Thought I saw something out here, Crusher."

"A stranger?"

"Looked like a kitty from where I was."

I shuddered, remembering Riossiti's evil green peepers. "Get a shape recognition?"

"Got away before I had a chance. But looked Siamese to me."

"Oh yeah?" I wondered why Lap would be prowling around— it didn't seem right—but I couldn't afford to loosen any secrets either. So I coughed. "You look after yourself, Bud. These are curly days."

"Sure are. Seen MacFluff yet?"

"I'm off the case. Not sure I was ever on it. You still running with the pack?"

"Just some retrieval work, that's all. Gonna miss you, Crusher."

"I'll be back, bigger and bitier than ever."

"Sure you will, Crusher."

Looking into Bud's sewage-brown eyes I couldn't help feeling a wave of yearning for the days, not a week ago, when he was my faithful sidepaw. But that was before Lap, before the dead 'weilers on the wharf, before I picked up my jangler. "Don't pick your teeth in Pugkeepsie," I sighed, noticing that Bud didn't have a toothpick in his snapper for the first time in memory.

"Catch ya later, investigator," he said, already slinking away.

When I got into the Rover something just didn't taste right, but I couldn't get my licker around it. I gunned the engine and turned into Duty Street.

I knew I was meant to stop at Pedro's but I wasn't sure if there was any point now. I still wasn't sure I should trust the Siamese anyway. Maybe he'd try another mind trick on me. Maybe he'd poison me. Maybe the safest thing to do was just go home and snooze.

But then again—I was almost at the bar now—why was I, Crusher McNash, running scared? I was a bull terrier, wasn't I? I never ran from anything. So why didn't I just storm into the bar, get some scruff between my choppers, and shake the truth out of him once and for all?

I hit the brakes.

Nothing happened.

I hit the brakes again.

Nothing.

I was already passing Pedro's and the Rover wasn't stopping. I kept hammering the pedal—the Rover kept going.

I swerved around a taxi and the tooter kept gaining speed. I overtook an ambulance. I hit the brakes again but the tooter only seemed to go faster.

The lights ahead were red. A bus full of greyhounds was inching across the intersection and I was headed for it like a missile.

I swung the wheel and the Rover squealed like a pig. I missed the bus by a few whiskerlengths and shot into Blithesome Street. I screeched off a Dumpster. I curled around traffic. I took out a fire hydrant in a geyser of water. My pumper was pounding so hard I thought it was going to punch through my chestcage. And the tooter just kept going.

In Yield Street I got chased down the street by some terriers trying to bite my back tires. In Devotion Street a pack of hoondogs in souped-up growlers tried to drag me. I swung into Squat Park, hoping the Rover would get caught in a pond, but there were so many hounds on the prowl in the darkness that I spent the whole time trying not to get anything caught under my wheels. I screeched into Conformist Way.

I was counting on an empty street—it was too late for shopping—but just my luck: There was a huge line of dogs queuing for tickets to the next Shagg Doggie Shagg concert.

But no sooner had these scattered from my path that I came across an even bigger queue, pups and grown-ups alike lined up outside a bookstore for the new Wizard Whelp novel.

Swerving around all of these I tried to map out an escape route, but all the streets branching off Conformist Way—Neurosis Alley, Depression Court, Futility Lane—were dead ends. I took out a billboard advertising a new snipe rag for bitches. I bounced off the front of Chew Toys "R" Us. And when I crossed into Appeasement Avenue I noticed another tooter racing alongside me.

It was a Jaguar. It was struggling to keep pace. Lap was at the wheel with a strange look on his mug. He was waving a gun. He was trying to shoot at me.

I swung the wheel, took a hard detour into Diversion Street, scraping parking meters. I heard bullets blowing apart my rear lights. I went faster. I actually pressed on the accelerator pedal. I wasn't going to let no cat see me die.

I hurtled down Deference Street, Orderly Road, and Obeisance Way. I was heading for Fly's Picnic, but that meant a detour down Submission Street. And I clean forgot about the fireworks to celebrate Democracy Day.

The road was thronged with families staring up at the sky

and jolting and barking at each new explosion. But the crowd was too thick, and I couldn't take it on. I swung the wheel wildly again.

I scraped down alleyways in showers of sparks. I ripped over asphalt and gravel. I tore through chain-link fences and jerked over railtracks. And finally I saw it—Wharf Twelve, where the whole thing had begun. Slinky Joe's Sardine Cannery. And beyond it the scummy black waters of Belvedere Bay.

I squeezed the wheel tight. I hunched my shoulders. Clamped my teeth. I plowed up the wharf, trundling over boards and rotting timbers. I passed the cannery and hit the end at 150 mph. I clenched my peepers. And for a few seconds I was sailing.

Then there was a great splash and I opened my eyes as the tooter filled with oily black water. A toothpick rose up and floated in front of my snout. I tried to wrestle open the door but it was jammed. The Rover was sinking. The headlights were lighting up swirling rubbish. My nostrils were full of water. I opened my snapper and liquid gushed down my gutchute.

I struggled but the steering wheel had bent and pinned me down—I couldn't budge. The Rover landed amid rusty wrecks and industrial waste. The headlights flickered. I was losing consciousness. It was a terrible way for a dog to die.

I sensed some movement, I turned, and the last thing I saw was a furry white-and-cinnamon face floating at the busted window beside me.

Then the lights went out.

ALL I REMEMBER are scraps. A sense of floating. Of getting hauled through slime. A conviction that my back was against wood. The feeling of something wet closing around my muzzle. The smell of tuna and soy milk blowing down my lungpipe. My great barrel chest getting pressed and pumped. And when my eyes flickered open—just briefly—I saw a dripping cat face coming down on me again as fireworks exploded in the sky. Nothing would ever be the same.

My brainpot drained like a sieve and when I came to my senses I was in a warm room with fresh blankets against my naked fur. There was a smell of overstarched sheets and drool-soaked pillows. Arranged on coat hangers in front of the radiator were my shirt, my pants, even my nut-huggers. My holster and Schnauzer were strung over the bedpost.

"We're in a hotel room."

It was Lap, blow-dried but still moist as a fairy cake, his whiskers drooping, his suit slick with water, and smelling like only a wet cat can.

"It's not the most salubrious of establishments admittedly," he went on, "but I believe it has a reputation for accepting inadequate identification."

"The In-Season?" I croaked.

"You know the place?"

"I've been here before."

207

How long ago was that? Last night? It seemed like a year. Since then I'd been to prison, to a movie set, and a fun park, I'd had a bullet ricochet off my skull and I'd dined with a mass murderer. I'd had my loyalties tugged like an old rope. I'd driven my tooter into Belvedere Bay. I'd almost drowned. And I'd been saved by a cat. By a Siamese cat. One who hated water more than I hated Siamese.

"How do you feel?" he asked, with more warmth than I ever got from my ex.

"Takes more than seawater to kill a bullie."

"You should've allowed me to shoot your tires. It would've saved us a whole lot of discomfort."

"Everything was moving so fast," I said. "I didn't know what I was doing."

"Your brakes were cut. Probably by Carlos the Jackal."

I shook my head. "It was Bud Borzoi."

"Officer Borzoi? Are you sure?"

"He left a calling card in my tooter."

Lap frowned. "Then this is even more serious than I thought. If they've infiltrated the Dog Force down to junior officers then they're truly throwing all caution to the breeze. Did MacFluff spin a yarn about me?"

"He said you were rabid."

"And you believed him, if only briefly?"

"I didn't know what to think."

Lap smiled. "The manufacture of lies makes artists of those who practice regularly."

He took it all so well, like he always did. It scared me, in fact, how much I liked him all of a sudden. It was all I could do not to hump his leg. So I distracted myself with anger.

"Just wait till I get a hold of that Borzoi. He won't have any teeth left to pick when I'm finished with him."

"Not now," warned Lap. "For the moment our enemies regard you as dead, which in many ways is a blessing. What we must do now is proceed covertly but boldly. Are you in any condition to continue when rested?"

"I can continue now." I tried to rise but a pain flashed down my flank.

"Nonsense. You'll most certainly need some time to recover. I'd call a vet but there's some urgent business to attend to."

"Where are you going?"

"To the island. I'm going to meet with my director at the FBI—the one I told you about."

"Sure you can trust him?"

"He's my sire."

As Lap turned to jangle ahead—he was arranging for some fresh clothes to be delivered—I wondered if I should tell him about Quentin Riossiti. Maybe the psychocat was stalking us right now. Maybe that was his plan all along. But then again maybe the whole thing was some sort of setup—probably they just wanted Riossiti loose so they could have an excuse to put him down. Run over him like an everyday stray.

"I've left a bowl of warm milk by the bed," Lap said, hanging up. "And some couch-grass in case you feel sickly. I dearly wish I didn't need to leave at all."

"How long will you be gone?"

"I'll be back mid-morning. In the meantime you can do nothing more constructive than sleep."

As he headed out I wanted desperately to follow him. I wanted to hug his heel, go into the wild with him, roam new territories. I couldn't have liked him more if he served up my dinner. Anything that attacked him now would never live to bite again.

But then he was in the corridor and closing the door. He was gone.

I don't know how much time slipped by—maybe three hours or more. I dreamed I was in a huge park, half of which was a muddy, overgrown field, where dogs were rolling, jumping, sniffing, and squatting. The other half was a neatly clipped garden, where cats were snoozing, sunbathing, and sharpening their claws on tree trunks. There were no barriers between the two halves—no hedges, fences, or marked territory. Dogs were cocking their legs in the cat half. Cats were pussyfooting through the dog half. I saw a Frisbee land in the lap of an old cat reading poetry—he smiled and handed it back to a young terrier. I saw a kitten chasing a butterfly through the tangled scrub and two mastiffs halt their ball game to let it pass. This was a place of respect. There were no hierarchies and no divisions, and nobody had an interest in inventing them.

But then a mighty lamb sprang from nowhere and bounded madly through the park. It flattened trees, smashed statues, plowed up the earth, scattered dogs and cats in every direction. Clinging to its golden fleece were Brewster Goodboy, Phineas Reynard, Doofus Rufus, and all sorts of clerics in silly hats. Riled, a few hounds started chasing it. Some herding dogs tried to contain it. Some cats tried to scratch at it. But the more attention it got, the bigger the lamb became. And the bigger it got, the more of the park it tore up, so that broken bodies were flung everywhere, mutts were fighting with moggies, and the air was full of dust and smoke.

But then a funny thing happened. Some of the dogs decided to ignore the lamb. Some of the cats decided to keep reading. And by their example many others got the courage to ignore the beast, too. It took great strength, because the lamb was stamping and bleating and sprinkling everywhere, but nobody paid it any attention. It ran in circles and bucked and wriggled and squealed but it kept getting smaller and smaller, until it faded into a puff of cotton wool and floated away. And Goodboy, Reynard, Rufus, and the clerics, all of them so high and mighty a few moments before, all bolted for cover like they never knew the lamb at all. And peace settled on the park again.

You can say I was dreaming—my paws were fluttering—but I'm not the only one.

So I woke with an unusual wag in my tail. I yawned and stretched, and was about to roll out of bed when I noticed a glinty-eyed figure sitting cross-legged in the darkness.

At first I thought it was still a dream—I hoped it was—but when I blinked my eyes he was still there, grinning.

I grappled for the bedpost but my Schnauzer was gone.

"Tallyho," said Phineas Reynard.

HE WAS WEARING a gherkin-green riding jacket and jodh-purs, like he'd just come in from a hunt, and his bushy tail—fake or not—was draped over the arm of the chair, swishing slightly. In one paw he was holding a rooster-headed cane, like a scepter, and he was looking down his pointed muzzle as if he was about to deliver a court verdict. His eyes smiled before his lips.

"My vixen assured me I'd find this place accommodating," he said. "'The desk clerk answers to money,' she claimed. A rather redundant observation, I would have thought. *Everyone* answers to money, surely? And if you have enough of it, as I do, you quickly learn that *any* dog—old, young, or in-between—can be taught new tricks."

I started across the bed. "Listen, foxfart, if you think—"

"*Ah ah,*" he said, holding up his cane like a magic wand. "Please don't get ahead of yourself. This is not the time for rash actions. I have two guards posted outside the door, another two in the stairwell, and still more in the street. And the very fact that I've not taken advantage of your vulnerability is proof, surely, of my good intentions?"

I stopped, simmering, and Reynard grinned.

"So please don't be alarmed. I'm not here to threaten you—not at all. Nor am I here to lie to you. I'm not even going to pretend that I'm anything but exactly what I am—a self-serving

212

old fox. But all that doesn't mean I wish you ill. Nothing of the sort. I want to apologize to you, in fact."

"Apologize?"

"Absolutely. And make you a generous offer."

I bristled. "If you think you can buy me, gingerbread—"

"*Ah ah*"—Reynard raised his cane again—"I told you not to get ahead of yourself. I just want to offer you something, that's all. Something very rare. Something very precious. Something I have the power to bestow upon those who impress me."

"Get to the point, pointy."

He smiled. "I want to give you *security*."

"*What?*"

"The most valuable commodity in the world. Even more expensive than respectability. Security."

"Security?"

"One check, one signature, and I can give you this invaluable gift."

"So you *are* trying to buy me?"

"I prefer to think of it as a donation. A little something to afford me a sense of charity. And assuage my tiny conscience."

I stared at him. "Aren't you supposed to be at your up-country estate?"

"Circumstances forced me to cancel."

"Got you on the run, have we?"

"I've not run for many years, Mr. McNash. From anything."

I chortled. "Not like a fox to run, is it?"

His voice flattened for a moment. "My running days ended when I bought the fourth estate, Mr. McNash. I can piss on presidents now. I can crack prime ministers like boiled eggs. I can swipe the crowns off kings. I can even elect the pope. I have immeasurable power. So just imagine what I could do, if it took my fancy, to a dog like you."

I threw back the sheet. "If you really wanna go tooth and nail—"

"Please"—Reynard gave a geckery little laugh—"I warned you not to get ahead of yourself. I'm telling you this in the hope that you appreciate the magnitude of my gift. Because you must surely recognize the parlous position you're in? You must know by now I'm in total control? You understand that, don't you? Or am I underestimating your canine intelligence?"

"You're underestimating my canine temper," I said, "if you don't tell me what all this is about. What do you want from me?"

"What makes you think I want anything?"

I killstared him.

Reynard chuckled faintly. "All right, there is something I'd like, of course. But it's very simple. Very simple and very easy."

"I'm listening."

"I just want you to leave town for a few weeks. Lie low. Have a good rest. Not so hard, is it?"

"You want me to run and hide?"

"The case is already over. You must accept it. Special Agent MacFluff will tie up the ends very neatly now. And you, Mr. McNash, have a clear-cut choice. Either you continue barking at thunder or you accept my offer of security. It's up to you."

"I don't want your filthy money," I said. "And I don't need any security."

"Oh, really?" Reynard looked me up and down with his foxy little eyes. "How old are you, may I ask?"

"What difference does it make?"

"Six years? Seven?"

"What of it?"

"And you mean to tell me you've never worried about your future? Never wondered what'll happen when you can't pay your vet bills? Never feared that you might be put down at the slightest infirmity? Or that you might be taken on one of those 'picnics' with your family and never return?" Reynard shook his head. "Well, with one simple check I can end all your worries. The greatest gift that money can buy, and I'm offering it to you now."

I shivered, because he'd hit a nerve, all right—bull terriers are prone to all sorts of complaints, the big C among them, and I knew I didn't have enough meat tickets to cover all those bases. I still had pups to raise. And palimony payments. And Chump's wasn't getting any cheaper.

Reynard reached into his riding jacket. "So why don't we get down to business?" He pulled out a checkbook and a pheasant quill. "Where will we start? Shall we say one million?"

I didn't answer.

"Two million?"

I stared at him.

"All right, let's make it even more—I admire hagglers."

And then he scratched away, tore the check neatly from its book, and pushed himself to his feet. "I won't even make you fetch it," he said, and came over to the bed, holding it out like a french fry.

In a daze I took the check from his hand—it was from the Reynard Finance Corporation—and stared at the row of figures: $5,000,000. More than I'd ever dreamed of. And I heard Reynard's voice: "Never have to beg for a scrap . . . never have to drink out of the gutter . . . never have to sleep on a busted armchair . . ."

I looked up at the smiling old fox. Into his amber eyes. At his swishing tail. His tense whiskers. And I smelled something.

Not charity. Not power. But *fear*.

He was scared. He was frightened of killing me all of a sudden. Not with the murder itself, but because things had gotten out of control. Because there was a loose link in his chain some-where. And he was trying to buy *himself* security.

And with that thought came all the power I needed.

I got to my feet, buck-naked, and stared him in the peepers. I scrunched the check into a ball. And I tossed it into my gob-bler.

"You got the power to write five-million-dollar checks," I said, swallowing. "I got the power to blow them out my butt-hole. Which is greater, you think?"

Reynard didn't look surprised. Didn't look disappointed. He simply raised his eyebrows a fraction—he was still wearing his barbed-wire smirk—and folded his checkbook into his pocket. "Ah well," he sniffed, "no one can say I didn't make a genuine offer."

I pointed to the door. "Out, fox. And take your tail with you."

"A mutt will always be a mutt, as they say."

"A fox will always be a pest." I shoved him into the corridor, where his guards jolted awake.

He gathered himself and narrowed his eyes. "I suppose you think populations are suppressed with infantilization, Mr. McNash—is that what Dr. Riossiti told you? Nothing of the sort. They suppress themselves. With consumerism. With trib-alism. With patriotism. And we in the media, far from being villains, are merely taking the edge off an insatiable hunger. Because if we didn't do it then someone truly dangerous—some dictator—surely would." He shook his head. "But clearly you don't deserve five million dollars, Mr. McNash, you've proved that now. You don't even deserve the paper it was written on."

"I'll send it back when it comes out the other end."

He tightened his foxgloves. "I hope you enjoy the show, in any case."

"Show?"

"There's to be a little fireworks display tonight. You should be able to view it from your window."

"Democracy Day? I already seen it."

"In Kathattan, I mean. It should start any moment." He tapped his cane to his forehead. "Cheerio, then—it was a pleasure doing insults with you."

"It was a pleasure banging the door on your snout."

I slammed the swinger shut—there was a dull clunk—and when I opened it again Reynard had his sniffer in his paws.

"Sorry," I said. "I must've got ahead of myself."

When he roared off in his Fuchswagen I was already at the window. The lights of Kathattan were blazing in the distance. I looked for Lap's building—Imperial Heights, he'd called it—and there it was, the giant ziggurat on the riverfront. I wondered what he'd say if he knew I'd just been yapping with Phineas Reynard. I wondered when he'd get back. And I wondered when the fireworks would start.

But then, as if on cue, there was a sudden flash at the side of Lap's building. A huge blossom of flame. Then, a few seconds later, the boom of an explosion rattled the In-Season's windows.

My hair immediately went stiff. My jaw locked.

I was out the door so fast I forgot to put on my clothes.

I HIT THE ground running on all fours. I ran like a bunny-chaser. I tore divots out of the sidewalk. I ran between toot-ers. I sprang over fences. My pumper was jackhammering. My windbag was working like bellows. My licker was flapping like a pennant.

At the Amity Bridge the black-and-tan mastiffs tried to stop me—I leapt over the boom gate and powered on. I jumped kelpielike from tooter to tooter. I bounded across the top of a semitrailer and speared over the last checkpoint into Kathattan. And I kept charging.

It was early morning. Sticky piles of the *Scratching Post* were getting dumped on the sidewalk. Dog street sweepers and gar-bage hounds were gathering up the night's kitty litter. Fat-cats in pinstripe suits were arriving at work. Kittens were getting dropped off at school. When they saw me they parted like seagulls. Some hunched up and hissed. Others jumped onto fences and scurried down driveways. A few covered their eyes. One cool cat laughed and cried, "Go, Hotdog, go!"

I ran down Sultan Street, Pharaoh Street, the Avenue of the Kings. When I reached Imperial Heights I was puffing like a steam engine. I could see fire trucks with huge ladders. There was a massive hole where an apartment used to be. Flames were licking up the side of the building. I could just make out the cats crowded onto ledges, many still in their pajamas. Some were clawing their way down the side of the building. Others were throwing themselves onto nets. A couple missed the nets, picked themselves off the sidewalk, looked left and right, and slinked away like nothing had ever happened.

There was a huge crowd of curious onlookers blocking the street. I was about to bite and bark my way through when I heard a high-pitched whistle. I looked around, up and down, heard a stage whisper—*"Here, boy"*—and finally located a Jaguar at the curb. The passenger door was wide open. In the driver's seat was Cassius Lap.

My pumper fluttered like dragonfly wings. I sprang into the tooter and had to stop myself from licking his face. He was alive. Cassius Lap was alive. My whole body wagged and trembled.

"I was lucky," he said, already launching into traffic and curling around some meat wagons, "though someone else, regrettably, was not."

I caught my breath. "What . . . what happened?"

"I called ahead to have a fresh suit laid out in my apartment. So it must have been some unfortunate cat from Laundry who triggered the explosive meant for me."

"Who did it?" I asked. "Carlos?"

"Or those behind him."

"Reynard," I said, thinking of the In-Season. "So they think you're dead now?"

"For a while at least. I was hoping to spot someone at Imperial Heights trying to verify my demise." He glanced at me. "But then a naked dog showed up."

I settled back in the seat, sniggering. "Where to now?"

He took a hard left. "Where I always meant to go—my sire's place. And from there, well, it's time to take full advantage of my regrettable death."

On the far side of town he steered his Jaguar down a back

alley and hid it behind some junglelike ferns. We squeezed through a cat-flap into the back entrance of a luxurious old tenement. As we climbed the carpeted stairs a 'wower maid yelped and dropped her bundle. I fell to all fours to hide my little tickler.

On the third floor Lap pressed a door dinger and a spyhole flickered. An owlish old Siamese in a tweed jacket and bow tie opened the door and surveyed us.

"Cassius, it's a pleasure to see you again."

"You, too, Sire."

"How is that investigation proceeding?"

"It's precisely what I'm here to see you about. May we come in?"

"You may."

It was a typical feline exchange, warm as overnight frost. As we moved into the place the two of them curled around each other, bumping hips, and the senior cat—he looked at least four years older than his son—took Lap aside.

"Son, how many times have I warned you about bringing dogs off the street?"

"Notwithstanding his appearance," Lap smiled, "this is no ordinary mongrel. It is in fact my partner in the investigation, Detective Max McNash of the Slaughter Unit."

"From the murder case?"

"That's me," I said, getting to my hind legs.

Lap Senior looked at me with sudden respect. "I've heard about you, Detective, of course. Your courage and tenacity precede you. You're welcome to make yourself at home, as long as you don't roll on the rug."

Lap said, "Our first priority is to change into something more fitting, Sire. Then we'll explain everything."

It was a cozy place full of antique furniture and cream-white carpets. Everything smelled of polish and wax. In a little chamber filled with trophies for harp playing and wood engraving—I guessed it was his old floproom—Lap slid open a wall closet filled with suits of panther-black.

"I was smaller and plumper in my youth," he said, selecting one off the rack. "I hope it fits you."

"I'll make it fit."

"As for me, I'll be in the next room for a quick spitgroom. If you find any cat hair on your suit, there's a bristle brush in the en suite."

I wasn't sure what an en suite looked like, so I just slid into Lap's mothball-smelling suit, laced up some shoes, and admired myself in a full-length mirror. The jacket was a bit tight at the chest, and I had to loosen the collar a bit, but all in all it felt like a second coat. In the bathroom, I found all sorts of shampoos, brushes, nail clippers, and fancy bottles of scent. I knotted a black tie, dampened my sniffer, and rolled some lynx juice into my sweatpits. In the corner was a funny-looking drinking bowl with a flip-top lid—I took a slurp of the blue-tinted water and went into the courtyard to drain myself against a tree.

When I got back inside I was surprised to find that Chief Kaiser Kessler had arrived, and was bowwowing gravely with the two Laps.

"I HAVEN'T LIKED it from the start."

Sitting on the spotless Naugahyde sofa in his cuff-bitten blue uniform, the chief didn't seem any more comfortable than I did. He was droopy-flewed and baggy-eyed, like he hadn't been snoozing well, and even from halfway across the room his breath would turn milk into yogurt. "The constant pressure from higher up," he said. "The veiled threats. The crazy accusations. The sense of panic—you could smell it—and the desperate lies."

He wasn't looking at me when he said all this, and this was no time to remind him that he'd been half a second away from selling out on Lap—that he'd been virtually begging me to make that call. But I couldn't blame him. With so much sewage flying around, he'd probably felt as buried in doodah as I did.

"But then, just a few hours ago, I overheard Agent MacFluff mewing in one of the grill rooms, not realizing the intercom was still on. He told Officer Borzoi that he didn't have the permission to make his own kills. He said Lap and McNash—I heard those two names clearly—would be taken care of by professionals, not by him." And now the chief managed a hangdog glance at both of us, maybe to assure himself we were still alive. "He even mentioned Carlos the Jackal. And something called 'Operation Pooper Scooper.'"

"Did he actually use those words?" Lap asked.

222

"You've heard of it?"

"It's the ultimate form of disposal. The most serious and the most ruthless. Elimination of not just individuals with direct knowledge of the conspiracy, but of all those immediately connected to them."

"Which includes me," his sire added. "And you, Chief. It's a real plop-and-drop operation."

"And further evidence," his son went on, "that the thread these murders have unraveled is connected to a much larger, even more sinister tapestry. Are you married, Chief?"

"With a fresh litter."

"Then you should make moves to protect your family immediately."

"They're already guarded day and night."

"It might not be sufficient. We're dealing with map-room fanatics here—the most ruthless ideologues of all. They kill with winks and twitches. They protect themselves with mazes of paper and fortresses of denial. They never see a kennel, let alone the Kennels. And what are the lives of a few unseen dogs to such types? What about you, Detective?" Lap looked at me. "I seem to remember from your file that you have a litter of your own?"

"Four mongrels and a bitch."

"Then they'll need to be hidden as well."

"I'll get them safe," I said, thinking of Spike's little fortress. "But what about your own family?"

Lap stiffened. "Since the passing of Cuddles," he said, "there's only my sire and myself left."

"My own queen"—the father gestured to the mantelpiece, where a tortoiseshell Cymric was stuffed and mounted above the fireplace—"passed away two years ago, after swallowing a snail pellet."

"Which at least," offered his son, "allows us to concentrate on the safety of others."

"Such as the feral himself," his father added. "We should never forget he's a citizen, too, with as many rights as anyone else, and a victim of manipulating forces."

"Plus, as our principal source of evidence, he remains the most at danger."

The chief spoke up. "MacFluff has called in the CAT Squad, you know. And he's made it clear the feral is to be shot on sight. No arguments. He's even got a written order from the governor."

Lap grunted. "Do they have any idea where the feral currently hides?"

"They're concentrating on the Flatear District, exactly as you directed."

"Which is where we might be in luck. Because when I plotted out the feral's most likely course I neglected one important factor, something that appeared in no survey map—the Cradles. And with the Flatear District already marked territorially, as it were, by waste dropped from above, the feral will most likely change course to avoid that region entirely. In fact, his appearance at Reynard Studios already gives an indication that he might be bending north."

"So they're looking in the wrong district?"

"They might be, but Carlos the Jackal might not. And Carlos, in his own way, is even more effective at hunting targets than the CAT Squad."

"What about Riossiti?"

"What about him?" .

The chief told him about Riossiti's escape from Cattica.

"Interesting," Lap said coolly. "Quentin must have known all along that he'd be signing his own death warrant—simply by speaking to us at all."

"It doesn't worry you that he might be pursuing you right now?"

"Riossiti will be unpredictable till the last, but I'm confident he won't kill us. In fact, his escape might well work in our favor. Another dangerous cat on the streets—another loose cannon— makes two mouths that will need to be silenced. And a possible distraction for Carlos, who'll no doubt be ordered to shoot them both."

I sniggered. "Kitty kitty bang bang?"

"But where it leaves us," Lap went on, ignoring me, "is in direct conflict with the official investigation. Completely at odds with it, in fact. An obstacle to its objectives. And working to an entirely different aim."

"Above the law?" the chief asked.

"Outside the law, if necessary." Lap stretched his neck. "It's not something that makes me feel comfortable."

"It need not be unethical," the older Lap argued. "I can even make it legal. For a start, I can authorize an independent investigation—one totally removed from external influences. And together with my trusted contacts at the CIA, and the Department of Order and Discipline for that matter, I can give it deep resources and far-reaching powers."

"And I can supply information as it comes in," the chief chipped in, "by secret line, if necessary."

"Then it's settled," said Cassius Lap, turning to me. "Detective McNash, we'll have to go back into the Kennels again. To catch and rescue a killer cat. We'll be alone. We'll be up against hired killers. Against immensely powerful forces with flush-button ethics. We'll have nothing on our side but our brains, our

225

brawn, and our total incorruptibility. So I must ask you again . . . are you willing to join me? Are you willing to stand by my side, whisker to whisker?"

It was a boneheaded question, and Lap knew it, but I took my time anyway, feeling the hope of everyone present: Lap One, Lap Two, the chief, even the stuffed mother on the shelf. I was aware that I was in a black cat suit. In a cozy cathouse. And that I owed my life to a cat. The irony was just chicken-delicious. Hours ago I'd wanted to give Lap a deathshake. Now we were inseparable. We were Truth's only hope. We were the Unscratchables.

I sprang off the sofa. "Let's scat, cat."

I was pawing at the door before Lap had even got to his feet.

IT'S TRUE I'M old-fashioned, but when it comes to pups—even my own—I reckon they should be smelled and not heard. I licked them when they were born; I let them nip at my ears; I showed them how to mark a tree; I even let them chase me in the park. I never bit them. I never gobbled their food. But my ex was always snarling that I was a lousy father. Not nurturing enough, she growled. Not attentive. She said I couldn't even remember their birthday. The snapping point came one day when I tied them to a post outside a bar while I ducked inside for a quick bite. When I came out, clutching a bag of scraps to toss to them, she was already standing there with lips curled. The marriage ended two weeks later.

Lousy or not, I had the pups at the front of my brainpot now as we crossed from Kathattan into the Kennels on the monorail. We were in a two-seat boxcar, sailing over the Old Yeller River. We'd already breezed through the outward checkpoint using some hastily cooked-up tags—Rusty Brown and Tom Katt—and now we were in sight of the Cradles, our secret hatchway to the Kennels below. And I had no time to be nervous.

"Ready, Detective?"

"Let's get it over with."

We jagged the car to a stop at a maintenance post and climbed onto a railing. The boxcar behind us swerved onto a

227

separate track, squealing and tooting. The fat-cat at the console stuck his mug out the window and shrieked an insult— *"Buttlicker!"*—but I didn't even glare at him.

This was the tricky part. There were about twenty rungs down the side of the pylon to the catwalks of the Cradles. Easy enough for a pussy; a nightmare for a mutt. Lap went first, claws out, folding and unfolding downward, step after step, nimble as a monkey. But when it came my turn I had to cling to each rung with my teeth, scratching for support, fighting for balance, struggling not to look down. It was a miracle I made it without wetting myself. And that was just the beginning.

The catwalk was made of wicker. It swayed like a clothesline in a hurricane. A hundred feet below—I knew it even without looking—were the tar-paper roofs of the Kennels. Down there I used to snarl at the flea-sized figures slinking along these walks—now I was one of them. I picked my way after Lap, gulping and shuddering, knowing one false move and they'd be scraping me off the pavement like last night's dinner.

We were heading for a huge nest of carpets, raincoats, pajamas, and bamboo—the palace at the center of the web, the converging point of twenty catwalks. Generator fans were whirling and clicking. Rain tanks were creaking and dripping. As we got closer I could hear cats hissing and spitting at me—they didn't want me there any more than I did.

"You'll need to wait outside a few moments," Lap said, "as I negotiate safe passage."

We stopped under a canopy of cheap rugs and palm-weave mats. Lap headed for a command post covered with mirror glass and camouflaging leaves. He miaowed a few times and a door peeled open wide enough for him to wriggle in. Waiting outside I clung to the railing, riding wind shifts, ignoring all the stinkeye. There were huge bird-catching nets beneath the walks. A few old-timers were skyfishing with nylon lines and hooks. A couple of wildcats on bungee lines were catching flappers in sacks. It was a whole new world to me, as weird as Kathattan, and I held my breath.

A greasy-looking Tonkinese brandishing a bird gun appeared to call me in. I plunged into the darkness, almost immediately gagging on the stink of incense and unlicked cats. It took seconds for my peepers to focus, and then I saw a posse of trigger-itchy guards ringing the joint with their tails twitching. And there was Lap, in the middle of the room, bowing. And at the back, wadded between feather pillows and sheepskins, was Don "Scarcheek" Gato—the first time I'd seen him in the fur.

"Dis is de first Yap dat's been up here since dat tax dog," he rumbled. "What happened t'him, Gomez?"

"Went sailin'," giggled a sniveling little tabby. "Didn't have no sails."

Don Gato smirked and eyed me like a canned herring. He was in hemp-weave pants and a tropical shirt covered with palm trees and toucans. His nails were unclipped and a huge gumleaf cigar was smoldering in his paw. "Maybe dis mutt here," he said, "he wants to go sailin', too?"

"Detective McNash seeks nothing more that to be lowered safely into the Kennels," Lap assured him. "We crossed from the island this morning. We have urgent business below."

Don Gato rolled his cigar unhappily. "Dis stinks of trouble. I already said too much."

"Your assistance so far has been most productive and appreciated," Lap told him, "but it has been mentioned officially to no one. I swear it on my mother's chemically treated hide."

"Did ya read the rags, like I said?"

"We did. And we picked up a thread. The thread led to a feral. A feral in the wrong place at the wrong time."

Don Gato flicked ash from his cigar. "Ferals were de original tenants of dis land, you know. Two thousand years ago, it was, before de arrival of de 'wowers.'"

"A matter of historical dispute, but we respect your convictions. And in any case we're not here for a debate. We ask only for your cooperation."

"What's in it for Don Gato?"

"Nothing but a warm heart."

"Cats don't have hearts. Dey got a muscle dat pumps blood. It ain't de same thing."

"Each of us, even the most hard-hearted cat, has in them somewhere a modicum of goodwill. A sense of justice. A hatred of exploitation. It's to those qualities that I appeal now."

Don Gato thought about it. He stared at me with slitted eyes. Behind him, a pigeon splattered against a pane of mirror glass and dropped into a net—he didn't even seem to notice.

"Why you say nuthin', Detective? Cat got your tongue?"

I shrugged. "Don't want to say nuthin'. Don't want to say something wrong."

"You gonna sink your teeth into a feral?"

"I'm gonna do my job."

"So you 'spect Don Gato to drop you into de Kennels just so you can chase a cat?"

"To *save* a cat, maybe. And my pups."

Don Gato squinted. "Pups?"

"They could be in danger, too."

Don Gato tilted his head, looking at me with a whole new expression. "Got a litter, Detective?"

"Five little scratchers."

"Proud of dem, are you?"

"Proud as a dog can be."

"Where are dey now?"

"In obedience school. That's where I wanna go now. To take them out, the whole litter. Before someone else does."

Suddenly Don Gato looked like he wanted to rub against my legs. He took a puff of his cigar and his eyes twinkled. "Family is everythin'," he said. "Nuthin' else matters. I sired ninety-seven kitties, you know. I only drowned forty-six of dem. Got some of dem in da crèche right now. Care to see 'em?"

But Lap chipped in. "With respect, Don Gato, we've not much time. Things are moving extremely fast down there. So may we be on our way, with your assistance and blessing?"

Don Gato didn't look completely happy—he must've been real proud of his scratchers—but at least we'd found some marrow in his bone-cased pumper.

WE WERE LUCKY and unlucky. There was a way of dropping into the Kennels unseen, through a giant chimney that reached almost as high as the catwalks. Problem was, it was in Dishlick just three blocks from the cophouse, where we all knew it well. Old Smoky, we called it. When it was pumping it made everyone sneeze.

We were lowered into the chimney by ropes. Lap went first, quickly swallowed by the darkness. But when it was my turn the Tonkinese reeling out the line had some fun, swinging the line so I banged around the sides of the shaft. I clamped my choppers so tight around the rope—thinking of Reynard, MacFluff, Carlos the Jackal, and everyone else who wanted me killed—that I bit right through it. I fell thirty feet into a feathery mountain of ash.

When I rose my suit was gray. My whiskers were singed. I had embers in my nostrils. But at least I was back on solid ground. And out of the Cradles.

"Your turn to lead the way," said Lap, also powdered white.

We spilled into Duty Street just in time to see Bud Borzoi whisk past in a squad tooter. I stared at him, ashen-faced, but he didn't even recognize us. Every sinew in me wanted to chase him and drag him through the window, but I reminded myself I had bigger gizzards to fry.

We ducked through the back of Pedro's and flashed our tags.

"We'd like a car," said Lap.

"And a soy milk?" asked the 'wower.

"Just a vehicle, if you have one."

We were lucky and unlucky again. Deported as illegal wetpaws, Poco and the Subwoofers had left their gig-mobile parked outside with a full tank. Problem was, it was a snarling little tooter, not much bigger than a Corgi, with an engine held together with rubber bands and bubble gum. The horn played "La Cucaracha." Squeezed ear to ear like two handbag hounds, Lap and I squirted through traffic to the Flagwag Expressway and spluttered across town to the Ever-Faithful off-ramp. In the sky, the thwuckers of the CAT Squad were already on the buzz, hunting the feral with super binoculars and audio-sensors.

We must've looked a sight when we got to the Rover Cleveland Elementary School. The principal, a prim Spitz bitch, looked dumbslapped when I demanded to see my puppies.

"It's not about Bitzer Chips, is it?"

"Listen, lambflap—"

"He's gone! He was shown the door!"

"I don't care if—"

"He wasn't appropriate! He didn't fit our standards! We have a new history teacher now!"

I had no idea what she was yapping about, but Lap chipped in:

"Excuse me, madam, are you saying that a history teacher wasn't appropriate?"

"That's correct!" The principal straightened, eager to impress.

"May I ask why, precisely?"

"He was too radical. He encouraged dissent. He made the pups confused . . . questioning . . . *ambivalent*."

"And these qualities are now regarded as inappropriate?"

The Spitz puffed up. "At Rover Cleveland we believe a happy

dog is a single-minded dog. We try to curb curiosity. We chastise independent thought. We hunt out disloyalty."

"You like to sing from the same songbook, in short?" In the background a choir was singing "It's a Short Life After All."

The Spitz looked guarded all of a sudden. "You could say that."

But I was losing patience. "What about my puppies?" I said. "I need to take 'em out."

The Spitz shook her head. "Classes are now in session. No one is permitted to leave until the bell sounds."

"I can't wait for no bell."

"It's a rule of conditioning here at Rover Cleveland—everyone answers to the bell. And it's only ten minutes."

I managed, at least, to find out where my pups were. Jip, the youngest, was in toilet-training class. Skip, slightly older, was in Alpha-rolling class. Rip was doing road crossing. Pip was learning how to be a good brood bitch. And Flip, the most acrobatic, was jumping through hoops for a visiting superintendent.

I paced the corridor. Above the door was an inscription: GIVE ME THE PUP AT SEVEN WEEKS AND I WILL GIVE YOU THE DOG. Lap picked up a little schoolbook and pawed through it with fascination. "Remarkable," he said. "Social steering on a massive scale. I had no idea it was so advanced. It's exactly what Quentin Riossiti was warning about."

"Don't mention that name," I said. "We got enough to worry about already."

"What really bothers me about Riossiti," Lap mused, putting the book down, "is that we failed to make sense of some of his puzzles."

"Some? I never made sense of him at all."

But just then the bell rang and doors slid back. Pups of all ages flooded into the corridor, blank-eyed, tight-tailed, moving obediently to the next class. I saw Jip and whistled him aside. I found Rip and grabbed him by the ear. I smelled Flip and hooked him by the collar. I spied Pip and separated her from a slow-moving pack. "Where's Skip?" I asked, looking around.

"Here I am!" said Skip, the brightest of all. "What's the meat, Pop?"

"I'm taking you to Uncle Spike's. And you know the rules— make with the lip and I give you a clip."

I rounded them up and herded them toward Lap, but the cat had the weirdest look on his mug, like he'd got his tail stuck in an electrical socket.

"Of course," he whispered, eyes wide as saucers. "Of course . . ."

But as usual he didn't explain himself.

"LET ME SEE if I understand this fully."

I knew Thomas Schrödinger from the quiz shows, where he answered all the flash-and-whistle questions and went home with the big biscuits. What I didn't know was that he was a law professor, a colleague and mentor of Lap's late wife, Cuddles, and a retired attorney famous for getting three border collies acquitted in the international sheepdog trials. Now with my pups and their mother safely squirreled away in Spike's doghouse, Lap and I were in Schrödinger's cramped little office in Cats 4 Dogs, a legal charity headquartered over a scraps kitchen in Gobbet.

"A secret department," he said, "part governmental and part corporate sector, is dedicated to Machiavellian manipulations of the public consciousness at both micro and macro levels. One manifestation of such is a plan to dent canine pride—and by extension dog status and aspirations—by proving in the boxing ring that cats are physically, and not just mentally, superior to their canine compatriots."

He was a shaggy-browed Kashmir wearing a carpet tie and a corduroy jacket with elbow patches. He was leaning back against a desk piled high with fat legal texts and seemed, like most lawyers, to be enjoying the music of his own miaows. Lap, like me, was itching to get to the gristle, but we knew we had to be patient—we had to give the old cat time to gather his wool.

236

"Two feral cats," Schrödinger went on, getting more and more fascinated, "are selected for grooming as champion prizefighters. The cats have already been tagged, not entirely respectfully, as 'Kitty' and 'the Cat.' In a highly secretive laboratory, hidden within the storehouse of an exotic bird-and-fish importer, the two unfortunate felines are conditioned over a matter of months to attack viciously the nearest dog upon the sounding of a simple bell—specifically the bell that signals the start of each round of a boxing contest. The better trained and more presentable of these ferals is transformed into 'Zeus Katsopoulos,' supposedly a championship contender from Greece, assiduously screened from all interfering noises by tight-fitting headphones. The less successful feral—'the Cat'—is maintained as an understudy until it's decided that his existence is redundant and possibly dangerous. Accordingly he is taken by two Rottweiler hoodlums to a wharf in Fly's Picnic, but before his assassination can be effected—"

"—a nearby factory bell rings," Lap said, "signaling the evening break."

Schrödinger smiled and nodded, as if Lap had just guessed something he hadn't gotten to yet. "The feral rises up in fury, dispatches the two hoodlums, and leaps for safety into Belvedere Bay, from where he enters the sewage system. But from there he doesn't lie low—he goes high. Using his experience as a rooftop predator, he ascends to the building tops of the Kennels and creeps noiselessly across the city toward his home in the woods. But as luck would have it, the night after the first killing he happens to be passing near a storage facility in Chitterling when a theft is attempted and—"

"—and a burglar alarm goes off—"

"—and the feral again goes into an uncontrollable rage. He sets eyes on an innocent dog, a Doberman Pinscher this time, and rips him apart before returning to the roofs and moving on. But the following night, alas, he is passing in the vicinity of a museum when yet another bell sounds—"

"—the bell warning of imminent closure—"

"—and by a twist of fate he tears apart a marketing manager whose company might well have financed, at least partly, his conditioning in the first place." Schrödinger was smiling again. "The feral then roams across the rooftops again, oblivious to the great controversy he's stirred up, ignorant of the hunt his actions have set in motion, and quite possibly confused as to why he has so much blood on his paws in the first place. Intent only on reaching familiar territory, he curls around the Cradles and is hiding within a film set when—"

"—when a bell rings to shut everyone up." It was me this time, wanting to get my muzzle in.

"—and the Cat kills yet again, his last-known murder, before bolting away, eluding hired assassins, and making his way back into the great maze of the Kennels, where he hides now. And where, by the grace of Our Master, he hears no more bells."

"The bells of sport, security, instruction, and popular entertainment." Lap shook his head. "I was looking for a link in the feral's victims. But the only connection was the prevalence of society's regulation by bells."

Schrödinger hooked his paws behind his lapels and launched himself from the desk, keen to take over again. "In any event, what we currently have is a mass-murdering feral on the loose, a cat who might conceivably kill again at any moment. And what you want from me, if I understand correctly, is a reason to find him completely innocent. You want me to turn him from an attacker into a victim. Poetically speaking, you want me to make him as sinless as a newborn kitten."

"What we want," said Lap, "is a reason to make his assassination unlawful. Because the governor's order is predicated on the assumption that the Cat is a clear-and-present danger to public safety. To the lives of innocent citizens. And as such he can be legally dispatched on sight, without even an attempt to capture him unharmed."

"Difficult." Schrödinger's shaggy brows creased at the thought. "If the Cat's murdering stimulus is simply the sound of bells, then there's a real possibility that he might become aggravated and unstoppable again—at the sound of a fire alarm, perhaps—and so there's every reason to support the principle of the governor's order."

"But *officially* the governor doesn't know about the bells," Lap argued.

"But *you* know," Schrödinger pointed out, "and so you can't argue the point without revealing your knowledge. And that brings us back to the start."

I butted in. "What if we clear him away from all bells?"

And Lap nodded. "Precisely. We can shut down the entire electricity grid for ten blocks around him, eliminating the possibility of bells and thus the whole murdering stimulus. And that makes him no more dangerous than any ordinary cat."

"Perhaps," said Schrödinger, "but you'd need to convince the governor that the Cat is not completely insane to begin with. Because technically the governor has decided he's a threat even without the bells."

"A completely conditioned response is a form of temporary insanity, surely? A loss of control? A reflex action? Remove the stimulus and you remove the insanity. It's exactly what Quentin Riossiti used to write in his books."

"Riossiti being a cat," Schrödinger noted with a smile, "whom you now suspect of being deeply involved in the conditioning process in the first place."

"Speculation, admittedly," Lap said, "but it certainly seems possible that Riossiti, as the unwitting architect of the whole brainwashing program, became the scapegoat for the murders committed by an unknown number of previous ferals—the test cases—and through his guilt and self-disgust he elected not to reveal the truth under oath. Because he wanted to protect the real killers—ferals he regarded as innocent victims."

Schrödinger was pacing back and forth, chin in paw, as he might once have done in front of the bench. "Guilty in action but not spirit," he mused. "A furry area for the law, which prefers to deal with absolutes. It reminds me of a legal thought experiment I used to put to my students—'Schrödinger's dog.' Imagine, if you will, a puppy ripped from its mother's teat and kept day and night in a sealed container. The puppy has no contact with the outside world other than the rubber tube through which it is fed. But through all its months of weaning and whelping the poor creature is subjected to daily bursts of electricity, blasts of hot and cold water, loud noises, and violent shaking of the container. The dog emerges after two years and promptly goes on a murder spree. So the question now is: Who is ultimately responsible for the murder? The murderer himself or the master who made him murderous?"

"The *master*," I gnashed, remembering my days in the madhouse. "It's gotta be."

"It must surely come down to a matter of intent," Lap added. "Because if the intention from the start is to control a subject's reflexes, and in so doing turn him into a weapon of propaganda— as is the case in this instance—then surely it *is* the master who absorbs the guilt? Making the murderer an innocent victim?"

"And yet it is all so difficult to prove, is it not?" Schrödinger looked happy to be tying us up in knots. "And such complexities have traditionally defeated the sharpest legal minds. What, for instance, if Schrödinger's dog were subjected to all those torments and humiliations not to rile him but to pacify him—to show him who's boss, for his own good? And what if the conditioning only backfired, even after the passage of years? Who is guilty then? The puppet or the puppetmaster? And what does that mean for societies that program its citizens to respond on reflex? Are they—the societies—then responsible when their puppies blunder around the world, chewing slippers and soiling welcome mats? It would take years to argue such a case."

"And yet we don't have years. We have one night, if even that. We have—"

But Lap was interrupted again by his pocket jangler. He answered and his whiskers stiffened. "Thank you—we'll be there immediately."

He rang off, fixed me with cold blue eyes, and spoke in a voice that had already sprung to action: "That was Chief Kessler," he said. "There's been a positive sighting of the Cat near the corner of Glory and Hallelujah."

I WAS ARMED with a Fido & Wesson; Lap had a small carton of full-cream milk.

The electricity went out as we left the expressway, just as Lap had arranged with a longhaired techno cat from the Cradles. The streetlights, the houselights, the porchlights, the night-lights, the neons, the advertising lamps, the insect zappers, everything that buzzed and belled in a three-sprint radius—all went off in a blink. I hit the horn to clear a path through the unlit streets as overhead the thwuckers of the CAT Squad roared toward Glory and Hallelujah.

But Lap, with a street map spread out before him like a board game, was counting on his logic and feline instincts to give us a head start. For days he'd been tracking the Cat's movements across the city grid; now he reckoned he could tell where the feral would be before the feral knew himself.

"Stop here," he said, and I slammed the brakes so hard the poco-wagon almost sprang off its chassis. "There's a bakery directly behind these tenements. The crumbs will attract birds and rats. Birds and rats will attract the Cat."

"Sure about this?"

"Skin me if I'm wrong."

We bustled up a fire escape just as residents started yapping about the blackout. Mounted at the top of the tenement was a huge REELECT GOODBOY/PALOMINE billboard. The sodium lamps were still smoking. Latching on to one of the stanchions Lap swung onto the roof and lowered a paw to drag me up as well.

I made sure I didn't whimper. Ahead was a vast rolling meadow of rooftops: slate, tiles, tin, corrugated iron, and all of it patched, gummed, daubed, crumbling, or plain missing— they didn't do a lot of roof repairs in the Kennels. But Lap didn't waste a second. He took to a narrow ledge in the center of the roof like it was a garden path, signaling that I should fan out. I lowered a foot onto a rusty sheet of metal, wasn't sure it would hold my weight, then gulped and lowered myself completely. But the roof didn't give way. I didn't fall through. I hugged the side of the building and inched my way around a row of oozing stink pipes.

To my left rose the Cathedral of Our Master, spires tall and black against the stars. Two blocks away the thwuckers of the CAT Squad were circling like dragonflies. Searchlights were probing Glory Street, Hallelujah Street, the alleys, the roof- tops. And everywhere mutts were spilling onto balconies, fling- ing open windows, growling, making a racket. Ahead I could just make out the silhouette of Lap, scrambling over a vent stack toward the bakery—I hoped he knew what he was doing.

I hadn't taken ten steps after him when my right leg suddenly disappeared through some rusty tin. There was a loud crash as plaster landed on the floor below. Someone started barking. I buttressed myself against a brick wall and dragged my leg free, shoeless. And suddenly I was hit by a blaze of light.

It was one of the thwuckers, curling around the cathedral towers, searchlights glaring. I shrank back behind the bricks and hunched up. The pool of light splashed over the top of the wall, lighting up stink pipes and cooling units and clouds of steam—swinging back and forth, up and down, over the chim- neys, around spinning fans, across the tar-papered roofs, and all the time the rotors were whacking and yammering, and I was pinned in place with ears flattened, hoping like hell that not a hair on my bobble was peeping over the wall.

Then a flare was thrown down on the roof, hissing and spraying, flashing between cracks. I had to roll up like a wood louse, my snout buried in my gut, frozen as a garden gnome.

There were a few more painful seconds of sparkling light, then the thwucker finally gave up and swung away, heading back to its mates a block away. I was safe again.

Or at least I thought I was.

Because the flare was still spluttering and giving off enough light for me to see, shining between a couple of busted water tanks, two yellow eyes as big as a tiger's.

I was pressed against the wall not ten leashlengths away. And the Cat was staring straight at me.

I could smell him now: grease, blood, rat guts, feathers, fear. But I couldn't move. I couldn't even think straight. All I could see was him ripping Jack Russell Crowe apart like a Twinkie. I was no longer a bullie—I was a titmouse.

The Cat started moving. His eyes were coming out of the darkness. I fumbled for my gun, hearing something rising up from the bottom of my windbag—a string of words, a prayer, a plea:

"Good kitty-kitty . . ."

"You found him!"

I jumped, but it was only Lap, returning to my side.

I pushed myself up, pointing. "There," I whispered, "between the tanks."

"I see him!"

Lap edged forward, fearless, shaming me. He stopped about two leashlengths distant and flipped his ID, like he was speaking to a mere bird smuggler. "I don't know your proper name," he said in his creamiest voice, "but I'm unarmed and mean you no harm. So please—"

But there was a screech from behind as someone lowered a fire escape. The Cat sprang out of hiding and ran for his life.

He loped across the rooftop on all fours—a lot smaller than I expected, and moving as fast as a weasel.

"Let's go!" said Lap before bolting off in pursuit, and I felt old instincts swell inside me—the thrill of the chase.

So I ran, too, bounding and scratching across the roof as bits and pieces of metal fell away beneath me in explosions of rust. Ahead, the Cat threw himself across an alley onto the roof of the bakery. Lap followed without a second thought. Flappers burst into the air, squeakers scampered. At the edge of the tenement I took a gulp of the yeasty air and sprang, too, landing on all fours and bounding forward before I had a chance to fall. In the darkness below, dogs were barking crazily.

A block away the flak-jacketed moggies of the CAT Squad were dropping like spiders from their thwuckers. Searchlights were waving everywhere. The Cat, seeing them, did a sudden U-turn. Lap swung around just as smoothly. I changed direction, too, bouncing off a cooling unit with a clang. The three of us scratched and scrambled across the roof, sprang across the alleyway again, and landed back on the tissue tin of the tenement, fighting for support.

But the Cat was limping all of a sudden—he'd damaged a leg on a jagged sheet of metal. He dragged himself around some exhaust fans and headed back for the safety of his water tanks, where the flare was still spluttering. Lap made for the center ledge as I struggled across the slope.

The Cat was between the water tanks. Lap, inching toward him, had pulled out his secret weapon.

"Here!" he said. "You must be thirsty!"

Cornelius Kane

He popped open the carton and splashed some milk into a small dish.

"I offer you this as a symbol of our goodwill!" he said. "We mean you no harm, I promise you—we can save you!"

The Cat's bloodshot peepers were glowing in the flare light. He stared at the dish. Half a block away more thwuckers were arriving.

"You need have no fear about the milk—it's unpasteurized and unhomogenized!"

As if to prove it, Lap got down on all fours and had a lick, lactose intolerance and all.

"Delicious," he said, "and all yours!"

And slowly something—trust or thirst—seemed to get the better of the Cat. He edged out from between the tanks. He headed for the ledge. Lap bowed and backed away.

"Please take some sustenance, take all the time you need, and we'll talk when you're finished."

The Cat reached the dish and sniffed the milk. And I saw, in the fluttering light, just how bony, scurfy, and matted he was—I almost felt sorry for him.

Lap looked at me and nodded—trust had been won.

The Cat stuck his licker into the milk and started slurping.

PING!

Something whanged off the ledge.

Lap looked up and cried, *"NO!"*

The feral got blown off his feet, squealing. Milk sprayed everywhere.

Another shot. The feral bolted off again into the darkness, bowling Lap aside.

I wheeled around and saw a pointy-eared shadow with a huge rifle in the cathedral tower—Carlos the Jackal.

I ripped out my Fido & Wesson and woofed off a couple of

shots just as Lap rolled past and over the edge of the tenement, clinging to the gutter with his claws.

Carlos meanwhile yelped like someone had stood on his tail. I fired off more shots—I emptied the whole chamber—until I saw him plunge into the tower. His rifle clattered down the cathedral roof.

I was reaching over to help Lap—the guttering was crumbling—when I heard it.

DING.

A sound like you'd hear at the end of the world.

DONG.

A bell like no other.

DING DONG.

The bell that ruled us all.

DING DONG DILL.

The bells of Our Master. The body of Carlos the Jackal had got tangled up in the ropes of the cathedral tower.

And I heard something else—a hiss like a busted steam pipe. But this sound came from the darkness. From a cat. From *the* Cat.

I turned, staring back across the roof, and froze. "Grab my tail," I breathed to Lap.

And then I saw him—the feral—creeping back over the ledge, leg after leg, like a giant tarantula. Coming back toward us.

DING.

He was three times the size he'd been a minute earlier.

DONG.

His hair was standing up like needles. His eyes were glaring like headlights. His fangs were bared and dripping. His claws were out like butcher hooks. And he was coming to take out the first dog in sight.

DING DONG DILL.

I stood in place, my gun empty, on the edge of the tenement with Lap clinging desperately to my tail. The Cat was oozing down the roof toward me, lit up by the fizzing flare. He was uncurling. He was rising. Towering over me. His saliva was dripping on me. Blood was jetting from the bullet wound on his shoulder. His eyes were as hot as barbecue coals. And I couldn't budge. There was nothing I could do but stare.

The bells were fading—*ding dong dill*—but nothing would stop the Cat from making his kill.

He roared at me like a lion, nearly blowing my whiskers off. He raised a paw—four grizzlylike claws—to cut me to ribbons, just like he'd done to the 'weilers. Just like he'd done to everyone else. I couldn't breathe.

I was two seconds away from being carved like a Peking duck.

But then—somewhere in the darkness—came another bell, a tinkle.

The Cat frowned. The tinkling stopped. In the blackness there was a presence.

The Cat blinked, tried to make him out.

A long, terrible pause—a cricket actually chirped—then a milk-curdling voice:

"Ding-dong dalemption
Pussy finds redemption."

Then the collar bell bounded forward. And a shape launched through the air.

The shape seized the feral and forced him off his feet.

The two cats, locked around each other like monkeys, flew over my bobble. They spun head over tail into the space between the cathedral and the tenement, plunging for what seemed half a minute before there was a splat like a couple of exploding watermelons.

Lap hauled himself to safety and together we peered over into the darkness. I picked up the fizzing flare and tossed it down into the alley, where it sprayed its light over a gruesome pasta of catguts.

We were silent for a minute, staring dumbslapped at the two bodies, as the thwuckers of the CAT Squad closed in.

"Fall must've killed 'em," I grunted.

"Not the fall."

"No?"

"No . . ." sighed Lap, straightening and shaking his head sadly. "'Twas Q. Riossiti killed the Cat."

EPILOGUE

WE DIDN'T DO anything rash. We never did anything rash. It was my very first lesson in the Unscratchables—that justice is a cheese that never grows mold.

Six months after the deaths of Q. Riossiti and the Cat there was a major bowwow at Phineas Reynard's country estate ninety sprints north of San Bernardo. Reynard himself was there along with Vice President Palomine, Ronald Chump, and a dozen fat-cats representing the press, television, motion pictures, music, publishing, theme parks, and the Internet. On the lunch table was a gobbler-watering mixture of marinated pheasant, pork crackling, lobster in hollandaise sauce, caramel truffles, Roquefort cheese, and mountains of whipped cream. Under discussion— we had the joint bugged—was a bold plan to take neoteny to an all new stage: to reduce the average dog IQ from thirty-four to twenty-six, the average nonfood-related attention span from ten seconds to five, and the average syllable-recognition capacity from two to one. The plan was called Operation Doofus, and everyone around the table cheetah-purred and hyena-chuckled with confidence about their eventual success.

What had happened was this. Between escaping from Cattica and saving us from certain death, Quentin Riossiti had plucked the tail feather from a raven, dipped the nib into some wet sidewalk tar, scrawled out the terrible history of Pavlov on the sides of a cracker container and dropped it into the nearest mailbox addressed to "Detective Max" of the San Bernardo Dog Force. Stampless, the container wandered around the postal system like a bamboozled Basenji before eventually landing at the Slaughter Unit, where Chesty White sniffed it out and passed it on to me.

It was ruff-tingling stuff. The grooming of wildcats and ferals to defeat dogs in a host of mutt-dominated sports: boxing, wrestling, tug-of-war, discus catching, dog paddle, bunny chasing, and the marathon. The ruthless training regime, often with fatal results. The strange habit of ferals to go mad in the experimental stage, especially when injected with growth hormones and performance-enhancing drugs. The loss of an untold number of "sparring partners"—usually junkies and Tom Does. The "disposal" of subjects who proved unsuccessful or uncooperative. The bottomless pit of "donations," sucked from antivivisection charities, to finance the operation. And all this being just one chapter in the unofficial history of the Office of Enforced Perspectives—the part Riossiti had time to scratch across a biscuit box before skedaddling away.

It was enough, anyway, to confront the governor and convince the DA to launch an official investigation. But by the time the case was ready for prosecution Pavlov had vanished like a blast of kettle steam. The warehouse in Loyalty Street had burned to the ground; the headquarters in Kathattan had nothing inside but a nail sharpener and a dead computer mouse; all bank accounts had been liquidated; the directors had gone to ground; the finance trail was a maze within a maze; and all associated companies, from Chump's to Reynard Media, stubbornly denied any knowledge. Legal advice slapped further doubts on Riossiti's testimony—the ramblings of a convicted killer who'd tried to plead insanity—and in the end it was decided to postpone all legal proceedings until better evidence could be rounded up.

Humphrey MacFluff retired with diabetes, Bud Borzoi got a mysterious promotion to a governmental security force, Nipper Sweeney was buried along with his research about Kitty and the Cat, and the carcass of Carlos the Jackal was never recovered. The escalating war between the Afghans and the Persians meanwhile made a barkfest out of the United Breeds, the foundations were laid for Babylon Towers, Brewster Goodboy and Lucky Palomine got reelected in a landslide, and my ex got engaged to my former friend Spike.

But something else happened at the same time. Oscar Lap of the FBI, in combination with Attorney General Barkus Bojangles and Justice Roxie Flowzer of the Department of Order and Discipline, made official his plan to set up a brand-new investigative unit, completely independent of existing law enforcement agencies. The first recruit was a Siamese cat called Cassius Lap. The second recruit was a hair-triggered bull terrier called Max McNash. The third recruit, our legal eagle, was a gasbagging old attorney called Thomas Schrödinger. Along with many others, herded together over the next few months, we made a fierce pack of incorruptible agents, desk hounds, tech noses, and dirt-diggers.

Officially we had no name. Unofficially we were the Unscratchables.

By January, we had the know-how—and the meat tickets—to infiltrate the retagged Pavlov and mike their conference rooms. And this was how, via the hired help, we got our sniffers into

Reynard's up-country manor that day and heard his guests mew and growl about their evil plans to reel back the national intelligence with reality television, game shows, snarl music, comic book movies, tinned news, hiss-and-poke editorials, celebrity scandals, sleaze sheets, humpshows, horoscopes, ghost yappers, stroke-and-tickle books, bitch-lit, thrillers by branded bulls, and especially muttonheaded mystery novels told by dog narrators.

Through hidden cameras we watched them toast each new suggestion with yak milk and blood-tainted springwater. We watched them chomp their food and lick their paws and toss catmints into their gobblers. We saw them slink off to the armory to choose weapons for the after-dinner hunt. We observed, at closer range, as they spilled out of the house and fanned out across the fields to hunt for the predrugged lambs. In particular, we tracked Phineas Reynard as he peeled off to a hedged-off corner of the estate, where the finest specimens had been hidden.

We watched him, dressed in his tweed jacket and galoshes, pass what he thought was a particularly ugly sheep. We watched him stop beside what he thought was a particularly empty tree.

We watched him raise his sheep-shooter. We watched him aim at a juicy lamb.

We watched him squint his eye.

We watched him start to squeeze the trigger.

Then—

"I wouldn't do that if I were you."

The voice came from behind and above.

Reynard stopped squeezing. His eye unsquinted.

"An unregistered fox firing an unregistered rifle? I can't tell you how many laws that violates."

Reynard didn't run, didn't flinch, didn't do anything at all—just lowered the weapon and looked around.

Cassius Lap spoke from the tree above. "Forgive me if I interrupted, Phineas, but I'm an incorrigible pedant when it comes to the law."

Reynard looked up, shielding his eyes against the sunlight. "Why it's Special Agent Lap," he said, as if welcoming an old friend. "Were you really on the guest list? It must have escaped my attention."

Lap smiled. "When necessary I bend the rules," he said, "but unlike you I never break them." He dropped nimbly from the branch to the grass.

"Break them?" Reynard shrugged innocently. "But I have no idea what you're talking about. An unregistered fox? What does that mean?"

"Come now." Lap straightened. "Your own media vigorously championed the compulsory registration of minorities, did it not?"

"That was for dog minorities, not foxes."

"I believe the legal definition was *canidae*, which includes foxes. And that means you've already broken the law, even without firing that weapon. Unless, of course, you've now officially—and not just surgically—become a cat?"

Reynard narrowed his little peepers. "I said you were an interesting cat. It seems I wasn't wrong."

"I like the word 'interesting.'"

"And yet"—Reynard slowly raised the sheep-shooter—"with that white fur . . . with the sun in my face . . . with the wind blowing . . . and with dust in my eyes . . ."

"Phineas"—Lap frowned—"you're not really going to say you mistook me for a lamb, are you?"

Reynard glanced around. "I believe we're all alone out here." He curled a digit around the trigger. "And no one would dare challenge me, in any event."

"As it happens you're wrong about that, I'm afraid."

"About being challenged?"

"About being alone." Now Lap nodded to me over Reynard's shoulder. "Have you never heard, dear Phineas, of the old adage, 'Beware the bull terrier in sheep's clothing'?"

It was at this point that I shucked off my sheepskins, stood up, and strode over to Reynard, resting my fat snout on his bony shoulder.

"Ding dong dite," I breathed, "Doggie likes to bite."

But again Reynard didn't squeal, didn't jolt, didn't look anything but amused. "My my," he said, glancing back, "I do seem to be outnumbered."

"And the firing pin of that rifle has been removed," Lap added, "as an added precaution."

"Well, well," Reynard said, lowering the weapon again. "Trespassing on private property *and* tampering with private firearms? I can't imagine how many laws *that* violates."

"I told you, Phineas, I don't break the rules. I have a warrant in my pocket if you really need to inspect it. And disabling an illegal firearm is a duty, not a crime."

"Is that a fact?"

"I'm afraid so. And in any case"—Lap smiled—"if you really wish to continue on the subject of lawbreaking we're more than willing to consult our voluminous surveillance records. We've been following you rather attentively, you see, for the last six months . . ."

"Oh?" For the first time Reynard actually looked ruffled.

"Indeed," said Lap. "And there's a multitude of places where we might begin. Perhaps, for instance, with that afternoon two months ago, when you strolled brazenly across the lawns of Cattery Park? You know, the one with the signs clearly stating NO CANINES ALLOWED?"

"Or maybe," I added, jabbing him in the back, "that morning last January when you were swishing through the clock market and couldn't help yourself. Remember, pal? When you stuck two spring-loaded chickens under your coat?"

"Or even," Lap said, "that night four months ago when you—how can I put this?—*unburdened* yourself on the sidewalk of Sovereign Street and failed to pick up the deposit?"

I frowned at Lap. "Remind me again—what's the sentence for minorities with three or more convictions?"

Lap grimaced. "Mandatory neutering, I believe."

"That's right," I sniggered. "Mandatory nutcracking."

Reynard's fox smirk slowly uncurled. He looked at me and he looked at Lap. And finally he nodded. "Well, well—it seems you've been busy out there."

"We take pride in our work," Lap said.

"And it seems you have me cornered—congratulations."

"We don't do it for plaudits."

"All right." Reynard grunted. "What is it that you want? A payoff, is that it?"

"We don't want your money, Phineas."

"Real estate, I suppose?"

"Real estate?"

"Every cat—every dog—wants territory. Let's not play games."

But Lap only shook his head. "We don't want your real estate, Phineas."

"Fame? You want to win ribbons?"

"We don't want any ribbons either."

"You want someone to stroke you—an all-day stroker?"

"Please, Phineas, we're not interested in personal gratification. We only wish to issue you with a polite caution, in fact."

"Of course you do."

"No, I mean it," said Lap. "We just want you to know that we'll always be stalking you. That we can't be corrupted. And we can't be shaken loose."

"Is that so?"

"And oh"—Lap acted like he'd just thought of something—"there is something you can do for us, yes. You might call it a demand. We'd much prefer to call it a request."

"I'm all ears."

Now Lap smiled. "We'd like you to go back to that manor, call in all your guests, and reconvene the meeting. And then we'd like you to make a special announcement. We'd like you to say that you're tired of dining with toads, wolves, weasels, and swine. You're tired of plotting in boardrooms. You're tired of trying to dominate the world with ropes, leashes, and command words. And you're especially tired of lowering the bar of intelligence, when what you really want to do is make everyone jump a little higher. It would help, by the way, if you spoke in a loud, clear voice, so there's no confusion when we transcribe your words from our tapes."

Reynard stared at him.

"And if anyone asks what brought about this change of heart," Lap went on smoothly, "you might say that you met a dog and cat while you were strolling in the fields. And that this dog and cat—who were unusually persuasive—convinced you that they were no longer interested in answering to bells and whistles. They would no longer be barked at, dogwhipped, scared by thunder, dragged through pits, rubbed in their own filth, locked up in cages, distracted by toys, or left out in the cold. They were no longer happy, in short, to be treated like pups and kittens."

Reynard shook his head. "My guests are not the types who respond to lectures."

"Then disguise it as news," Lap said. "I'm sure you can find a way."

Reynard sniffed. "Is that all?"

"Indeed." Lap gave a slight bow. "But we're extremely grateful to you for hearing us out. For welcoming us onto your magnificent estate. We'd love to accept your invitation to supper, of course, but regrettably we have much work to attend to."

I poked him in the back again. "Catch ya later, manipulator."

"Unless," added Lap, turning, "you give us no reason to catch you at all. *Vulpem te esse memento.*"

We started heading across the field toward a break in the hedge, but Reynard hadn't finished.

"I must say I'm disappointed, Detective," he called out. "A bull terrier side by side with a cat? Working in tandem with a Siamese? Sniffing through the same garbage? Lapping from the same bowl? Whatever's happened to the world?"

I looked back just long enough to give him my crocodile smirk. "Must've got me confused with a creature of instinct," I muttered, and jerked my bobble at the tooter. "Let's scat, Cass."

"You got it, Crusher."

Off the leash. On your tail. Unscratchable.